GRAVE OF ROBIN HOOD

A MADDIE JONES MYSTERY BOOK 2

MARK DOUGLAS, JR.

*This book is dedicated to my gorgeous wife, Hollind.
Thank you for listening when I talk about Maddie Jones. She is a
stronger character because of you.*

Prologue

Summer 1191
Holy Lands of Jerusalem

THEY ONCE CALLED ME a lady.

Now they called me a knight.

I sat astride a bloodied warhorse as it lumbered through the slaughter of battle. An arrow had pierced the animal's muscled leg during the skirmish, so we moved slowly through corpses littering the field. Among the dead, I recognized my Christian brethren, but also the Muslims we'd fought to defeat. My passage stirred a wake of vultures feeding off the dead. They flew into the air like a billowing cloud of smoke. Human scavengers also disturbed the corpses. They yanked off boots, removed rings from fingers, and rummaged through pockets in search of loose coins. A few scraggly faces turned to stare as I passed, but they quickly grew disinterested and resumed their desecration of the dead.

I knew how they perceived me. As another knight. Another *man*.

My bosom lay flattened beneath a leather jerkin and links of heavy chainmail. My ginger hair had been shaved. To further hide my womanly features, I'd shrouded my beardless face behind a helmet with a visor.

Very few knew I was a woman. *None* knew what I had come to retrieve.

I steered my warhorse onto a rutted road. The double-edged broadsword strapped to my waist rattled against my thigh. I gripped its hilt to steady the blade, then cantered up the path toward a stone keep the Christians had dubbed the Tower of David. The massive structure, a citadel with battlements and turrets designed to withstand a siege, looked as if it had been chiseled from a mountain. Despite its fortitude, I found the gate broken and splintered, torn apart by a battering ram the size of a tree.

A knight with a white scar across his eye guarded the entrance. He wore the outfit of our Order, a surcoat with a crimson cross sewn across his chest.

"Have you seen the king?" I asked, projecting my voice as deep as I could.

The scarred knight nodded. "He went straight for the crypt."

Of course he did, I thought.

Over the past decade, we'd raided countless crypts and tombs throughout Egypt and the Holy Lands in search of powerful relics. We'd found a few items of importance—like the Mandylion, a square cloth with the miraculous imprint of the face of Jesus. But the artifact paled in comparison to the elusive Holy Grail and Ark of the Covenant. Both the Grail and Ark were still missing, but if the rumors were true, then I was about to lay my hands on an artifact of power.

Finally, after all these years . . .

I tilted my helmet's visor to get a better view of the stone keep. Its tower stretched to dizzying heights. A blood-red sun loomed low on the horizon. Smoke from the battle drifted into the sky, making me think a thunderstorm brewed in the distance.

"Should I tell the king ye've arrived?" asked the scarred knight.

My warhorse snorted. I dismounted and handed the knight my reins. "No," I said. "I shall speak to him personally."

I strode past the knight and into the keep. Corpses grew in number the farther I went. Christians, yes, but mostly Muslim martyrs who died trying to defend the tower. I walked with my sword still sheathed at my side. There was no need to fear attack, not anymore. We had won the Tower of David with blood. And despite King Richard's faults, his policy on survivors was simple.

Take none.

As a testament to this, I found the dead piled in heaps like logs for a fire.

Another knight guarded a stairwell descending into darkness. I grabbed a torch from a nearby sconce, gave the knight a curt nod, then hurried down the worn stone steps as flames crackled and spit, shifting shadows. My heart beat harder with each passing step.

Will it be here? Have we found it at last?

The stairwell leveled out. I entered a long chamber with stone coffins lining the walls. Hebrew writing had been etched into their lids. I swept past them, eager to join two figures bathed in torchlight at the far end of the crypt. One held a sharpened broadsword. The other was on his knees, unarmed save a folded woolen cloth squeezed tightly in his hands.

No, not a he, I observed as I crossed the distance toward them. The one kneeling was a woman. Wiry black hair shrouded her features, but her bosom was unmistakable.

"Ah, I am pleased to see you," King Richard said. He wore a bloodied surcoat with the crest of a lion emblazoned on his chest. He stood a sword's hilt taller than me. His ginger hair and freckled complexion mirrored my own—a clue to any who might pry into our shared ancestry.

I ignored the king. Instead, I knelt and peered into the face of the woman. Her skin was tanned and leathery like a field laborer. A crow's feet of wrinkles framed pale gray eyes that gleamed in the torchlight.

King Richard knelt beside me, almost like he sensed something of great importance was unfolding. "Marian . . ." he started.

The woman's gaze narrowed. She must've understood our language if she recognized my name to be a lady's. Her stare tried to pierce through my closed visor's slits to see my face.

King Richard continued, unaware of his loose-tongued mistake. "Based on your orders, we sieged the tower. Upon your command, we attacked the keep. Many lives were lost and *this* is all we find—a woman guarding a simple woolen cloth. Why?"

I did not answer the king. I spoke to the woman. "How old are you?"

The woman didn't respond, so I asked again, this time using an ancient dialect of Hebrew. "When were you born?"

The woman inhaled deeply. When she spoke, her words came out raspy and thin. "I was born in Nazareth during the older years of zero and three."

King Richard understood enough Hebrew to scoff. "The third year of our Lord? But that would make her over a thousand years old. Impossible."

I tried to imagine what this woman had *seen* throughout the centuries and millennia. How many cities had she witnessed crumble to dust? How many loved ones had she lost to the passage of time? To live such a life would be a curse . . . and a blessing. My eyes darted to the cloth gripped tightly in her hands.

She hugged the cloth close, protecting it. "The world is not ready for miracles," she rasped, her tone coming across as a warning. "What you seek should remain hidden."

I refused to listen. This powerful relic could do wonders for mankind. "Perhaps so," I said. "But this relic is no longer yours to wield."

"B-but, Marian," the king stammered, his eyes wide.

I faced him fully, annoyed he had divulged my name twice now in the presence of a stranger. He fell back at my gaze, not frightened of me, his cousin, but appearing ashamed at such a foolish mistake.

"Bring the woman," I commanded. "Keep her age hidden."

"Aye," the king replied. "But, please, I have earned the right to know. What does she carry?"

I wrenched the woolen cloth from the prisoner's hands, then admired its simple artistry and weaving. "This cloth is an artifact of power," I whispered, my fingers tingling from touching the mystical relic. "It was once worn by a Hebrew rabbi the world now calls the Messiah. It is the Klok Kyoor, the traveling cloak of Jesus Christ."

Part One
TREASURE MAP

Chapter 1

Present day

LOOK, I DIDN'T MEAN TO blow up my dad's museum. It wasn't my fault, I swear. It all began when a mysterious package arrived one gloomy afternoon addressed to my dad. Even weirder, the package's shipping label had numerous stamps from countries all over the world with dates going back to the early 2,000s.

The package was beaten up and worn with water stains and crumpled corners. It appeared a secret benefactor had sent something to my dad, which meant the box was likely filled with a priceless artifact or a fat stack of cash. Definitely a box I should take to him personally.

So.

I hoisted the box from the museum's front steps, grunting from the effort. The package was frigging heavy.

"Everything okay, Maddie?"

The voice came from my phone, which I'd set on top of the box so I could lift the package. My screen showed a video call with a girl of dark complexion. Her brown eyes were stylishly painted in purple mascara like an Egyptian princess. Her head was skin bald.

Amira Raja. A girl so cool she made bald a fashion statement.

It's not like Amira *wanted* to be bald, but when chemotherapy treatments steal your gorgeous locks, you don a pretty scarf and accent your eyes with a splash of color. Unfortunately, Amira's cancer was so bad she lived in a children's hospital located in Boston. To make matters worse, her father died last year trying to find the fabled Elixir of Life from the tomb of the First Qin Emperor of China. He had hoped the Elixir would cure Amira's cancer. I don't have time to explain all of it now, but let's just say it's a pretty wild story.

"A bizarre package arrived for my dad," I explained, nudging the museum's front door open with a black combat boot. The main lobby was empty. Museum banners hung from a twenty-foot ceiling to showcase major attractions: Nature photography by Ansel Adams, dinosaur fossils of a brachiosaurus, and a magnificent painting of a Spanish galleon out at sea.

"The face your making is ridiculous right now," Amira said. "It looks like you have to poop, but can't."

I blew brown hair with mint green highlights from my eyes. "You try carrying this thing. It feels like it's loaded with bricks."

I reached the elevators and pressed the UP button using my hip. My reflection stared back at me from the closed metallic doors. A skinny girl of fifteen with a studded nose ring, leather jacket, and a blue jean miniskirt with torn fishnet stockings.

"What'd you think it is?" asked Amira.

"I dunno, but if its value is based on weight, it's worth a fortune."

A chime sounded and the elevator doors opened. I stepped inside and set the heavy package down with a thud. Then I jammed the button for the third floor. "We still on for tonight?" I asked as the elevator jolted into movement.

Amira's face lit up in a smile. "You bet," she said. "I managed to sneak some junk food from the hospital's gift shop."

"Amira," I scolded.

"Hey, you can't watch a Harry Potter movie without snacks."

Amira just finished reading the final book in the series, and like we'd promised each other during our first meeting (a few days after her dad passed away), we planned to watch the movies together over FaceTime after she finished each book.

The elevator bounced to a stop. Its doors opened, and I picked up the package and lumbered down the hall to my dad's office. As I nudged his office door open with my shoulder, the package slipped from my hands and I nearly dropped it. My cell phone fell off the top of the box and skittered onto a Persian rug. I hurried to Dad's desk, which was cluttered with research papers, memos, and an iron box that had a tree carved on its lid. I shoved them aside and dropped the package down.

My elbow bumped a picture frame and knocked it over. It was a photograph of my mom. Her auburn hair flowed in the wind and her bright, sea-green eyes matched the water in the background. The picture was taken at the beach a few months before she died. I was only four years old at the time. Gently, I set the picture frame back on Dad's desk in the place he liked to keep it.

The room was dark so I flicked on a desk lamp. Its warm glow illuminated bookcases, miniature Native American statues, a suit of knight's armor in the corner, and framed paintings of Spanish conquistadors hanging on the walls. A sticky note on the blank computer screen drew my attention.

Kleopatra,

Went to New Mexico. Tried to call. Please watch the kids while I'm away. Shouldn't be gone more than a week. Thanks!

~Dr. Hank

"Fetch," I groaned.

"What's wrong?" Amira's tiny voice sounded from my phone.

I snatched it up from the carpet. "My dad's outta town. He got us a babysitter."

"Who?"

"His intern. She's the worst."

"Why can't you stay home alone?"

"Because my dad thinks I'm irresponsible. He says my pranks are getting out of hand."

"Are they?" asked Amira.

I smirked. "Only if I'm caught."

"What are you gonna do with the box?"

I grabbed a pair of scissors from a nearby pencil cup. "Open it."

"Should you? Will your dad get mad?"

"Yeah, but he left me with Kleo so who cares?"

I set my phone down on the desk. Then I used the scissors to slice the box's packing tape along the seam. The packing tape came free. Slowly, I pulled back a cardboard flap. Part of me expected to find a crystal skull or a tarnished magical lamp. Instead, I found . . .

"Oh, my God" I gasped.

"What?"

I grabbed my phone and showed Amira what I was seeing. The box was filled with wires—red, blue, and green ones—and they were all connected to a small propane tank. Tubes stretched from the propane tank and were attached to clear containers with golden liquid inside. It smelled like gasoline. A digital clock with big, red numbers counted down the seconds—*blinking* with each change of the number.

Holy frigging crap! In less than one minute, this bomb was going to detonate.

"M-Maddie," Amira sounded scared.

My brain wasn't functioning properly. I needed to run, but all I could focus on was the red numbers counting down.

Fifty-three.

Fifty-two.

Fifty-one.

"Maddie!"

Amira's loud voice snapped me back to the present. I shoved my phone into my pocket and lifted the box. Then, as quickly as my legs could carry me, I rushed out of Dad's office and down the hallway toward the girl's bathroom. On the way, I passed a fire alarm—so I skidded on my heels and yanked down its handle. Immediately, an alarm blared throughout the museum. A prerecorded voice spoke through the intercoms.

"Please exit the museum," it was my dad's deep baritone. *"Follow all exit signs and listen to your tour guide as you safely exit the building."*

"Maddie—what's going on?" Amira spoke from my pocket.

"I'm getting people outta here," I said.

"And the bomb?"

"I'm flushing it."

"You're *what?*"

I burst into the girl's bathroom with the package gripped awkwardly in my hands.

Chapter 2

A FLOATER SLOSHED AROUND in the bowl, and my cheeks puffed out as I nearly vomited from the smell. "Ngggh," I gagged. "Oh, that's nasty."

"What is it?" asked Amira.

"You don't want to know."

I lifted the toilet seat with the toe of my boot, then dropped the package into the water. *Splash!* Yellow-brown water spilled over the rim, wetting the tops of my boots.

"Ngggh," I gagged again.

The bomb's clock kept counting down, now at twenty-eight seconds. Its blinking numbers didn't make any noise, but each passing second sent a jolt to my heart. I had hoped the water would short-circuit the bomb, causing it to malfunction.

Boy, was I wrong.

"Did it work?"

"Nope," I said. "Wait—lemme try something." I flushed the toilet. Water swirled around in the bowl, but nothing happened other than the turd smearing across the box. "Yeah, this was a dumb idea."

"You can't flush a bomb, Maddie."

"Now you tell me?!"

The bomb's countdown was now at twenty-two seconds. Twenty-one! I didn't know what to do. How could I disarm a bomb?

"Get outta there!" Amira's voice was so loud my cell phone's speaker rattled with static.

I turned and bolted out of the bathroom, my wet boots squeaking across the tile floor. I sprinted down the hallway and burst into the stairwell, then bounded down three flights of stairs using the handrails to help me leap two, and sometimes three, steps at a time.

"Hurry, Maddie."

I barely registered Amira's voice as I crashed through a door and entered the main lobby. I looked left and right, but I didn't see anyone. The welcome desk was vacant. TV monitors behind the security desk showed museum galleries of dinosaurs, Spanish conquistadors, terracotta warriors, and Native Americans—all empty of museum guests. Water burbled from a fountain in the center of the expansive room. The fire alarm continued blaring.

"Please exit the museum," my dad's voice droned over the intercom. *"Follow all exit signs and listen to your tour guide as you safely exit the building."*

"Yeah, yeah, Dad, I hear you."

I raced for the exit and slammed into glass doors embossed with fancy letters reading EVANSVILLE HISTORY MUSEUM. Outside, a throng of people milled about in the parking lot. They shielded their eyes from the early morning sun as they stared at me bursting out of the museum. A plump man with an overly tight shirt tucked into his pants towered over everyone else—security guard Jimmy. He clapped his hand on his forehead when he saw me. I knew what he was probably thinking: *Oh, great—what's Maddie done now?*

"Run!" I yelled, darting down the stairs leading up to the museum and waving my hands frantically at everyone in the vicinity. "It's gonna—"

BOOOOM!

I was catapulted into the air as the blast sent stone, wood, and marble debris hurtling violently forward. Black smoke and bright flames engulfed the sky.

Chapter 3

FIERY HEAT SUCKED THE BREATH from my lungs. The world spun, and I landed on my back with a painful *oomph*! My ears rang. It felt like something wet dripped down my neck. I touched my fingers to the wetness and flinched from a sharp sting. A gash beneath my ear dripped with blood. I wiped bloody fingers on my leather jacket, coughing as clouds of dark smoke choked the air.

I rolled onto my side to see what happened to the museum. "No," I cried upon seeing the destruction.

The building was in ruins. Angry fire licked the air and black smoke billowed into the sky. The main lobby's magnificent entrance, which had been flanked by two marble Grecian columns, had collapsed and was now barred with large slabs of busted marble, stone, and burning wood. The entire east wing where my dad's office was located looked completely demolished.

My heart sank. Dad would probably have a stroke when he saw all of this.

I climbed to my feet and glanced down at my clothes. They were torn, shredded, and covered in ash and soot. Cuts and scrapes marred my skin. I didn't feel most of them—chalk it up to adrenaline, I guess—but the few gashes I did feel stung as if I'd walked through a hornet's nest.

I looked around the parking lot. Museum guests and employees all appeared stunned. They stared at the destroyed museum, mouths agape and wide-eyed, though not nearly covered in as much soot as me. It seemed I'd taken the brunt of the explosion since I was closest to the building when it blew.

Security guard Jimmy broke away from the crowd of survivors. He hurried to my side and grabbed me gently by the shoulders. As he worried over my injuries, his lips moved, but I couldn't make out what he said because of my buzzing ears.

"What?" I asked, but I couldn't even hear my own voice.

"Are you okay?" his words finally reached my ears, but they were muffled like he spoke through a tin can.

I nodded. "Jimmy, it was an accident," I began.

His gaze hardened. "Accident? Don't tell me you dropped another cherry bomb down the toilet."

"No, it wasn't like that," I said. "Well, I *did* drop a bomb down the toilet, but it's not what you think. Someone sent a strange package to the museum."

Jimmy sighed heavily. He pinched the bridge of his nose. "I'm not buying it this time, Maddie. The last time you pulled a prank like this you nearly killed an old lady. But now—" he looked up at the destroyed building, "—you nearly killed *everyone.*"

"I swear, Jimmy. This isn't my fault."

"That's not up to me to decide," he grunted. "The cops will get to the bottom of this."

"The cops? Nobody needs to call the cops!"

He scoffed, then walked away while shaking his head.

The next hour was a blur. Firetrucks, police cars, and ambulances raced into the parking lot with sirens blaring and lights flashing. Firemen worked to extinguish the blaze. Paramedics went from person to person and checked them for injuries. A paramedic with bushy eyebrows and a bald head with brown hair on the sides led me to a nearby ambulance. As I sat on its rear bumper, he tended my wounds.

Then the news crews arrived.

Reporters stood in front of cameras and filmed the chaos and destruction. A blond reporter in black high heels shoved a microphone into my face as the paramedic applied a bandage to my bleeding neck. "Can you tell our viewers what happened?" she asked.

"No comment," I said, waving the microphone away.

The reporter *tsk*ed, then she stormed off, her high heels clacking on the asphalt as she searched for someone to interview.

"Maddie, are you there? Helloooo . . ."

The voice came from my pocket. Oh, fetch—I'd completely forgotten about Amira. I reached into my pocket and pulled out my phone. She was still live on FaceTime.

"Geez," she whistled when she saw my ash-covered face. "You look like you just survived an atomic blast."

"I kinda did," I said.

"Really? So it was an actual bomb?"

"Yeah—half the museum blew up." I angled my phone so she could see the destroyed building.

"Oh, Maddie, I'm so sorry. At least you made it out in one piece."

"For now," I grumbled. "When my dad hears about this, I'm dead meat."

An unmarked police car pulled up and parked. Its driver's side door opened and a middle-aged woman in her late thirties got out. She wore blue jeans and a leather jacket with a badge clipped to her belt. Her brown hair was pulled back in a severe ponytail.

"Fetch," I swore. "Amira, I'm gonna have to call you back."

"Why? What's happened now?"

I sighed. "Detective Murphy just showed up."

Chapter 4

IF YOU HAVEN'T FIGURED IT out already, I'm a prankster. I love playing jokes on people, businesses, or the government. Once, and this is hilarious, I modified a drone to look like a UFO and flew it in restricted air space. The media had a field day. They couldn't figure out who the perpetrator was, or how the drone could say, "We come in peace!" in the voice of a Martian.

So when something goes wrong in the community—like the museum blowing up on a bright, sunny day—Detective Murphy is the first to knock on my home's front door or visit my school. She is determined to catch me in the act and bust me for a prank. Although we share a mutual respect for one another (we saved each other's life last year after mercenaries crashed their van into her cruiser), she's married to her job. I guess the law is her husband and I'm flirting with disaster.

"Well, well, if it isn't Maddie Jones," Detective Murphy said as the paramedic continued patching me up, each swab of his disinfectant sharp and stinging on my cuts. "When I heard the police scanners say the museum was on fire, I thought to myself: I bet Maddie Jones is the culprit behind it." She *tsk*ed as she looked me up and down. "And here I find you, covered in more soot than anybody else."

"Hey, Detective," I said sheepishly.

She sighed and removed a small notebook with a little pencil stuck inside its spirals from her back pocket. "So what'd you do this time?" she asked in a dull tone, flipping to a blank page and starting to record notes. "Ignite a stink bomb and hit a gas line?"

"No—it wasn't like that."

"Another cherry bomb down the toilet, then? You're lucky the old lady you nearly blew up last time didn't press charges."

"Ugh," I groaned. "Believe it or not, this isn't my fault, Detective!"

"I checked with Principal Watson today. She said you weren't at school. Skipping again?"

Fetch. Busted.

"Look," I said, my voice rising. "I didn't skip school to blow up my dad's museum. I was dodging a math test."

"Mm-hmm. Why don't you tell me what happened? Let's start from the top."

I massaged my temples to ease the migraine starting to form. Then I told Detective Murphy what happened while she recorded my story in her little notebook. I explained how a strange package arrived addressed to my dad, and what the bomb looked like, but I left out the bit about me trying to flush the bomb. You know how everyone keeps referring to a cherry bomb incident and a poor, old lady?

Yeah, that really happened.

I flushed one down a toilet right before an elderly woman rushed in to drop a number two. Thankfully, the toilet exploded *after* she finished.

I love pranks, but I never want to hurt anyone.

Detective Murphy didn't speak during my story, but I could tell from her expression that she wasn't buying it. She finished scribbling something into her notebook. "I'm gonna mark this down as *Maddie Jones blew up her dad's museum* for the time being."

I groaned. The Evansville History Museum was as much my home as the house I lived in. Detective Murphy had gotten to know me pretty well over the past year, so why couldn't she see that?

Familiar voices shouted my name. I looked up to see my brothers ducking beneath yellow police tape and rushing toward me. Jason, a handsome teenager of thirteen, wore glasses with black rims and had stylishly spiked blond hair. Both middle and high school girls crushed on him, and it drove me nuts. If they only knew how nerdy he was.

I'm serious.

He's captain of the chess club, the Dungeons and Dragons club, and the anime club. He also plays the weirdest video games. I'm talking about the ones with knights, wizards, goblins, and junk.

Zac's freckled face looked flushed like he'd just come from football practice—which was probably true. Although he was only eleven years old, he played varsity sports in football, basketball, baseball, soccer, golf—pretty much anything with a ball. High school coaches had even started scouting his games.

Let me give you a fair warning about my brothers before you officially meet them. You might think they're cute, you might think they're lovable, but they'll annoy the baked beans out of you.

"Wow, Maddie," Jason said as he scanned the museum rubble. "I think it's safe to say your pranks have finally gotten out of hand."

"I didn't do it," I grumbled.

"Are you okay?" asked Zac. His eyes raked over my newly bandaged wounds and soot-covered face. "You look horrible."

"Thanks, it's good to see you too."

"No—I'm serious. You're not hurt or anything?"

I ruffled Zac's curly, brown hair. "Not at all, big guy. A few cuts and bruises, but I'll survive. How'd you guys get here?"

"Kleopatra," Jason said. "She has a suitcase and says she'll be our babysitter for the next few days."

"You're in a lot of trouble," Zac informed. "She knows you skipped school."

"Trouble seems to be my middle name today," I sighed.

Detective Murphy kept writing in her notebook. I didn't know what was worse: the detective's investigation or the wrath of my babysitter.

"Lemme through!" someone shouted. "I—am—their—babysitter!"

I glanced up to see a dark-skinned woman yelling at a uniformed police officer just beyond the yellow tape marking the area as a crime scene. The officer let her pass, and the woman ducked beneath the tape and stormed closer, her high heels clicking forcefully against the pavement.

I cringed. Here came my babysitter's wrath.

Chapter 5

MY BABYSITTER WAS FROM Cairo, Egypt.

Most people might think that's pretty cool, but not me. Kleopatra was Dad's newest intern and studying to be an archaeologist. As a part-time job, she'd agreed to house-sit when my father traveled. The job included the added responsibility of watching me and my younger brothers. Despite my complaints that I was old enough to stay home alone and that Kleopatra was only five years older than me, Dad hired her anyways.

And that's why I didn't like her.

Every time she stayed at our house, I increased my pranks from one to three just to make Kleopatra's life more difficult. Was it a jerk move? Sure. Did I care? Not in the slightest. There was something about the wannabe archaeologist that irked me. Perhaps it was her effortless beauty or her constant travel stories, but whatever it was, I think I simply didn't like a strange woman living in my home who wasn't Mom.

"I can't *believe* you skipped school, Maddie Jones," my babysitter wagged a finger at me as she approached. Her exotic skin was dark and she had a rich Egyptian accent. She wore a fashionable blue jean jacket with jewels for buttons, dark pants, and a purple hijab—a head scarf worn in public by many Muslim women. "Just wait until your father hears about this—"

"Kleo!" I said, trying to muster as much cheer as I could. "It's so good to see you."

"Don't *dare* pretend everything is normal." Kleopatra's eyes were clear gray under a smoky fringe of lashes. At the corner of her lavender-painted lips, she had a mole—a fake beauty mark. It wasn't real. I forgot to mention Kleopatra was not only an archaeologist in training, but a makeup artist on YouTube. She had, like, sixty-thousand followers and several videos with over a hundred-thousand views. "Tomorrow, I'm handcuffing you to Jason and forcing you to go to school."

"That won't stop me," I said under my breath.

"What'd you say?" asked Kleopatra.

Detective Murphy pocketed her notebook and stuck out a hand. "Ma'am—I'm with Evansville PD."

"I know who you are," Kleopatra spat, her anger at me spilling over to the detective. "We spoke on the phone about Maddie's prank at school."

"Hey," I protested. "Nothing has been proven."

Which was partially true. The investigation was still ongoing. I'd stolen five pigs from a local farmer, then painted numbers on them. One. Three. Four. Five. Six. Then I set them loose on campus. Hilarity ensued as Principal Watson and the entire teaching staff scoured the grounds for elusive pig number two. I'd never seen so many adults yelling at one another to, "Find the missing pig!"

"Be that as it may," the detective said. "We have an ongoing issue with Maddie. Her pranks are getting more and more serious. I'm afraid she may end up in a juvenile correction center if her behavior does not change."

Kleopatra glared at me. "Perhaps a correction center will do Maddie some good."

"Guys," I said. "I didn't blow up the museum."

"Hush," my babysitter said; and the detective added, "The adults are speaking, Miss Jones."

I threw my hands up and walked away. Stupid adults. It didn't matter how many times I told them about the mysterious package and its bomb, they simply wouldn't believe me. Sometimes it sucks to be a teenager.

"Maddie," the detective called me back over once she and Kleopatra finished speaking. "If my criminal investigation team discovers that a toilet was at the center of this explosion—I'll have your head."

Just great, I thought.

Evansville PD would likely discover scorch marks inside the toilet I'd flushed the bomb in, and knowing my luck, all evidence of the bomb was probably incinerated by the blast. Maybe I should have told Detective Murphy about the attempted flushing. Not that it would've mattered. Nothing I said could convince her of my innocence. Man, it looked like I would be going to juvie.

Again.

Talk about the worst luck ever.

Chapter 6

I'M SURE YOU'VE HEARD OF bad drivers. Heck, I'm sure you've seen them on the road. They tailgate other cars, honk at random people, and drive way too fast. That's Kleopatra.

My babysitter gunned her convertible Ford Mustang and peeled out of the museum's parking lot. She shot down Eleventh Street doing close to sixty. Then she proceeded to ignore stop signs, traffic lights, and nearly struck a pedestrian.

"You wanna go back and run over that guy?" I asked, gripping the dash with white knuckles. "Because I'm pretty sure he was worth fifty points for a direct hit."

Kleopatra didn't answer me. Instead, she took a hand off the wheel to glance down at her phone. At the same time, we turned onto Lincoln Avenue. Well, it was more like we *drifted* onto Lincoln Avenue like Tokyo street racers.

"Please slow down!" Jason clung to his seatbelt as the Mustang straightened out. "I'm gonna blow chunks."

"What're you talking about? This is *awesome*!" shouted Zac. Every time we hit a curve or raced over a bridge, he tossed his hands in the air like he rode a roller coaster. "Faster! Faster!"

"You guys," said Kleopatra. "Your dad just texted me and asked how our day went. I don't think he's heard about the museum."

My stomach lurched. "Maybe you should call and tell him. He might take the news better if it comes from you."

"Me? No way, kiddo. He'll kill me."

"Nah, he won't kill you. He might fire you, though."

"That's even worse!"

"How's that worse?"

"I don't know—but it is. This is all your fault, Maddie."

"How's it *my* fault?"

She yanked the wheel. We swerved across traffic, hopped a curb, drove across the medium, and merged onto Highway 62—just barely missing the yellow and black impact barrels.

BEEEEEP! BEEP—BEEEEEP!

I glanced over my shoulder and spotted an angry driver honking as his sedan was driven off the road and into the grass. Geez, Kleopatra drove like a madwoman.

"Can you drop us off here?" I asked, not wanting to die in a car crash. "We'll call a cab and meet you at home."

"Not happening, kiddo. You skipped school *and* blew up your father's museum—all on the same day. The least you can do is tell me what happened."

"Where should I begin?" I asked. "With the strange package sent to the museum? Or the scary bomb inside? Maybe I could start with trying to flush the bomb down a toilet with a squishy turd."

My brothers chuckled.

Kleopatra scowled. "That's gross. Who is dumb enough to try something like that?"

"Me, apparently," I said.

"Sounds pretty unbelievable if you ask me. Why would someone want to blow up a museum?"

"I don't know—somebody must *really* hate history."

"Unless," Jason said, drawing our attention. "The bomb wasn't meant for the building."

"What'd you mean?" I asked.

"What if the bomb was meant for Dad?"

Wait, that was a good question—and one I hadn't considered due to all of the craziness over the past few hours. Jason was right. The package had been sent *to* Dad. Somebody had tried to *kill* him. I got a sinking feeling in the pit of my stomach.

Our lives were about to get a lot more dangerous.

Chapter 7

THE NEXT DAY, I WAS determined to prove my innocence so I did something that under normal circumstances you'd have to pay me a million dollars to do.

I got up before sunrise.

Hey, don't judge me. I realize it's not an amazing accomplishment or anything, but for someone who loves sleeping past noon, it was quite a feat.

I opened bleary eyes as my cell phone's alarm buzzed. Pale moonlight streamed through my bedroom window. The musty smell of dirty clothes filled the room. I glanced over at my hamper. Blue jeans, tank tops, T-shirts, and, ahem, my unmentionables overflowed the rim. Crap, in the chaos of yesterday I'd forgotten it was my turn to do laundry.

My cell phone kept chirping. I reached over and silenced the phone. It looked like I'd gotten a few texts in the middle of the night.

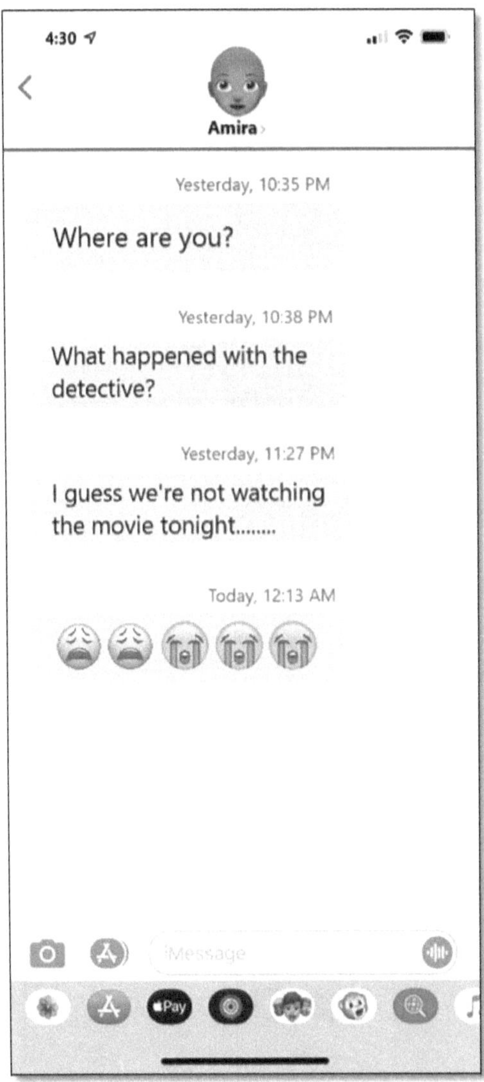

Double crap. I'd forgotten about my date with Amira to watch Harry Potter movies and gorge on junk food. I typed out a quick text. *Whoosh*, my phone sounded as I hit the send button.

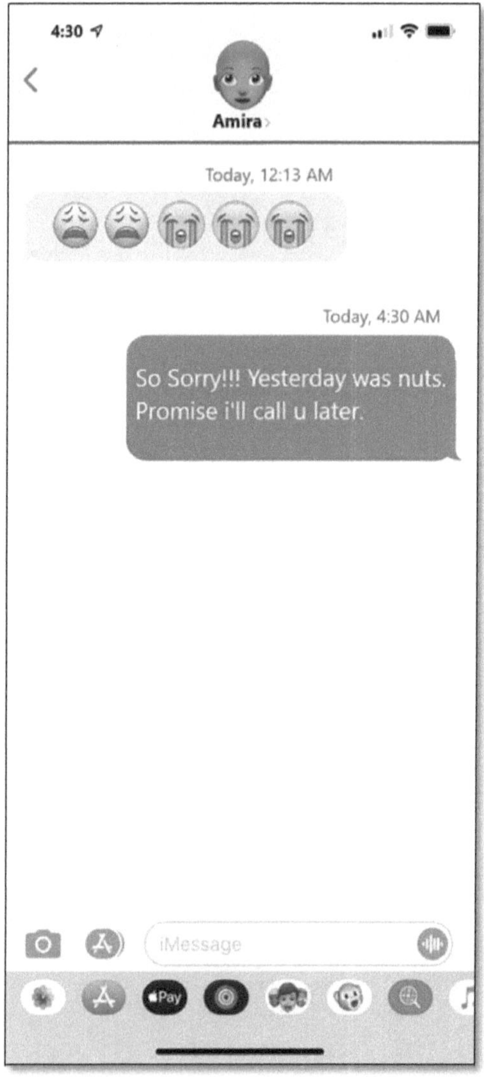

Groggy, I sat up and rubbed my eyes. Before going to sleep, I researched Evansville's bus routes and discovered that we had a stop just outside of our neighborhood. The bus station's itinerary said the earliest stop was at 5:00 AM.

According to my phone's clock, that was thirty minutes from now.

Time to get moving, Maddie.

I threw back my Walt Disney *Tangled* blanket. It had a painting of Rapunzel's tower and a picture of the main character with long, golden hair. A pretty childish blanket for a teenager, but the movie was my absolute fave.

Again, don't judge me.

I crawled out of bed and lumbered down the hall to the bathroom, the hardwood floor cold against my bare feet. After brushing my teeth and gargling mouthwash, I slicked back my brown and mint green hair with gel to manage the bedhead. Then I dressed in blue jeans with rips in the knees, a white tank top with a graphic of Bigfoot and a caption reading HIDE AND SEEK WORLD CHAMPION, Converse tennis shoes, and a leather jacket with zippers up and down the sleeves. I completed the outfit with a studded nose ring, hoop earrings shaped like emerald stars (to match the mint green highlights in my hair), and my all-time favorite necklace—a mini-compass tied to a black cord.

The compass necklace was my most prized piece of jewelry. Mom had given it to Dad before she passed away, but I owned it now. Dad told me I reminded him so much of her that I should wear it from now on.

So I did, every day.

Downstairs, I pressed my ear against the guest bedroom door and listened. Inside, I heard the most un-lady-like snoring coming from Kleopatra.

"Squonnk-sheeeooo!"

"Squo-ha-ha-honk, she-hee-hee-ooo!"

Geez, my babysitter might be pretty, but she certainly didn't sleep pretty.

Convinced she wouldn't catch me sneaking out, I grabbed a pack of strawberry Pop-Tarts from the kitchen pantry, took a swig of orange juice from the container, then tip-toed outside onto the front porch.

Zac was in the yard wearing a red tracksuit and sneakers. He stopped mid-stretch to gawk at me. "Have I gone insane?" he asked. "Is Maddie Jones seriously out of bed before sunrise?"

I halted in my tracks. "What the heck are you doing out here?" I whispered, afraid we might wake Kleopatra.

He popped his neck left and right while bouncing spritely on his toes. "I'm training for a track meet. Figured I'd warm up with a light run before breakfast."

"I always knew you were a psychopath," I said. "Nobody in their right mind gets up early to exercise."

"Erm, I'm pretty sure healthy people do."

I rolled my eyes.

The front door suddenly opened. Jason walked out. He wore long sleeve pajamas and was yawning.

"You've got to be kidding," I grumbled. "Can I not sneak out of the house without the two of you catching me?"

"Not when you gargle mouthwash like a spitting desert camel," said Jason.

"Oh, shut up."

"Where are you going, anyways?"

"Into the city," I said.

"Why?"

I groaned. The bus would arrive in less than ten minutes. I didn't have time for this nonsense. I glanced up at the sky. The stars were still out. Cool morning air felt damp against my skin. The whole point of getting up early was so I could visit the museum to look for remnants of the bomb. It might be the only way to clear my name before Detective Murphy arrested me for the explosion.

But my brothers threatened to ruin all of that. Did they not realize I might end up back in juvie?

"Look," I said, trying hard to keep the edge out of my voice. "I'm going to the museum to try and clear my name. Maybe if I'm lucky, I'll also find out who sent Dad that bomb."

The boys both flinched at the word *bomb*. They knew how dangerous things could get if Dad was in trouble again. We'd learned that lesson the hard way last year after a business tycoon kidnapped him for his expertise in all things antiquities.

I didn't wait for my brothers to respond. I stormed down the porch's steps and marched across the yard. Wet grass clung to my Converse tennis shoes.

"Maddie, wait—"

I stopped at the edge of the driveway.

"Do you need help?" asked Zac.

I whirled around to face him. "What about your *light run before breakfast?*"

"*Pssh,*" he scoffed. "I can win today's race in my sleep."

"What about you?" I glared at Jason. "Do you wanna help?"

Jason blinked. He seemed hesitant. "Kleo," he began.

"Isn't family," I said. "This doesn't involve her."

"Yeah, but—"

I turned around to march toward the bus stop.

"Okay, I'm coming," Jason blurted out.

I stopped. Before turning around, I stifled a smile. Secretly, I had hoped my brothers would want to tag along. With their help, we could search more museum rubble and increase our odds of finding bomb remnants. Plus, if we found it early enough, we could still make it in time for school—which would keep Kleopatra off our backs.

Win, win, for all of us.

"Grab your things, knuckleheads," I said. "The bus leaves in a few minutes."

Chapter 8

THE SUN WAS RISING WHEN we arrived at the Evansville History Museum. Its warm glow slanted through the clouds, casting ruddy hues across the museum rubble. City traffic bustled as taxis, sedans, and limos sped through the streets. A few early morning pedestrians walked the sidewalks. They carried battered briefcases, held Starbucks coffee, or stared at their cell phones as they traveled to work.

Nobody seemed to even notice the destroyed museum.

Part of me hated them for it. I mean, come on, this place had been a staple of the community since before I was born. Why didn't anybody care that the museum was now in ruins?

But part of me was also thankful they weren't paying attention. It would be much easier to sneak beneath the yellow police tape marking the area as a crime scene without people watching.

I ducked beneath the police tape and marched up the stairs leading to the demolished museum entrance. Huge slabs of busted stone debris blocked the way forward. Seeing the rubble made me realize how lucky I was to be alive. If I had been a couple of seconds slower . . .

"Where was the package when the bomb went off?" asked Jason as he scanned the destruction. His glasses were askew on his nose.

"Girl's bathroom, third floor," I said.

"Maddie exploded a bomb in the bathroom?" said Zac, chuckling. "Talk about explosive diarrhea."

Jason giggled. "Yeah, Maddie dropped a deuce and it exploded."

"Will you both shut up?" I said.

"C'mon, that was funny."

"You guys are dorks."

I hoisted myself onto a slab of busted stone. After the boys stopped laughing at their stupid poop jokes, they followed me up the rubble. The broken concrete slabs were shifty and unstable. One misplaced step and we might snap an ankle or cause a rubble avalanche. None of us spoke as we focused on our footing. I hopped from a block of marble to a charred wooden beam—and it rolled beneath my feet. I fell forward and stumbled to my hands and knees.

Jason hopped closer and helped me up. "Are you okay?"

I brushed bits of pebbles and charred wood from my palms. "Yeah, thanks."

We hiked through the rubble for ten more minutes. Finally, we reached a spot where I thought the third-floor girl's bathroom might have been. The only clue we were in the right location was a shard of black and white tile—the same color of tile found in the third-floor bathrooms. I scanned the surrounding debris, then I closed my eyes and tried to envision what the administration hallway looked like. In my memory, I could see the stairwell, elevators, Dad's office, the fire alarm near the drinking fountain, and the restrooms. I opened my eyes and looked around at the rubble. This had to be the spot.

"Now what?" asked Zac.

"What else?" I said. "We dig."

Over the next hour, we busied ourselves uncovering debris. We moved marble light enough to pick up, and countless pieces of charred wood. The strong scent of wood smoke filled my nostrils. Ash and soot blackened my hands.

"Hey, I found something?"

I dropped a heavy stone and glanced up at Jason. He was bent over a beam of blackened, burnt wood. I climbed over to him, sweat dripping down my brow despite the cool morning air. My lower back felt sore from crouching and lifting. Beneath the beam Jason leaned over, a metallic object gleamed in the sun. I knelt to inspect the object, which was covered mostly in soot except for a small section that reflected the sunlight.

"Does it look like part of the bomb?" asked Jason.

"I can't tell," I said.

"Can you remove it?"

I grasped the metal object and tugged—but it wouldn't come free. It was pinned beneath the rubble. "Zac!" I called. "Come help us with this."

Together, the three of us lifted the blackened beam and rolled it off of the object. The beam thudded down onto a slab of busted concrete and twisted metal. We knelt to inspect the object. I pulled it from the ashes.

It was an iron box. Heavy, weighing around ten pounds.

I blew on its lid, and ash and dust rose like little clouds of smoke, then rained down like flecks of snow. The lid had an ornate design on its surface—a grand oak tree embossed on brushed metal. The tree's bony branches wrapped around the box's sides and bottom. A thin seam ran between the box's lid and the container itself.

"Please tell me this is part of the bomb," said Jason.

"It's not," I said.

"Fetch," he swore. "I'm not digging anymore. This sucks!"

I turned the box over in my hands. "We must be closer to Dad's office than the bathrooms."

"What makes you say that?" asked Zac.

"I saw this box on his desk yesterday."

"What is it?"

"It's a piece of crap relic, that's what," said Jason. "Probably one of Dad's dumb pet projects to try and save the museum."

"Whoa, hold up," I said. "What do you mean: *save the museum?*"

Jason cleared his throat. He averted his gaze from mine. "Nothing. Forget I said anything."

"Like hell, I will. What'd you know that we don't? What're you hiding?"

Jason shook his head.

"Because if you don't tell me, I'm going to beat the living crap out of—"

"We're gonna lose the museum," Jason said, tears now swelling in his eyes. His emotional reaction punched me in the stomach like a heavyweight fighter. He meant it, every word.

Chapter 9

"WHADDYA MEAN WE'RE gonna lose the museum?"

"Dad's trip to New Mexico," Jason explained, wiping his cheeks dry with the sleeve of his shirt. "He traveled to an auction hoping to buy a relic that might be famous enough to bring in visitors. The museum's numbers are down. It's not making money. Dad tried to get government funding to keep the place open, but they denied his request. I overheard him on the phone right before his trip."

"The museum is gonna close?" said Zac, his voice higher than usual. Tears blurred his bright, blue eyes. "Where will people go to learn about history?"

Jason shrugged. "People don't care about history anymore, Zac. They're too distracted with cell phones, Netflix, and video games. Museums are becoming a relic of the past."

I slumped onto a slab of concrete. This was a lot to take in. The museum was more than a place where my father worked. It was our home. Dad had taken Mom here on their very first date. He proposed to her one year later in the museum's planetarium. I'd learned to walk in the dinosaur exhibit. Heck, every day after school my brothers and I would do our homework in the food court, then sneak off to play hide and seek throughout the museum's expansive rooms. If we lost this place, it would be like losing a member of our family. Not to mention we'd likely lose our real home if Dad's income was cut.

"What about insurance money?" I said, trying to brainstorm a solution. "Maybe the payout will be large enough to repair damages *and* save the museum."

Jason shook his head. "It's highly unlikely. Plus, I doubt an insurance company will want to give money to a failing business."

"We're going to lose everything?" asked Zac, and now the tears blurring his eyes streaked down his cheeks.

I bit my lip to keep from crying myself. My brothers needed me to be strong right now. Shedding tears would show them I was worried. Don't get me wrong, I was flipping out on the inside, but there wasn't anything we could do about this situation right now.

"Let's get to school," I said with a heavy sigh. "We can talk about this later."

The boys both wiped away tears, and nodded. Then we clambered down the rubble and back onto the sidewalk. A few minutes later, we stood at the bus stop waiting for it to arrive.

"What's in the box?" asked Zac.

I wiped away soot from the iron box with the hem of my Bigfoot shirt. "I honestly haven't thought about it," I said. "Not after hearing Jason's depressing news."

"Well, open it. Let's see what's inside."

I sat down on a nearby bench and tried to pry open the box. My fingers scrabbled along its edges, scraping at the lid, but no matter how hard I pulled I couldn't get the box opened.

"You're such a wimp." Zac snatched the box from my hands and strained to open it. "Nggghhh!"

"Give it up before you accidentally fart," I said, taking the box back.

"We're screwed," he said. "If I can't open it, nobody can."

"Whatever. You're not Captain America, you know?"

"Maybe not the Captain, but I'm definitely as strong as the Incredible Hulk. How old do you think that box is, anyways?"

"Hundreds of years old," said Jason.

"How'd you know?"

"Because we just pulled the box from a museum of frigging history. Everything in that place is hundreds of years old."

"Oh, har-har."

Movement across the street caught my attention. A hooded figure emerged from an alleyway. He wore a green cloak that stretched to his ankles. A bow and quiver of arrows were strapped to his back.

What the fetch?!

The guy looked like he'd just time-traveled straight out of medieval times. His strange attire reminded me of a woodland archer from one of Jason's nerdy role-playing video games.

Pedestrians flowed past him, not seeming to notice his presence, and he was staring right at me. My breath caught in my throat. Something about the cloaked man promised danger. The way he stood seemed predatory, like a black panther crouching amongst the brush, stalking its prey.

I started to warn my brothers, but the city bus came to a stop right in front of me, blocking my view.

"Maddie—let's go!" shouted Jason.

I rushed to the bus and boarded. Then I quickly found a seat and pressed my face against the glass to find the cloaked figure—but he was gone.

Who the heck was that guy?

Chapter 10

SCHOOL WAS BORING.

Teachers droned on and on about math, science, English, and junk. The only class I halfway enjoyed was history—and only because Mr. Weaver was teaching about ancient Chinese dynasties. I guess my time fighting the mummy of China's first emperor alongside an army of terracotta warriors last year made the subject somewhat bearable.

In between classes, I slipped away to the girl's bathroom where nobody would bother me, and hid in a stall. I sat on a closed toilet seat and removed the iron box from my backpack, then I attempt to open it.

Every effort was a waste of time.

No matter what I tried, I couldn't get the box opened. But I did learn something interesting about the box. Each branch on the box's sculpted tree pressed in like a button, twisted, or slid into a different position.

Maybe it's a puzzle box, I thought. *One of those boxes that can only be opened if you solve a riddle.*

The toilet in the stall next to me flushed. I gathered my things and cleaned up at the sink. In the mirror, I noticed I still had soot on my face. I splashed some water on my cheeks, wiped a smudge off my neck, then I tied my brown and mint green hair into a ponytail and rushed off to gym class.

As usual, Coach Sinclair tortured students by making them run a mile, climb the rock wall, and do thirty pushups—all within one hour. Unlike my brother Zac, who exercised every day, I only ran if scary things chased me—like bears, clowns, or school mascots. Thankfully, Coach Sinclair didn't see me fudging most of the exercises by only putting in half effort.

After it felt like I'd served a life sentence in prison, the last bell of the school day rang. I joined the throng of students pushing toward the front of campus and found my brothers in the car pick-up line.

They were whispering.

"Why are you guys being secretive?" I asked.

Jason stopped talking. He glanced around at nearby students to make sure no one was listening. "We're discussing the iron box. Zac says one of the decorative tree branches *moved* when he tried opening it this morning."

"He's right," I confirmed. "The branches appear to be buttons or switches of some kind. I think it's a puzzle box."

"That's wicked cool. When we get home, let's try and open it again. After we do our homework, of course."

I scoffed. "Whatever, nerd. I'm opening the box."

"I see Kleo," said Zac.

I scanned the line of cars for Kleopatra's convertible Mustang. The sports car's top was down. Kleopatra's sun visor was also down, and she used its tiny mirror to reapply mascara.

I groaned.

Another thing I found annoying about Kleopatra was how she constantly tried to appear pretty. She even suggested that I needed to wear *more* makeup. The nerve!

"Do you want a boyfriend, Maddie?" she had asked.

"No, I mean yes. Look, I don't care about stuff like that."

"Whatever, kiddo. I'm just saying, you'd look pretty if you wore some lipstick every once in a while."

"I am pretty!"

Dad told me almost daily I reminded him of my beautiful mom. Even so, I didn't care for dresses and all of that girly stuff. The small amount of makeup I did wear sometimes felt like it was too much. Maybe if Mom were still around I'd feel less tomboyish and more like a lady. But the truth was: I was raised by a single father and constantly surrounded by my two younger brothers. Our house had enough testosterone to make lumberjacks look like sissies.

" 'Ey, you guys," Kleopatra called from her car, which was now parked beside us in the pick-up line. She stared into the rearview mirror, adjusting her pink hijab and batting her newly painted eyes. "I don't have all day, you know. Your dad called and he wants me to take pictures of the damaged museum—for insurance purposes or something."

Eek, Dad now knew about the explosion? I wondered how he reacted when he heard the news.

We piled into the convertible Mustang with the boys in the backseat, and myself in the front. Kleopatra started to pull forward, but she slammed on the brakes and my seatbelt wrung my neck.

"Ack!" I choked. "What's wrong?"

"My nails," she said, glancing at them on the steering wheel. "They've gotten dirty."

"Seriously," I complained. "You're an archaeologist for crying out loud!"

"Not by choice, kiddo."

I blinked. An archaeologist who hated dirt and didn't choose the profession? Interesting.

We started moving again. Kleopatra drove her Mustang from the car pick-up line into the traffic leaving school.

But not before I saw Detective Murphy.

The detective stood in the middle of an intersection beside a uniformed police officer who directed traffic. She smiled and waved as we drove by, a simple gesture to let me know she'd been keeping tabs on me throughout the day.

"Piece of crap—" I sighed under my breath, disgruntled that I was being watched by the cops like this. I glanced into my passenger-side mirror and watched as the detective got on her police radio and started speaking. I could just imagine her calling reinforcements to tail me to my next destination.

Dang it, why'd Detective Murphy have to be so dedicated to her job?

Chapter 11

NO SURPRISE, KLEOPATRA DROVE like a maniac. She did sixty in a forty-five, jumped curbs, and drifted around corners like she fled from a bank robbery. All the while, Egyptian rock music blared from the speakers.

"Whaddya guys think?" she shouted over the music, banging her head in time to the beat. Speakers rattled with static each time the bass thumped. "The band is called Bad Apple and they seriously rock!"

I thought the band wasn't all that bad, even with Arabian lyrics I couldn't understand. But the music was so loud it felt like my ears might bleed.

"Can you turn it down?" I yelled.

"What?" Kleopatra punched the gas as a traffic light turned yellow. We didn't make it. The light turned red and we barreled through the intersection.

"Can you turn the music down?!"

"Oh." She turned the volume down a few notches. Not loud enough to make your ears bleed, but still loud enough to bust an eardrum.

"I like them," said Jason, leaning forward from the back seat so Kleopatra could hear him over the music. Wind whipping through the convertible also added to the noise. "Have you seen them in concert?"

Kleopatra took her eyes off the road to smile at Jason. And she didn't look back. "Oh, my God—I have. Lemme tell you about it!"

"Erm, Kleo," I said, spotting a stop sign fast approaching.

"I saw them in concert last summer, and their lead singer is so frigging cool."

"Kleo—the sign—"

"He looked right at me standing in the front row, and as he sang Evolution Incarnate, we made eye contact. Like, we totally had a moment. You know what I'm saying?"

"Arggghh!" I screamed as we ran the stop sign, causing cars to slam on brakes and swerve to avoid a collision, their horns blaring.

Kleopatra returned her focus to the road, completely unaware of the chaos left in her wake.

"That was *awesome!*" hooted Zac.

My stomach felt queasy all of a sudden. "Oh, man, I think I'm going to be sick."

Jason kept talking as though we hadn't just died. "Maybe we can go see the band together sometime."

"That would be a lot of fun," said Kleopatra.

"Then it's a d-date."

I scoffed. Jason was blushing. Wait a minute, he didn't even flinch as Kleopatra ran that last stop sign. What the fetch? Was my weirdo brother crushing on our babysitter? Was he attempting to *flirt*?

"I see what's going on here," I said to him.

"What?"

"You—like—her—" I mouthed.

"No, I don't."

"I'm gonna tell."

"Don't you dare!"

"Hey, Kleo," I reached over and turned the music's volume down a little more. "Jason has something he wants to tell you."

Kleopatra adjusted her rearview mirror so she could see him in the reflection. "Oh, yeah? What's up, kiddo?"

Jason glared daggers at me.

"He can pirate music." I winked at him as his face dawned with the realization that I wasn't about to spill the beans on his bizarre feelings.

"Is that true?" Kleopatra asked.

Jason cleared his throat. "Erm—y-yeah."

"Including Bad Apple, even their uncensored album?"

"S-sure, anything you want."

"Wicked," she said. "Now *that* sounds like a date." Kleopatra turned up the rock music's volume and banged her head. I must say, watching a beautiful Muslim woman in a stylish hijab rock out like she was a hardcore punk rocker was a strange sight.

I glanced at Jason. His face had turned red. I stuck my tongue out at him.

EERRRRRRKKKKKK! Kleopatra slammed on the brakes and the Mustang skidded to a stop. My seatbelt locked as my entire momentum thrust forward. My heart pounded in my pants—because I was pretty sure I'd just pooped myself.

"What happened?! Why'd we stop?" I asked, short of breath.

"The light turned red," Kleopatra said. "What, did you think I'd run it?"

"Traffic lights haven't stopped you before."

I glanced around. We were stopped at the intersection of First and W. Illinois Street. The Mustang idled like a cheetah's throaty purr. A beautifully constructed red brick building with arched windows, a tower, and white trim loomed across the intersection on the corner.

The historic Willard Library.

I'd never checked out books from the place, but it was a great resource for Dad whenever he worked on boring history reports or needed information about recently discovered artifacts.

Wait a minute . . .

The iron box we found was an artifact. The library might be a perfect place to learn more about the puzzle box.

"Erm—I need to get out here." I popped open my door.

"Huh? Hey, wait—" said Kleopatra.

"Sorry, Kleo," I said. "But I have a history project due tomorrow, and I need to visit *that* library." I pointed.

She glanced across the street at the historic building.

"*Pshh*," Jason scoffed. "Since when have you ever visited a library?"

"Since when has she ever done homework?" chuckled Zac.

I gave them a threatening look. "My *project*," I said through gritted teeth, "is on the history of puzzle boxes."

"The history of puzzle boxes," Kleopatra repeated. "Is that even a thing?"

I looked at Jason for help.

"Erm—yes—" he stammered, finally catching on. "Yes, it is. And Maddie's grade depends on it. Didn't you say you'll fail the class if you don't finish the project?"

"Big fat F," I lied.

Kleopatra arched a heavily manicured eyebrow. "I don't know . . ."

"Look," I said, as the light turned green and the cars behind us started honking. "We'll just be an hour. We can meet you at the museum when we're finished." My brothers climbed out of the backseat. Kleopatra protested, but now she had a line of angry drivers yelling at her to go.

"Hey, I'm talking here!" She flicked an obscene hand gesture that needs no introduction. Then she looked at me. "One hour, Maddie. I mean it."

"Kleo—you're the best!"

She punched the gas and the Mustang's engine growled as its rear tires peeled out, leaving skid marks on the road.

Jason shook his head. "I'm one hundred percent confident Kleo doesn't have a valid driver's license."

"I know, isn't it great?" said Zac.

Chapter 12

ONE OF THE COOLEST THINGS I'd ever heard about the Willard Library was that the place was haunted. Our town's local ghost story began when a Lady in Gray was caught roaming an aisle of books on a webcam a few years ago. The grainy video footage even went viral with national news networks reporting on the story and YouTube views reaching the millions.

Heck, every Halloween since the ghost sighting began, our town held a Lady in Gray festival. The Willard Library redecorated and became a haunted house. Trick-or-treaters paid money to tour its rooms while a madman chased them around with a chainsaw. The last scare of the night was always a Lady in Gray who jumped out from behind a bookshelf to scare the bejesus out of people. I must admit, the event is a lot of fun.

And guess what the best part is?

Nobody has ever figured out that *I* am the Lady in Gray. Even my brothers didn't know the ghost had been me. Not to brag or anything, but the Willard Library prank was my best one to date.

I'm really frigging good.

We now sat in a dark corner of the library with half a dozen books on puzzle boxes propped up on the table.

Jason clacked away on his laptop's keyboard while I leaned back in my chair and admired a framed picture hanging on the wall of myself dressed as a ghostly woman in a tattered cloak. My face was blurry in the picture, partly because it was a still image taken by a library security camera, but also because I had worn a mask. A bronze plaque beneath the frame read: LADY IN GRAY.

"Did you know a ghost once sat in this very chair?" I asked. This was partially true since I was the ghost. In the picture, I wore nasty bedsheets shredded to look like an old garment.

"Ghosts aren't real," said Jason. He shoved a book into my chest. "Now stop loafing and help me figure out how to open the iron box. And you—" he directed his frustration at Zac, whose head was propped on his arms as he snoozed with drool pooling beneath him. "Wake up!"

"Geez, what's gotten into you?" I asked.

"What's gotten into me? Look at this mess. We've got six books and countless web pages detailing how to open puzzle boxes. And what're you guys doing? Talking about ghosts and sleeping on the table. Hey, wake up—" he tossed a book at Zac. It thumped him in the head.

"Huh? Wh—" Zac stammered, rubbing his forehead where the book struck him.

"*Read!*"

"*Sshhh,*" said a librarian pushing a cart of books.

Jason blanched. "Sorry, Mrs. Harriett."

"Wow, you know the librarians here by name?" I said. "You really are a dork."

"Shut up."

Zac frowned. "This is boring."

"Well, if you help we can be done in less than an hour," said Jason.

"Wait a minute," I said. "That's why you're so uptight. You want to see Kleo again because you *like* her."

"No, I don't. We promised we wouldn't take long."

"Whatever, lover boy. I know the truth."

Jason rolled his eyes. He resumed typing, this time smacking the keys in frustration.

I glared at the stack of library books. Homework sucks, and researching puzzle boxes certainly felt like homework. Despite my teasing, I really did want to know what was hidden inside the iron box, so I cracked open the book Jason had shoved into my chest.

"What am I looking for?" I asked in a bored tone.

"Anything on puzzle boxes with decorations that move," he answered.

I sighed, then got to work.

Over the next half hour, I combed through pages of text in search of anything that might help us open the iron box. Since the box's sculpted tree branches pressed in like buttons, I figured there must be others like it, but most of the information I read was pretty basic.

Except for one book I found.

The cover showed a picture of an intricate wooden box with a maze design carved onto its opened lid. The title of the book was in golden letters: UNLOCKING RIDDLES. I scanned the table of contents, and I found a chapter that sounded promising. I thumbed to the page.

CHAPTER 5: PUZZLE BOXES
& THEIR TREASURES

Puzzle boxes originated in Japan, but many cultures throughout history have used them. They can be opened through a series of complex moves. Some boxes only require one or two moves, while more complicated boxes can require up to one hundred. Regardless of how many moves are required, the mechanics are typically the same: sliding, lifting, and pressing the box's decorative designs until a hidden compartment is opened.

"Hey, I think I found something." I set the book down on the table, then rummaged in my backpack until I found the iron box. I fidgeted with the box's tree branches by pressing, lifting, and sliding them into different positions.

Jason glanced up from his laptop. "What?"

I explained what I'd just read.

He nodded and hooked a thumb at his computer. "I read a similar article. It said some puzzle boxes can only be unlocked if you press buttons in the right sequence."

"Whaddya mean?"

"I think we have to move the box's branches in a particular order."

Zac groaned. I glanced at him and—nope, he hadn't groaned. He was snoring. Oh, brother!

Jason shook his head. "Let's start at the bottom of the

tree and work our way up."

"Why at the bottom?"

"Theoretically, those branches would've been first to grow."

"First to grow. First to move. Gotcha," I said.

Together, we fiddled with the box's decorative tree branches by lifting, sliding, pressing, and pushing branches into different positions. After a few minutes of fumbling with the box, we still hadn't opened it, but we didn't give up. We continued to move tree branches until the unexpected happened—one of the branches *clicked* and locked into place. We could no longer move it.

Jason and I looked at each other and smiled.

Then we turned our attention back to the iron box and worked to manipulate the tree branches, now with more gusto than before. We pressed twigs. Slid limbs. Lifted stems. Occasionally, one of the branches *clicked* and locked, so we moved to a new section of the box to explore. Anticipation made my fingers tremble. Excitement made my heart flutter. A final stem with a tuft of leaves was the only remaining branch that could move . . .

It clicked into place and the iron box shook, vibrating in our hands.

"Whoa!" said Jason.

Grinding gears sounded from inside the box and a compartment popped open. A wrought-iron key tumbled out.

Chapter 13

THE KEY WAS COVERED IN orange-red rust and appeared extremely old. It weighed at least a pound and its length was the size of my hand. The handle was shaped like a lion's head with a king's crown worn on its mane.

I handed the key to Jason, then I glanced inside the iron box and discovered that the key wasn't the only treasure. Folded, yellowing parchments were tucked deep inside. I pulled them out. They felt thin, soft, and brittle. As I unfolded them, I feared they might tear apart in my hands.

Wow, the parchments were ancient letters. The script was flowing, loopy, and looked like cursive. Dang—I couldn't read cursive. I never learned, but Jason was such a nerd, maybe he could read the letters.

"Does this look like English to you?" I asked.

He took the letters from me. "Amazing," he gasped. "These papers and this key are living history, Maddie."

"Yeah, yeah, but can you read them?"

His eyes roamed over the top letter. "Yeah," he said. "I learned how to read and write cursive for extra credit in elementary school."

"How are we related? You're such an overachiever."

Jason shrugged. "What can I say? I like being smart."

"Well, right now I'm thankful for it. What'd the letters

say?"

He read the first page. "They appear to be written in Old English," he explained. "And they're addressed to a king."

"A king, no way?"

"Yeah—look here," he showed me the parchment. "King Richard the Lionheart." We both stared at the lion-head key that had tumbled out of the box.

"Okay, read the letter," I prompted. I suddenly felt excited like we'd discovered a secret treasure.

Jason cleared his throat and read aloud:

> *King Richard the Lionheart,*
>
> *I regret to inform you that your dear friend, Robert of Loxley, died of treachery a fortnight past. Suffering from illness, I half-carried him to his Aunt the Prioress of Kirklees, scarcely knowing it was a trap.*
>
> *The Prioress, as it became clear but only too late, was the mistress of Sir Roger of Doncaster, a longstanding enemy of Robert's. Under the pretense of bloodletting to alleviate his ills, the Prioress cut one of Robert's veins and left him to slowly bleed out and die.*

"Whoa, this letter is talking about murder," I interrupted.

Jason nodded. "It seems that way."

"Who was Robert of Loxley?"

"Beats me, but the name sounds familiar."

"Look it up."

Jason turned to his laptop and pulled up Google. He typed *Robert of Loxley* and hit enter. Images of Robin Hood appeared onscreen. Some showed Robin Hood shooting a bow and arrow. Others were of a green-cloaked archer surrounded by a band of merry men. One of the images looked like a modern-day Robin Hood, stylish and threatening with a bow and quiver of arrows slung over a shoulder. The image reminded me of the cloaked figure I saw this morning at the bus stop.

"Holy crap!" I said.

"*Sshhh,*" the librarian quieted.

I snapped my gaze onto the elderly woman, prepared to say something smart, but she glared at me like a WWE wrestler ready to power-slam my skinny butt. I gulped and turned my attention back to Jason.

I lowered my voice to a whisper. "These letters are talking about the murder of Robin Hood."

"That's not possible," said Jason. "Robin Hood wasn't real. He was a fictional character like James Bond or Sherlock Holmes."

"But these letters . . ." I pointed at our discovery.

He waved my comment away. "Robin Hood was a legend, Maddie. Plain and simple."

"But Dad says legends are often based on facts."

Jason shook his head.

"What if Robert of Loxley was the *real* name of Robin Hood?" I asked. "It would mean he wasn't a fictional character. Look, let's not argue about this right now. I want to hear more."

"All right, all right." Jason took a deep breath, then continued reading:

> *Aware that he would soon die, Robert requested I write Your Grace regarding his final will and testament. His vast wealth, amassed from his time in the Holy Lands of Jerusalem during the Crusades, will be buried with him at a site designated holy.*
>
> *In a show of unrelenting loyalty to the Crown, Robert left Your Grace a key that will grant access to his tomb and the treasures locked inside. Robert assured me that this was the right thing to do for the good and true King of England. I seek your wisdom so will be traveling posthaste. Please look for my return.*
>
> *Yours forever in the Year of our Lord, 1196.*
>
> *John Little*

Jason looked up from the parchment, a surprised expression across his face. "This letter was written by Little John."

"Oh, my gosh, Jason. Do you realize how crazy this is?"

Let me pause and rewind for those of you who have never seen a Robin Hood movie or read a story about him.

Robin Hood was a noble thief who robbed the rich and gave to the poor. John Little, AKA Little John, was Robin's most faithful companion—and he was a man considered a giant despite his *little* name. How would I know? Well, my dad is a huge fan of Kevin Costner, an actor who played Robin Hood in the nineties. Needless to say, I've seen the movie a dozen times.

I sat back in disbelief. "The famed Robin Hood was killed by his aunt."

"No, he wasn't," said Jason.

"What a dysfunctional family."

"He wasn't a real person."

"What do the rest of the letters say?"

Jason thumbed through the remaining pages and skimmed over their texts. "Pretty much the same thing," he said. "They each allude to Robert of Loxley's murder, his grave, and a vast treasure hidden inside of his tomb. Wait—there's something else."

I sat bolt upright. "What?"

"There's a drawing—a sketch—and a poem is written beneath it." He handed me the drawing.

I looked down at the delicate parchment. The sketch depicted a grand oak tree with a man and woman carved into its trunk. They were kissing or getting married—it was hard to tell. A graveyard was located beside the tree. One of the tombstones read RIP. A lonely church sat on a hill in the background. In the foreground, an arrow was sticking out of the grass. There was more going on in the drawing—too much to describe—so let me just show it to you.

Finally, the poem read:

In the canopy of a tree, seek the way.
For the treasure you seek, lies deep in a grave.

In the land of Kirklees, you shall find a tomb.
Empty and barren, except for a clue.

There the first step, is where the arrow flies.
Dig where it lands, and you shall be wise.

"Do you realize what this is?" I said, my voice barely containing my excitement. "It's a treasure map!"

"*Sshhh!*"

"Oh, shush yourself!" I snapped.

"Out!" the librarian yelled, dropping a book she was about to stack onto a shelf. The book banged against the floor and echoed loudly throughout the library, along with her voice.

"Geez," I cringed. "I thought there was no yelling in the library."

"Out—GET OUT!"

We quickly gathered our things. Jason apologized to Mrs. Harriett as we walked past her, promising he would never bring his siblings to the library ever again. Meanwhile, Zac rubbed bleary eyes, not sure why we were being kicked out to begin with.

"Man, what's her problem?" he mumbled sleepily.

Chapter 14

OUTSIDE, THE SUN HAD NEARLY set and the last of its rays cast the city into shades of blood-red. It gave me an eerie feeling as we walked the streets toward the Evansville History Museum. I felt like we were being watched, maybe followed.

I glanced behind me, but all I saw was a patrol car parked across the street. The cop was on the corner buying a pretzel from a food vendor. He wasn't paying attention to us, so I didn't know if he was just hungry, or if he was slacking on the job when he should've been tailing me for Detective Murphy.

"Let's go this way," I said, and I cut down an alleyway to get out of the cop's line of sight.

"But this is the long way," Zac groaned.

The alleyway was dirty and darkened in shadow. Dumpsters overflowed with trash. A feral cat lapped a puddle of water, but she skirted up a fire escape ladder as we walked by. I glanced back the way we came. I didn't see the cop. Even so, paranoia told me we were still being watched.

It's just your jittery nerves, I told myself, trying to shake the feeling away. *You found a treasure map and now you're feeling suspicious. That's all.*

"It's gotta be fake," Jason said. "There's no way Robin

Hood was real."

I stepped around a pile of garbage. "The letters called him Robert," I argued. "They never called him Robin Hood. As far as we know, the guy could've been a real person."

"What're you talking about?" asked Zac, still oblivious to our discovery since he slept through it.

"We were able to open the iron box," Jason explained.

"And we found a treasure map inside," I said, smiling.

"Wow, that's awesome," said Zac.

Jason smacked his forehead. "C'mon, Maddie. Be reasonable. It's not a treasure map."

"Then how'd you explain the key with a lion-head handle? Or the old letters describing Robert's grave and how it's loaded with cash? Or the bit talking about his murder?"

"Murder?" said Zac.

"Yeah, Robin Hood died a bloody death."

"No, he didn't," Jason said. "He died of bloodletting. It was an ancient medical practice perfected by the Egyptians. Doctors would put leeches all over your body to cleanse you of bad blood. It's how George Washington died."

"Are you finished with the boring history lesson?" I asked. "Because we're talking about how Robert of Loxley might've been Robin Hood."

"Oh, I love that movie," said Zac.

"Me, too. It's one of the few movies Dad watches I actually enjoy."

Jason groaned. "Robert is not the same as Robin," he pointed out.

"Well, maybe it was a nickname," I said, thinking hard. "Maybe it's what people called him because he was, like, always *robin* from the hood—as in stealing from the neighborhood." I chuckled at my corny joke.

Jason didn't laugh.

Man, I thought my nickname theory was pretty good. "Look," I said, taking my phone out of my back pocket and swiping left to unlock its camera. "I'm not giving this up so stop arguing with me. If you want to be useful, then help me do one of those Google image search thingies."

"Image search thingies?"

"You know what I mean." I dug the letters out of my backpack and rifled through them until I found the one with the drawing and poem. I snapped a picture of it. "How do I search Google for images that are similar to—"

A cloaked figure suddenly plummeted from the sky and landed right in front of us. I jumped back, startled. It was the archer I saw this morning at the bus stop. He was crouched in a ninja stance with one hand planted against the ground. The other hand gripped a bow. He stood to his full height, and I was surprised to see that he was only an inch taller than me.

A green hood covered his head, cloaking his face in shadow. A mask covered his mouth and nose. The only features I could make out were his dark, ebony eyes. His gaze darted to the Robin Hood letters in my hand, and before I could kick my brain into gear, he snatched them lightning-fast.

"Hey!" I shouted. "Those are mine!"

The archer tucked the letters into his cloak and ran.

"Whoa!" breathed Zac. The awe in his voice made it sound like the archer was the coolest thing he'd ever seen.

"What the fetch?!" Jason stammered.

But I knew what was going on. "He stole the treasure map!" I yelled. "After him!"

Chapter 15

FAST DOESN'T BEGIN TO DESCRIBE how quickly the archer ran. Lightning might've been a better word. He flew down the dark alleyway and hurtled a chain-link fence, his green cloak billowing out behind him.

I took after him like a pent-up racehorse. We'd only just discovered those letters and I wasn't about to let them go. I certainly wasn't about to let a stranger with weird fashion taste steal them from us. I jumped the chain-link fence and landed on the other side. My brothers crashed into the fence and began climbing just as I resumed sprinting after the archer.

Good, I thought. *The three of us should be able to catch this guy.*

But I tripped over my stupid foot and went sprawling.

A jarring buzz of pain shot through my chin as it ricocheted off the ground. Zac whizzed past me and I scrambled to my feet. I tasted blood in my mouth, but I charged forward, my arms pumping, my legs protesting under the sudden strain.

We bolted down the alleyway. Zac ran so fast he nearly caught the archer, but the cloaked figure cut right and bounded down a new alleyway—and my brother crashed into a metal trash can. Garbage sprayed into the air and he tumbled to the ground. I ran past my brother covered in banana peels and spaghetti noodles.

Gross!

I turned the corner and glanced ahead. The archer was already half a football field away. I panted and wheezed as I ran after him. A sharp pang pinched my side. Curious where Jason was, I glanced back to see him running a few paces behind me—wheezing like me. In the distance, Zac climbed out of the pile of garbage, picking gunk from his curly hair. I returned my attention to the archer, and I witnessed him do something insanely impressive.

He shot an arrow at the rooftops.

Hey, I know what you're thinking: Whoop-de-frigging-doo, Maddie Jones. Why's that such a big deal? Well, there was a rope attached to the end of his arrow as it soared through the air. The arrow *clunked* into the brick wall of a three-story apartment building and stuck. The archer slung his bow across his shoulder—

—and he leapt up the side of the building while shimmying up the rope. He reached the rooftop and swung over the ledge.

I slammed into the building's brick wall and lunged for the rope, but the archer pulled it up before I could grab it. He glanced down at us in the alleyway and gave us a mock salute. The jerk was taunting us! He turned and bolted out of sight.

"We're losing him!" I shouted, panic filling my voice. "Our letters are getting away!"

Jason finally caught up and I tossed him my backpack, which held the iron box and lion-head key. Then I darted to a chain-link fence blocking street access to the back of the apartment building, and I began to climb. Beyond the fence, cars zipped past as they drove down a busy street.

"What're you doing?" panted Jason.

"I'm not letting that archer get away!"

I landed on the other side of the fence. I ran to the end of the alley and emerged onto the sidewalk near the street. As soon as I exited the confined space of the alleyway, the sounds of honking cars and distant sirens filled my ears. I glanced up at the rooftops to get my bearings on where the archer might've gone—and I saw him jumping from building to building and soaring over alleyways as he sprinted to escape.

Insane! The archer was like a real-life version of an Assassin's Creed video game character.

I ran down the sidewalk and sprinted in the direction the archer traveled. My lungs screamed for air, but I didn't let up. Not even when the archer leapt from one rooftop to another right over my head and I had to cut across four lanes of busy traffic. Cars honked and a taxi slammed on its brakes. I bumped into the taxi's hood and rolled across it, but I landed on the other side and kept on running.

Ow, that's going to leave a bruise.

How much longer could I keep up with this guy? Leaping from rooftop to rooftop, he didn't have to deal with obstacles like people, food vendors, parked cars, or moving traffic. Not to mention the fruit stand I just barreled through. Apples and oranges flew everywhere.

"Hey, what's your problem lady?!" an angry food vendor yelled.

"Sorry," I said, but I didn't stop running.

My phone rang. For the briefest moment, I thought the archer was calling to say: "Stop chasing me!" Then I remembered he didn't have my phone number, so I grabbed my phone from my back pocket and glanced at the screen.

It was Amira Raja.

She wanted to FaceTime. Part of me didn't want to answer in the middle of a chase, but I also didn't want to leave her hanging for the second time in a row, so I answered the call.

"Hello?"

"Maddie?" said Amira. My screen showed her sitting in a hospital bed with pillows fluffed behind her back. Her expression appeared worried. "Are you okay? You didn't call me back. After the museum explosion I thought—"

"I'm fine—" I cut her off, sprinting through an intersection as the archer leapt to a new building. "I'm sorry about missing the movie last night."

"No worries, I'm just thankful you're alive." She paused. "Are you exercising? Your screen is bouncing around a lot."

"Running," I panted. "I'm chasing an archer who stole Robin Hood's letters."

"Erm, okay . . ." she said slowly.

"I'm not making this up. Look—" I pointed my cell phone toward the archer as he leapt a wide gap between rooftops, his cloak fluttering and his knees tucked like a parkour ninja warrior.

"Whoa!" Amira said. "Is he the person who sent the bomb?"

"No idea, but I'm gonna catch him and find out."

The archer was running out of buildings to jump. Two blocks ahead, a walking park opened up with trails and soccer fields. He would have to come down. As we reached the last building overlooking the park, the archer leapt from the rooftop, spun in midair, and he threw a grappling hook. The grappling hook latched onto a chimney and its rope snapped tight. The archer repelled down three stories to the sidewalk. He started to retrieve his rope, but then he saw me charging straight at him.

"Dang, girl," he said, his young baritone voice slightly muffled behind his mask. "You lit as hell if you can keep up with me." Then he turned and sprinted into the street, leaving the grappling hook and rope behind.

"Stop!" I yelled, wheezing for air and pinching my side. "Gimme back my letters!"

A black SUV suddenly collided with the archer, striking him hard. He tumbled onto the SUV's hood and crunched into the windshield as its driver slammed on the brakes. The vehicle's rear tires locked, screeching loudly, and the archer went flying forward. He smacked the asphalt.

And he didn't get up.

"Holy crap, Amira," I breathed into my phone. "I think I just witnessed vehicular manslaughter."

Chapter 16

THE BLACK SUV'S DOORS opened.

Three women in dark suits and ties stepped out. They were young, possibly early twenties. One of them had dark skin with braided, black hair pulled back in a tight ponytail. The second was a curly redhead with a freckled complexion, and the third was blonde with hair cropped to her chin. Ponytail strode calmly toward the archer and knelt beside him. She touched his neck, presumably to check his vitals to see if he was still alive. Meanwhile, Blondie and Redhead stood guard and scanned the park, soccer fields, and buildings as if searching for threats.

I gulped. The women reminded me of Secret Service agents prepared to throw themselves in front of a bullet if necessary.

Pedestrians who had seen the accident rushed forward, but the agents intervened. "Nothing to see here, folks," said Redhead, as she and Blondie ushered people back. "Clear the way and let us do our jobs."

"Maddie—why'd you stop running?" Amira's tiny voice asked from my phone. "Did you catch the guy?"

"*Shhh.*" I slipped quietly behind some metallic trash cans to hide and watch events unfold. It stank of rotten meat and soured fruit. I breathed through my mouth to try and avoid the stink. Then I angled my phone's screen so Amira could see what I was seeing.

Ponytail looked up from the archer and nodded at the others, once.

Blondie opened the SUV's passenger door. A frail-looking, elderly woman stepped out. Her skin was wrinkled and leathery. Thin wisps of gray hair clung to her balding scalp. Her back was stooped like the Hunchback of Notre Dame. She wore a black leather duster with a star-shaped badge pinned to its breast.

A sheriff, I thought.

But she couldn't be. The woman was too old to be a police officer. Strapped to her arms were elbow crutches, which she used to hobble toward the unconscious (or maybe dead) archer.

"Who is that woman?" asked Amira. "She looks ancient."

Goosebumps crawled up my spine, making the hairs on my neck stand on end. Something about the old woman unsettled me, and I didn't know why. Maybe it was because she looked like a walking corpse.

The old woman reached the archer. She used the heel of her crutch to turn him over. "Remove his m-m-mask," she stuttered. Her voice was hoarse, but it still carried loud enough for me to hear.

The archer's hood and mask were ripped from his head. He was a black boy, probably fifteen or sixteen years old, and he was seriously good-looking. His hair was cropped close on the sides with mini-dreadlocks on top. He had a strong jawline, and when he blinked open his eyes, I saw a stylish gash across one of his eyebrows.

"Wow—model much?" said Amira.

"I know, right?" I said.

The old woman croaked: "Does he have the l-l-letters?"

Ponytail rummaged inside the archer's cloak. When she pulled out Robin Hood's letters, the black boy stirred. He swiped at the parchments, but missed. The old woman struck him in the head with her crutch and he passed out again.

"Leave the boy alone!" A muscled man in a tight T-shirt shoved past Redhead and rushed to help, but she removed a Glock pistol from her suit jacket and shot him in the back of the leg.

BANG! The gun went off.

The muscled man fell to the ground, screaming and clutching his leg.

"Stay back," Blondie said to onlookers in a calm tone, as if her companion didn't just shoot a guy in broad daylight. "Allow us to do our jobs and nobody else will get hurt."

Bystanders on both sides of the street shifted restlessly, but they kept their distance. A mother with a stroller ran away with her baby.

I ground my teeth. As much as I wanted to get Robin Hood's letters back, they meant nothing compared to people's lives. These women needed to be stopped before they killed someone, but what could I do?

Ponytail and Blondie dragged the unconscious archer toward the SUV's open door.

"Maddie, they're kidnapping him," said Amira.

What the fetch was going on? Who were these people? Part of me wanted to stay hidden behind the safety of my trash cans, but I couldn't sit aside while someone was being kidnapped. I felt its sting last year when my father had been taken by bad guys with guns.

I swiped my phone's screen to unlock its camera, while still keeping Amira on the line with FaceTime, then I jumped to my feet and revealed myself. "Hey, over here!" I shouted.

The agents and old woman turned to stare in my direction. I snapped a photo of them.

"Oh, good one," Amira said.

Redhead aimed her pistol at me and fired, fired, fired. I ducked behind the trash cans and covered my head. Bullets pinged against the metal cans. A few wild shots struck the brick wall behind me. I cowered and screamed, in shock that anyone would try to murder someone for taking a photo.

The gunfire ceased. In the distance, I heard the faint sounds of sirens, but they sounded several blocks away.

Thunk! Thunk! An unusual noise came from the direction of the SUV.

I stole a glance around my trash can—and I saw two arrows now sticking out of the SUV's rear tire. It deflated down to the rim. I whirled around to find the arrows' source, and I spotted a couple of archers standing on a nearby rooftop. They wore green cloaks with hoods. Masks covered their mouth and nose. They were also armed with bows and arrows. As I watched, they each nocked an arrow and fired.

The arrows struck the SUV's front tires, deflating them.

BANG! BANG! BANG! Blondie and Redhead fired their guns at the rooftop archers. Meanwhile, Ponytail shoved the black boy into the back seat of the SUV while the old woman climbed into the passenger side and slammed the door.

"Let's g-g-go!" the old woman stammered, yelling at the agents through the open driver's side door.

The agents piled into the SUV. They continued shooting from open windows while arrows thwacked into their vehicle's side. The SUV peeled out, its deflated tires thumping on rims as they sped down the street. I started to come out from my hiding spot, when a gang of Kawasaki Ninja motorcycles zoomed past, their bike engines screaming. I caught a glimpse of the riders. They wore green cloaks with hoods covering their heads. Bows were strapped to their backs.

What the fetch? More archers?

The SUV swerved around a corner. The motorcycles sped in pursuit. Overhead, the two rooftop archers ran in the same direction, jumping from building to building. They all disappeared from view, leaving me and the other bystanders standing around in a daze of confusion.

"Erm, Amira—" I said, my heart hammering in my throat from nearly being shot. "Please tell me you saw all of that."

"I did," she breathed.

"Oh, thank goodness," I said. "For a moment I thought I'd gone insane."

Chapter 17

"THE LETTERS WERE STOLEN," I told my brothers when I finally reached the Evansville History Museum half an hour later.

Nighttime had fallen. Neon signs lit up nearby bars and restaurants. Pedestrians walked the sidewalks, some heading home after a long day of work, others dressed up for a night on the town. None of them gave the destroyed museum a second glance. It was further confirmation the place wasn't making money.

"We know they were stolen," said Jason. He and Zac sat on a slab of busted concrete near the museum's entrance. Nearby, Kleopatra paced back and forth while she spoke on the phone. "We were with you when it happened."

I sat beside my brothers, zombie-like. My eyes were set in a faraway gaze. "Not by the archer. Somebody stole the letters from *him*."

"What?!" they said together.

I explained what happened, and how the archer was struck by a black SUV driven by an all-female version of the Secret Service, led by an old woman who looked like a walking corpse. I told them about the kidnapping and the shootout between the agents and a gang of archers who rode insanely fast motorcycles. My brothers couldn't believe it.

"That explains why we heard sirens a while ago," said Zac.

I nodded. "The place was crawling with cops when I left."

"What'd the old woman look like?" asked Jason.

I pulled my phone out of my back pocket and showed him the picture. "I think she was a sheriff or a retired sheriff," I said. "She had a badge of some kind."

"She looks like she's a hundred years old. No, older than that."

"Who do you think the archer was?" asked Zac.

"He must be an ex-soldier, probably a former Army Ranger or Navy Seal," said Jason. "Did you see how he ran up the side of that building? Training like that only comes from the military."

"He was just a kid," I said.

"What? No way!"

I shrugged, not bothering to share how handsome I thought the black boy had been. I still felt sick to my stomach that I hadn't been able to save him. The things he was able to do—like scaling a three-story building and leaping rooftops—were extremely impressive.

Too bad his training didn't involve looking both ways before crossing the road.

Kleopatra hung up her call. "You guys, I have some seriously bad news." She looked flustered. Her hijab wasn't perfect on her head. "Your dad just got off the phone with the insurance company—and they aren't going to pay for the museum's damages. Apparently, bombs aren't something their company covers."

"That's not fair," I protested.

"What about the artifact Dad traveled to New Mexico for?" asked Jason. "The one that might bring visitors back to the museum. If visitors return, we might earn enough money to save the place."

"I'm sorry, kiddo," Kleopatra said. "Your dad stopped bidding on the artifact the moment he heard about the explosion." She looked at the museum, her eyes scanning the rubble with a sad expression across her face, and sighed. "I hate to say it, guys, but the museum is going to close."

None of us spoke on the ride home.

Kleopatra didn't lower the top of her Mustang convertible, nor did she play her favorite rock band Bad Apple. She drove slowly and stopped at all the appropriate traffic signals. It was almost as though she were in a trance, mindlessly driving home while her mind raced with ideas of how we could save the museum.

At least, that's what was going on in my head.

How could we acquire enough money to pay for damages caused by the explosion, and keep the place afloat financially for years to come? How could we pay our family's bills if Dad was out of work? What would happen if we lost our home? Despite my attempts to avoid it, my thoughts kept going to one solution—one dangerous and absolutely nuts solution.

But we can't do that, I told myself. *It would be suicide to even try.*

Zac finally broke the quiet, his voice choked with

emotion. "What're we gonna to do?"

As much as it scared me, I thought I knew the answer .

. .

Chapter 18

"WE'RE GOING AFTER ROBIN HOOD'S treasure," I said.

It now neared midnight. My brothers and I were huddled around a flashlight in my bedroom. Beyond the light's edge, my room was darkened in shadow, but some things were visible. A nightstand with my compass necklace hanging from a lamp, a cluttered dresser with clothes sticking out of the drawers, and a table near the window where a tiny orange fish swam in an aquarium.

Neon lights illuminated the fish tank, changing different colors every few seconds. It cast an additional luminescent glow about the room. Wink, wink—it was the same fish I'd stolen from school last year during one of my pranks. Principal Watson still eyed me suspiciously anytime I walked past the front office's aquarium.

"That's why you woke us up?" Jason's hair was messy with bedhead. "Your grand plan to save the museum is Robin Hood's treasure?"

"Well, yeah," I said. "How else are we gonna come up with the money?"

Jason rose to leave.

"Wait—here me out."

He pinched the bridge of his nose. "Maddie, there isn't

secret money buried in a grave somewhere because Robin Hood wasn't real."

"But the letters, Jason. They're proof that he lived."

"Pssh," he scoffed. "That's not proof!"

I cringed at his loud voice. "Geez, keep your voice down before you wake up Kleo."

Zac yawned. "Is that why we're sitting in the dark with nothing but a flashlight? You don't have to worry about Kleo. She's downstairs in the guest room snoring like a grizzly bear in hibernation."

I got up and flicked on the lights. "Fine," I said, exasperated. "I don't have proof the treasure is real, but there are facts you guys haven't considered."

"Such as . . ." Jason said.

"Well, for one, who were those archers today? If the stories are true, then Robin Hood was one of the best archers of his time."

Jason put his hands up, conceding my point. "Okay, yeah, Robin Hood was an archer. And, yes, it's strange those archers showed up. But it was just a coincidence, Maddie."

"What about the Secret Service women?" I pressed on, determined to convince my brothers the treasure was real. "Why'd they show up and steal the letters? Why'd they shoot a guy in broad daylight and kidnap someone? I'll tell you why. Because the letters are *real* and they're willing to kill for them."

"They didn't kill anybody," said Jason.

"As far as we know," I pointed out.

Zac shuddered. "But they *did* shoot a guy. I'm kinda glad we don't have those letters anymore. Imagine what they'd do to us if we had something they wanted."

"I think you're forgetting something," I said.

"What?"

"We *do* have something they want. I just don't think they realize it yet."

My brothers blinked in confusion so I rummaged inside my backpack and pulled out the iron box. I opened it and removed the lion-head key. "When the agents read those letters, they'll realize they're missing *this key*."

Zac groaned. "Wait, does that mean they're gonna come after us now?"

His words lingered in the air. Searching for Robin Hood's treasure wouldn't be as simple as I made it out to be, not if other, more dangerous parties also sought the noble outlaw's buried riches. But if we could find Robin Hood's treasure before the agents or archers, then we might have enough money to pay for the museum's damages caused by the bomb.

The treasure could save our home.

"*We* have the key." I brandished the heavy lion-head key like it was the ticket to solving all of our problems. "Which means *we* have the advantage. If we can find the treasure before anybody else, we'll be rich. The museum will be saved."

My brothers didn't say anything.

"Look," I said. "You guys might not remember what life was like after Mom passed away, but I do—and the museum saved Dad's life! His work became a distraction from the grief. Imagine how depressed Dad will be if he loses the place now."

"Whoa, hold up," said Jason. "Just because Zac and I don't remember Mom as well as you doesn't mean we love her any less."

"I know. Sorry, I didn't mean it like that." I took a deep breath. "All I'm saying is . . . if we lose the museum, we might as well amputate Dad's legs. He'll be crippled without the place."

The boys exchanged looks. I knew my brothers well enough to read their expressions. Their eyes glimmered with understanding.

"She's right," Zac finally spoke. "The museum means everything to Dad."

"Yeah, but . . ." Jason began.

"I want to go after Robin Hood's treasure," I said. "I know it will be dangerous, but I can't do it alone."

Jason shook his head. "Maddie, I'm not convinced the treasure is real, or that Robin Hood was a real person, but when it comes to our family—" he sighed. "You can count on me."

I smiled, then I glanced at Zac.

He yawned. "I never needed convincing, sis. I'm with you."

"Great," I said. "Then let's get to work."

Chapter 19

WE GOT TO WORK RIGHT away.

If this were a movie, a music montage of Fall Out Boy's song "Immortals" would play in the background—just like in *Big Hero Six* when the heroes prepared for the final confrontation with the story's villain. Although we weren't crafting cool weapons or programming robots to fly, we did spend the next couple of hours researching everything we could about Robin Hood.

We searched the internet for information on Robert of Loxley, King Richard the Lionheart, and Little John. We analyzed the lion-head key and read a Wikipedia article about skeleton keys. We even studied the picture I'd taken on my phone of the drawing and poem. While the stolen letters had been interesting because they alluded to Robin Hood's murder, the drawing and poem seemed to be the most important clue. Each time I read the poem or stared at the image of a grand oak tree with a kissing couple carved into its trunk, the more I realized what it reminded me of.

"It's like a pirate's treasure map," I said.

"What?" asked Jason.

I pointed at my phone's screen. "The drawing must be a map and the poem must be its key."

"How?" asked Zac. "It doesn't look like a map to me."

"Listen to the poem's first verse: *In the canopy of a tree, seek the way.* I think it's saying to search the drawing, and to look at the oak tree's canopy for an answer."

Jason adjusted his black-rimmed glasses. "That kinda makes sense. Let's look at the drawing and see if anything unusual stands out."

We huddled around my phone's tiny screen and examined the drawing. We stared at the image from every possible angle. I zoomed in on the oak tree's canopy and searched the image for . . . something. But nothing stood out.

"We could try a Google image search," Zac suggested.

But the only results that popped up were maps of Great Britain.

"That's strange," Jason noted as he scrutinized the maps and compared them to the drawing.

I sat back with a sigh and raked fingers through my brown and mint green hair. "Man, I thought we were on to something."

"Aha!" Jason glanced up from the drawing. "We *are* on to something. Look!" He clicked on a map of Great Britain to enlarge the image, then showed it to us.

"Okay . . ." I said slowly. "I'm not following you."

"The canopy of the tree in the drawing," he explained, "forms the shape of Great Britain." He placed the Robin Hood drawing on its side, then he set it next to the map of Great Britain. Sure enough, the two images were a near-perfect match.

"Holy fetch," I said.

"I know. Crazy, right?"

"So lemme get this straight," said Zac. "The clue is saying to seek the way in Great Britain?"

"That's exactly what it's saying," I said.

"And it makes perfect sense," Jason added. "All of the Robin Hood stories took place in England."

"Do you believe he was a real person now?" I asked.

"No," he shook his head. "But I do admit this is pretty cool."

"Well, that's the end of our treasure hunt," Zac said.

"What? Why?" I asked.

"We can't travel to England. It's so far away."

I ruffled his curly hair. "Did you think the treasure would be buried here in Evansville?"

"No," he shoved my hand aside. "But how will we travel? It's not like we can stow away in a crate of mummies again. We're going to need . . ."

"An adult," Jason finished. "An adult who doesn't mind being our chaperone and is gullible enough to pay for plane tickets, food, and travel expenses. Somebody who owns a credit card and won't ask too many questions."

"Where will we find an adult like that?" asked Zac. "It's not like we can buy one on eBay."

From the hallway, reaching us all the way upstairs and through a closed door, we heard the nasally wheeze of Kleopatra snoring like a lumberjack sawing through wood.

"Kleo!" we said together. We rushed from my bedroom and sprinted downstairs, then stormed inside her room.

Chapter 20

YOU'D BE SURPRISED HOW difficult it can be to wake an Egyptian intern. Kleopatra was sprawled in her bed with a mask covering her eyes, the blanket knotted around her legs, and drool hanging from her bottom lip.

"Ew, gross," said Zac.

"Do you still think she's cute?" I asked Jason.

"Shut up," he said.

I nudged Kleopatra gently on the shoulder. "Hey, sleepy head," I whispered. She didn't move so I tapped her a little harder and raised my voice. "Rise and shine, Queen of the Nile."

"Squonnk-sheeeooo!"

I blew hair from my eyes and scanned the room. A stack of *Cosmopolitan* magazines sat on a nightstand beside the bed. The top magazine read: GIRLS JUST WANT TO HAVE FUN. Oh, brother. All right, time to get rough. I snatched it up and rolled it into a tube.

Then I whacked Kleopatra over the head with it.

"Maddie!" Jason protested. "Don't be a jack-hole."

But Kleopatra kept snoring. "Squo-ha-ha-honk, she-hee-hee-ooo!"

Zac chuckled. "Man, it's like she's dead or something."

I dropped the rolled magazine. "That's it, she leaves me

no choice." I stuck my finger in my mouth."

"Oh, no," said Zac. "Not a wet willy."

"Wep," I said, which was supposed to sound like *yep*, but it came out funny because I was drooling on my hand. I pulled a slobbery finger from my mouth, and as I leaned in close toward my babysitter's ear, spit dribbled from my finger onto her earlobe.

Kleopatra flinched.

I smirked.

Then, just as I was about to stick my finger in her ear and wriggle it around—

—Kleopatra sat bolt upright and lashed out.

SMACK! Her open palm slapped me on the side of my head. Stinging pain lanced through my temple and I fell from the bed and went sprawling to the floor. Jason and Zac laughed.

"Shut up," I groaned as I climbed to my feet.

"At least we know how to wake our babysitter now," said Zac. "Wet willies."

I rubbed the spot where Kleopatra struck me. "Yeah, and I'll never do it again. Fetch, that hurt."

Kleopatra removed her blindfold. She blinked, and I realized it was the first time I'd seen her without glitter mascara. "Kids?" she said groggily. "Is everything okay?"

"We need to talk," I said.

"What's wrong?" She glanced at the time. "It's almost five AM. Is it urgent?"

"Yes, kind of. Well, no, not really."

"Which is it, kiddo?"

Ugh, I hated it when she called me kiddo. It was almost

as bad as my father calling me baby girl, sweetie pie, or pooh giggles. "It's about the museum," I said, trying to make my voice pleasant. "The boys and I were talking and—"

Kleopatra yawned.

"—and we think we figured out how to save the place."

"Oh, yeah?"

"Yeah . . . but it won't be easy. We have a proposition for you. A new job offer—sort of. It pays more money than what you make now."

That got her attention. She yanked off her sleeping mask and scooted to the edge of the bed. Three things always worked with Kleopatra: Egyptian rock music, makeup, and money.

She stood up. Her satin nightgown was embroidered with pink flowers. Her black hair stretched to the small of her back in a healthy sheen, long and straight. She grabbed a hijab from the dresser and wrapped her hair, hiding it from view.

Jason cleared his throat. I glanced at him and caught him blushing. None of us had seen Kleopatra's hair before, and I don't think we were supposed to. I felt embarrassed all of a sudden.

Kleopatra folded her arms and looked down at me. "Okay. What's your proposition?"

I'd never considered Kleopatra to be an intimidating person. But now that we needed her help, she seemed more intimidating than all of Dad's previous interns combined. "Erm—it's a trip," I said. "You'd be our chaperone."

Kleopatra frowned. "What kind of trip? And why isn't your dad asking me about this?"

"Because he doesn't know about it," Zac blurted out.

If I could smack my brother upside the head, I would. The boy needed to zip his mouth before he ruined the whole thing.

"If your dad doesn't know about it, then go to bed," Kleopatra said. "You're ruining my beauty rest."

Jason stepped forward. "He doesn't know about it because we want to surprise him."

Kleopatra's gaze narrowed.

I was worried Jason might freeze up under her glare, but he swallowed and kept going. "Dad is under a lot of stress," he said. "And since we know how to make the museum a lot of money, we thought it might be better if we leave him out of it. But there's a slight problem."

"What kind of problem?"

"It would require us to travel to England."

"*England?*" Kleopatra yelled.

I cringed. "M-my Aunt Heather lives there," I added to the story. "She works at Cambridge University and she's loaded." That last part, at least, was true. Our Aunt Heather *did* work at Cambridge University and she *did* earn a good living.

"Then call her and ask for a money transfer," Kleopatra said.

"We can't do that," Jason said. "We haven't seen her in a couple of years so it wouldn't look good if we called and asked for money."

"We already have passports," I said. "And we figured the trip will only take a few days. Usually, when we go to England we stop at a few extra places."

Kleopatra looked suspicious. "What places?"

I thought about the treasure map and poem, and how the second stanza alluded to a place called Kirklees. "Oh, you know, the touristy places. English castles, pubs, and we might even visit the place where Harry and Meghan got married."

Kleopatra's eyes widened. "Windsor Castle?! I just read an article about royal weddings in my latest *Cosmo*."

"Y-yeah," I chuckled nervously. "Wouldn't that be fun? Maybe you could visit Windsor Castle while we meet with Aunt Heather."

Kleopatra was cool and all, but the last thing we needed was for her to follow us around as we searched for Robin Hood's treasure.

"What about the money you mentioned?" Kleopatra asked. "You said the job pays a lot?"

"Oh, of course. Aunt Heather will cover your travel expenses no questions asked."

Kleopatra looked pleased with this.

"The only problem is paying for the trip," Jason said. "We don't have any money, but we know Aunt Heather will compensate you for whatever you dish out."

"Wait a minute," Kleopatra said. "You want *me* to pay for this trip?"

"You'll earn interest," I said. "Consider it an investment."

"And you're positive Aunt Heather is good for it?"

I crossed my heart and hoped to die. "Girl Scout's honor."

Zac snickered. "When were you in Girl Scouts?"

"I wasn't," I said. "But the point is—Aunt Heather will pay Kleo back and then some. Plus, think how thrilled Dad's gonna be when he learns that his intern saved the museum."

Kleopatra stared at me for a good, long minute. Then she picked up her cell phone and dialed.

"It's five in the morning," Jason said. "Who the heck are you calling?"

"Hello, Papa," Kleopatra said when a deep, muffled voice spoke on the other end. "How are things in Egypt?"

I tensed. Why was she calling her father? I had visions of her telling on us and of my dad bursting into the room to strangle me.

"Yeah, Papa, the desert sand does get into everything. Listen—I've got a new job for the museum."

She paused.

"Of course, it pays more money. But the job requires me to travel and I'll need to use the credit card. No, the museum will reimburse me for all of my expenses—plus interest!" Kleopatra picked up the nearest *Cosmopolitan* magazine and thumbed through its pages until she found an article on royal weddings. "How much? Erm . . . we're traveling to England so maybe a few thousand. Could be more."

The voice on the other end of the line started yelling. Kleopatra yanked the phone away from her ear. "Papa," she said. "The museum is under construction and it might not reopen for months. This new job will allow me to continue my internship. I could just use the credit card and—"

More yelling.

"Well, if you'd let me go to cosmetology school instead

of doing this stupid archaeology stuff—"

Her father's yelling blared like a foghorn signaling an approaching storm.

"Papa?!" Kleopatra said. "What'd you say? The connection is breaking up. I guess I'll have to call you later. Love you!"

She hung up.

"He's totally cool with it," she announced. "Let's go to England."

Part Two

GRAVE OF ROBIN HOOD

Chapter 21

"WHAT CAN I GET FOR YOU?" she asked.

I looked up at the flight attendant, feeling tired and bored. She and her drink cart had finally made it back to me and my brothers. Kleopatra sat across the aisle from us, her sleeping mask covering her eyes with a pillow fluffed behind her neck.

"I'll have a Dr. Pepper," I said.

"Oh, I'm sorry, I just gave out my last one. Something else?"

"How about a Sprite?"

Her eyes darted to the opened green cans on top of her cart. All empty.

I sighed. "What do you have?"

"Do you like Ginger Ale?"

Yuck, I thought. "Forget it, I'll take a cup of water."

She poured Dasani into a plastic cup and handed it over with a small bag of pretzels. After serving Ginger Ale to the boys, she wheeled the cart off. I popped a mini-pretzel into my mouth and tried to move my legs. No luck. With my tray table down they were wedged in from every angle. Plus, I was crammed into the middle seat between my brothers.

Yes, indeed. Sixteen hours of travel was horrible for your health. But I had to admit, this was far better than traveling in a crate of mummies like we did last year when we stowed away in a cargo plane headed for China.

This was our final leg to London. We'd already had one layover, napped in an airport, and flown on two planes. Traveling to a country across the Atlantic Ocean was exhausting.

Zac elbowed me in the ribs as he shifted in his seat.

"Ow," I said.

"Sorry, it's cramped in here."

The pilot spoke through the intercom: "Ladies and gentlemen, we are approximately one hour away from our destination. The weather today in London is cloudy with a slight chance of rain. Temperatures are in the mid-sixties. Should be smooth flying as we make our descent."

"Finally, almost there," said Zac. "I can't wait to get off this plane."

"You and me both," I said.

Jason set his plastic cup of ginger ale down on his tray table and grabbed a tourist map of England from a seat pocket. "Any idea where we're going after we land in London?" he asked as he opened the map. "England is an awfully big place."

"Kirklees," I said.

"Kirklees?" he repeated.

"It's in the poem," I said, which I had read so many times I'd memorized by now. I recited the verse, "In the land of Kirklees, you shall find a tomb. Empty and barren, except for a clue."

"So, what, we just walk around until we find something?" asked Zac.

I shook my head. "Kirklees is a small town north of London. The poem not only tells us the place, but also the destination—a tomb. We're searching for a cemetery."

"We're looking for a *graveyard?*"

"That makes sense," said Jason. "I wonder what we'll find there."

I touched the heavy lion-head key now dangling from my necklace. I had looped it through the same black cord my mini-compass was attached to. The combined weight of the compass and key resting against my chest gave me a sinking feeling in the pit of my stomach. Images of the dangerous shootout between the archers and agents filled my thoughts—arrows soaring all over the place and bullets whistling invisibly through the air.

"Either a clue that could make us rich," I said, "or get us killed."

Zac shuddered.

Jason pointed at the map. "Well, I've got some bad news. The only Kirklees I see on this map is Kirklees Hall, and it's in a village called Clifton."

"Why's that bad news?" I asked.

"The village is two hundred miles from the airport. It's at least a three-hour drive."

"*Three hours?*" I said a little louder than intended. I glanced at Kleopatra to make sure I hadn't woken her. Her mouth hung open with drool running down her chin. She sounded like a dying moose. "I was hoping to ditch Kleo in London," I whispered.

Jason shook his head. "Not advisable. We're going to need a rental car."

I groaned. Things were already getting complicated with Kleopatra. And the longer we kept our lie going, the harder it would be to make it believable.

"What about Aunt Heather?" asked Zac. "Don't you think Kleo will get suspicious if we don't meet up with her?"

When we had hastily planned this trip, I'd spoken with confidence that Aunt Heather would greet us with open arms. But I had yet to call her. What if she told Dad we were in England when we were supposed to be in Evansville? Not to mention we were skipping school just to go on this trip.

"I'll think of something," I said.

Chapter 22

I PRETENDED TO BE TALKING on the phone when Kleopatra came out of the rental car place. "We can't wait to see you, Aunt Heather," I said loudly. "Please save us some of your delicious pot roast. We haven't eaten a decent meal since Evansville." I paused for dramatic effect as Kleopatra joined us. "Oh, of course, I'll let her know. See you soon!"

I hung up.

Kleopatra raised purple glitter mascara eyes. "What will you let me know?" She twirled a new set of car keys on her finger.

"Well," I chuckled nervously, "Aunt Heather isn't in Cambridge this week. She wants to meet us in Clifton."

"Clifton?" Kleopatra said. "I've never heard of it."

"That's not surprising," said Jason. "It's a small village, usually avoided by most tourists."

"Does that mean we can't visit Windsor Castle today?"

"Not if we want to meet Aunt Heather for dinner," I said. "She's serving pot roast. Yum."

Kleopatra adjusted her purple hijab. "Whatever. Stay right here. I'll bring the car around." She left us standing there with the bags.

"I don't like lying to her," Zac said once Kleopatra was

out of earshot. "It feels wrong."

"I don't like it, either," I said. "But we need a ride to Kirklees, don't we? Let's keep the story going a little longer. Okay?"

My brothers didn't answer me.

"Okay?" I asked again.

They both grumbled in agreement.

"Good, now where's Kleo with the car?"

EERRRRRRKKKKKK! A car careened around the corner and into the parking lot. It accelerated right toward us. *Beep, beep, beep* its horn bleeped weakly. I took a step back, afraid the car wasn't going to stop, but right before it hit the curb, Kleopatra slammed on the brakes. The vehicle drifted into a parking spot right in front of us.

" 'Ey, you guys," Kleopatra greeted us through a rolled-down window. "What'd you think?"

I thought the car looked like a micro-machine. It was tiny and red with two doors and a British flag painted on its roof.

"They call it a Mini-Cooper," Kleopatra said.

"More like a Mini-Pooper," said Zac. "This thing is lame."

"I like it," Jason said. "I call—"

"Shotgun," I blurted out.

He gave me a disgruntled look.

"Hey, you know the rules. I get the front seat."

The boys squeezed into the cramped backseat. I sat in the roomy front. My legs stretched comfortably in front of me.

"Erm—Maddie," said Jason. "Can you please scoot

your chair forward? It's like a clown car back here."

"Nope," I said.

Hey, don't judge me. I said it with a smile.

"Buckle up, kiddos," Kleopatra said. She donned a pair of stylish mirrored sunglasses, then shifted the gearstick to drive. I was still in the process of buckling my seatbelt when she punched the gas. The Mini-Cooper jerked forward, and my heart lurched to my throat as we rocketed down the street.

I swallowed. Here goes another round of Kleopatra's suicidal driving—British style.

Chapter 23

MY FATHER DROVE THE SPEED limit wherever we traveled. He obeyed all traffic signals and made sure we arrived at our destinations safely. I always thought his slow-paced driving was super annoying.

Until I met Kleopatra.

Even in England, she drove like a maniac. She raced around corners, gunned the gas through intersections, and drove on the right when she was supposed to drive on the left.

"Whoa—whoa—slow down!" I yelled as Kleopatra sped through a loopy traffic circle called a roundabout. I braced my hands on the dash, but momentum slammed my body into the door and my cheek pressed into the cold glass.

"Sorry, you guys," Kleopatra said, accelerating faster as the road straightened out. "But I want to reach Clifton before sunset. Gotta see the sights, you know?"

I peeled my face from the window and stared ahead. We were on the M-1 Motorway heading into the countryside. I would've thought the scenery outside my window beautiful if I'd had enough time to enjoy it. Instead, cows and pastures and cute little cottages zipped past as Kleopatra sped like a Formula One racecar driver.

My nose ring felt crooked after having my face smashed

against the window. I lowered the sun visor so I could see my reflection in its tiny mirror. I adjusted the sparkling pink stud, raked fingers through my mussed brown and mint green hair, and was about to close the visor when I noticed something strange in the mirror.

A black SUV drove right behind us.

Hey, I get it, that's not unusual back home in the States. But here in England, the SUV stuck out among all the little British cars driving around. Its front windshield was tinted, so all I could see of the driver were hands on the steering wheel. Kleopatra swerved to the right. The black SUV did the same. She made a fast turn to the left. The SUV followed suit. A prickling sensation crept up my neck.

We were being followed.

I snapped the sun visor closed. "Hey, Kleo," I said. "I'm kind of bored. Got any music we can listen to?"

"Giiirrrl," she drawled. "I've got the best Egyptian rock you can imagine. Here, plug this in." She handed me a phone adapter. The Mini-Cooper had the latest tech gadgets, including a digital interface with USB ports. I plugged in her phone.

Rock music blared, loud and shrill in a language I couldn't understand. Kleopatra banged her head in time to the beat. I twisted in my seat and faced my brothers.

"Behind us," I mouthed. "Black SUV."

The boys stole glances, just as Kleopatra swerved around a blue sedan and the SUV accelerated to stay with us.

"Do you think it's the Secret Service women?" asked Zac.

"It's gotta be," I said.

Jason tensed. "How do we lose them?"

I sat forward and tried to think.

"Not bad, huh?" said Kleopatra. "They performed in Cairo once. Their bass player is so unbelievably gorgeous."

"Zac's gotta use the bathroom," I blurted out.

"What?" Kleopatra turned down the music. She adjusted her rearview mirror so she could see Zac in its reflection. "You gotta pee, kid?"

He shook his head.

"Number two, then?"

He nodded.

"Can you hold it? I wasn't planning to stop until we reached Clifton."

"I don't think he can," I said. "Weak bladder."

"Weak bladder?" Kleopatra repeated, eyeing Zac. "Is that even a thing? You're like, what, eight years old?"

"Eleven," Zac said.

"Old enough to hold it," she said.

"Nggghh," Zac grunted. "I'm about to fart."

"Kid, you fart in this car and I will seriously kick your—"

BRRRRT! Zac ripped a huge one. How could he do that on cue? So disgusting.

"Ah, man," Jason said, waving the stench of rotten eggs away.

"Please pull over," Zac said. "The next one might be the real thing."

"Ugh, gross." Kleopatra rolled down her window. Brisk winds blew into the car and wafted the smelly fart around the interior. "Okay, lemme find an exit."

Ahead, I saw an exit ramp approaching, but we were traveling too fast to make it. *Wait, that might work out perfectly,* I realized.

"Take that exit!" I yelled.

"Are you crazy, kiddo?" Kleopatra said. "We'll catch the next one."

BRRRRT!

"All right—fine!" Kleopatra yanked the wheel to the right and the Mini-Cooper careened across three lanes of traffic. Jason and Zac yelled. I held on tight to the dash. Right before we were about to slam into the safety impact barrels, we slipped onto the exit ramp.

Behind us, a deafening *crash* sounded. I whirled around in my seat—and saw water spraying violently as the black SUV slammed into the impact barrels. "Whoa," I breathed.

"Geez," Kleopatra whistled, adjusting her mirror so she could see the accident. "The Brits sure are crazy drivers, huh?"

Chapter 24

OUR FIRST STOP IN CLIFTON was a bathroom. After forcing farts Zac ended up *really* needing to go. Oh, brother! Afterward, we drove to our final destination—the Kirklees Hall estate.

It was a privately owned stone manor in the middle of eighteen acres of land. The entire place was gated with high brick walls. A guard stationed near the driveway paced back and forth in front of an iron gate. He gripped the butt of a rifle with its barrel resting on his shoulder.

Jason groaned. "I thought this place was a public park."

"Is there a problem, kiddo?" asked Kleopatra.

"Nope. No problem," I said, clearing my throat. We drove slowly past the driveway and guard. "Take a right at the stop sign up there."

Kleopatra turned at the stop sign. The brick wall guarding the estate continued onward as far as I could see, snaking its way with the road. I faced Jason, and said through gritted teeth, "Where is the graveyard?"

He shrugged. "How am I supposed to know? The map on the plane only showed a black dot with Kirklees Hall written beside it. The cemetery is probably on the other side of this wall."

"Are you serious?"

"Where do I park, guys?" Kleopatra asked. "I'm ready to meet this Aunt Heather of yours."

I noticed an oak tree. Its gnarled branches overhung the wall, perfect for climbing. "Pull over here," I said, motioning to the tree.

"Here? In the middle of nowhere? Kiddo—I was hoping to freshen up in a hotel room and maybe get a shower to wash off the plane ride."

"And we will," I said.

"Perhaps I should ask that guard where to park?"

"NO!" Jason and I said together, a little too forcefully.

Kleopatra eyed us suspiciously.

"Erm—we want to surprise Aunt Heather," I formed a lie quickly. "If we let the guard know, he'll phone up to the big house and the whole thing will be ruined." I pointed at the oak tree with its thick branches overhanging the brick wall. "But if you let us climb this tree and jump over the wall, we can show up at the manor unannounced. Aunt Heather will flip out."

"You want to *sneak* onto the property?" Kleopatra scoffed. "Sounds a little sketchy to me."

Jason cleared his throat. "You don't know Aunt Heather like we do. She loves surprises."

Kleopatra didn't say anything for a good, long minute. She stared past me at the oak tree and wall, biting the bottom of her lavender-painted lips. This was a make-or-break moment for our trip. If she said no, would our treasure hunt be stopped before it ever got started?

"All right," she said. "But make it quick. I'm tired of sitting in this car."

"Deal," I said.

I climbed out of the Mini-Cooper. The boys joined me. Outside, the air was damp and a light fog misted the ground. Gray clouds blanketed the sky. I strode toward the oak tree.

Jason jogged up beside me, glancing back nervously at Kleopatra sitting by herself in the car. "What are we doing, Maddie?" he asked.

"We're gonna hop over this wall so we can search for the cemetery."

"Yeah, but . . ."

"No buts, Jason. We don't have much time. You heard Kleo."

"Yeah, but the guard. He had a gun."

"He's probably just a rent-a-cop," I said.

"And if he's not?"

I touched the oak tree's rough bark and glanced up. The thick trunk spread out into twisted branches and a leafy canopy that overhung the brick wall. I hopped onto the lowest branch and began climbing.

"Just don't let him spot you," I said.

Chapter 25

I LANDED ON THE OTHER SIDE of the wall with a thud. Thick grass softened my fall. My brothers hit the ground beside me. There were bushes nearby. We crouched behind them and peered ahead.

A stone manor loomed a hundred yards in the distance. The mansion looked like a miniature castle. A driveway the length of a football field was lined with expensive cars: Mercedes, Ashton Martins, Ferraris, Hummers, you name it. Whoever owned this place was seriously loaded.

It looked like a gala was taking place. If you're an unsophisticated person like me and don't know what a gala is, think of it as an exquisite party for rich people. I only knew the word because my dad often attended galas for the museum.

A white limousine turned into the driveway as we watched. The expensive car parked in front of the mansion. A chauffeur exited the driver's side and rushed around the limo to open the door for a handsome couple dressed in a tux and glimmering dress. They were escorted inside the mansion, right past a trio of guards.

"Fetch," I swore.

The guards were armed with rifles and binoculars. What is more, half a dozen more guards patrolled the property, some watching the cars, others marching around the perimeter of the estate.

"I'm getting a drug lord kind of vibe here," said Zac.

"For reals," I said. "Let's just find the graveyard and get out of here."

"Can you see it from here?"

I peered past the mansion. Behind the building were gardens and fields of green grass. But there weren't any cemeteries as far as I could tell. "Man, I thought we'd see the graveyard as soon as we jumped the wall."

Jason stared at me like I was an idiot. "You're joking, right? Did you seriously think it would be that easy?"

"Yes, actually, I did."

He groaned. "Why do I have to be the responsible one?"

"Because you're good at it," I said, giving him two condescending thumbs-up and a fake smile.

He rolled his eyes, then pulled his cell phone from his pocket. He input his passcode and opened an app.

"What're you doing?"

"This property is huge," he said. "So I'm gonna check Kirklees on Google Earth. The app will let me scan the property from a bird's eye view."

"Ooh, smart thinking."

As he searched, I studied the guards' patrols. One of them was overweight with a big belly. I figured if push came to shove we could outrun him, but the other guards were all lean and fit. There was no way I could beat any of them in a race.

"Okay—" Jason showed us his phone and the Google

Earth image. He pointed to a building located on the opposite side of the mansion, then zoomed in so we could get a better view. All I could see of the building was its roof, but in its shadow, there was something that resembled a series of tombstones.

"Looks like we need to head here." He tapped his screen and the image zoomed out. Several acres of land was between the mansion and the cemetery.

I groaned. "Gee, that's not going to be difficult or anything. It's pretty far away."

"And we have these guards to worry about," Zac said.

I nodded.

"We came all this way, didn't we?" said Jason. "Might as well check it out."

"What about Kleo?" asked Zac.

"Kleo will have to wait," I said. "We're too close to Robin Hood's grave to turn back now."

"She's going to be mad."

"Not if we hurry," I said. "Let's just focus on the hard part." I turned my attention to the guards and the apparent drug lord gala taking place at the mansion. "How do we sneak past these guys?"

Chapter 26

WOULD DRUG LORD GUARDS shoot unarmed kids? Boy, I hoped not.

Whoa, Maddie, I thought. *Don't worry about getting shot. Worry about not getting caught.*

If we were going to sneak around the mansion and avoid the rent-a-cops, then I needed to utilize all of my skills. And what am I good at? Well, I'm not athletic or fast like Zac. I don't have brains like Jason.

But I'm pretty good at dodging authority.

Why do you think my pranks have been so successful all these years? It's because I don't get caught. Plus, a lot of my pranks have required me to sneak in and out of places undetected.

"Do you have a plan?" asked Jason.

"I'm thinking," I said.

My brothers often looked up to me in times of trouble. They knew I could be depended on to get us out of it. I studied the mansion and watched as another fancy couple was escorted inside. A valet parked their Rolls Royce. I noticed a copse of oak trees to the left of the mansion. Perhaps we could sneak through those trees. It looked shady enough. But getting there would be difficult with so many guards about.

"We need a distraction," I said.

"On it," said Zac. He reached underneath the bushes and picked up a rock the size of his fist.

"What're you doing? Hey, wait—"

Zac chucked the rock as far as he could. It sailed right over the fat guard's head, struck a yellow Ferrari's windshield, and busted the glass.

Weee-wooo! Weee-wooo! Weee-wooo! The car alarm blared.

Zac looked at me and smiled. "You're welcome."

"You idiot," I breathed. "I wasn't finished planning our mission."

"Oh," he said.

Geez, the kid never strategized. Only reacted. Now I had to figure out a new—

"Hey, it's working," said Jason.

I looked out toward the mansion. The guards were all rushing to inspect the Ferrari.

"If we're going to do something, now's the time."

"All right, let's move," I groaned.

We rushed from our hiding spot and dashed for the copse of trees. As we ran, I scanned the manor and driveway of cars. Guards were circling the Ferrari as they inspected its busted windshield. One of the mansion's side doors opened.

Another guard walked out.

But before he could look up to see us running, his walkie-talkie crackled with static. "Check the security cameras," a voice sounded from the walkie-talkie. "We found a rock."

The guard said, "Roger," and rushed back inside the mansion. The door slammed shut behind him.

Phew!

We reached the copse of trees. I ducked behind a thick trunk and stole a glance toward the driveway. The guards spread out as they searched for whoever threw the rock.

"There it is," panted Jason. His hands were on his knees as he inhaled large gulps of air. "That rundown building over there."

I glanced through the trees toward the building. It looked hundreds of years old with stone walls overgrown in moss. A single-story roof was covered in shingles pocked with wood rot. For all I knew, the building had been constructed during medieval times. The cemetery must've been on the other side of the ruined building because I couldn't see it from here.

"How far do you think it is?" I asked. There was nothing but gardens and a field of green grass between us and the building.

"Probably two football fields," said Zac. "We need to hurry."

"He's right," Jason said. "If they have security cameras they'll spot us in the footage."

"Do you think they'll see me throwing that rock?"

"Who cares?" I said. "Hopefully we'll be long gone by then."

I eased to the edge of the copse of trees and peeked out. There weren't any guards on the far side of the mansion. Now was our chance to make a run for it while the guards were distracted with their investigation. "You guys ready?"

My brothers were sweating and their expressions looked nervous, but they nodded.

"Last one to the graveyard has to lick the gum off my shoe," I said.

And, not waiting for *ready, set, go*, I burst from the copse of trees and raced for the rundown building.

Chapter 27

I RAN SO FAST IT FELT LIKE my feet moved 88 miles an hour and I would disappear in time like the DeLorean from Back to the Future.

Despite my speed, Zac bounded past me as if the scary clown Pennywise chased him with a red balloon. Meanwhile, Jason lagged behind us with his glasses fogging over from heavy, labored breaths. Perhaps he should've spent less time on computers and more time outdoors. But who was I to judge? The farther we ran the more it felt like I might pass out.

The rundown building was getting closer. We slowed down to hop a low, wooden fence then darted behind the building to hide from the mansion's view.

"Did they—see us—?" Jason wheezed, pinching his side.

I breathed in a large lungful of air, my side aching. "Dunno," I panted. "Lemme check—"

The rundown building was made of brown and gray stone. Moss crawled up its walls and thick vines reached from the grass to strangle the building. It must've been a medieval family's home a long time ago because its size reminded me of a single-room house people from the past used to live in.

I leaned against the building's wall, feeling rough moss between my fingers and inhaling a strong earthy aroma, and peered around the corner. Back at the mansion, guards were fanning out to search around the manor for signs of an intruder. None of them chased us, as far as I could tell.

"I think we're safe," I said. "For now."

"Guys—look—," said Zac. He didn't even sound winded. "I think we found it."

I whirled around.

A small cemetery loomed in the shade of an oak tree. Rows of worn tombstones had been erected in an area no wider than my backyard. Beyond the tombstones, just on the edge of the Kirklees estate, loomed a monument. The monument was an eerie sight—a mess of twisted railings and crumbling stonework rotting beneath the tree's canopy. The graves had all been left to wrack and ruin.

Inside the monument's walls, we found a cracked stone the size of a spare tire resting on a bed of dead leaves and moss. Just past the stone, a plaque read:

Here beneath this little stone,
lays Robert, Earl of Huntingdon.

Never was an archer so good as he,
and people called him Robin Hood.

Such outlaws as he and his men,
will England never see again.

"Holy crap, you guys," I said. "We found the grave of Robin Hood!"

Chapter 28

"THERE ARE ABOUT A THOUSAND places all around Britain believed to be the grave of Robin Hood," said Jason. "How do we know *this* grave is the one?"

I pulled my phone out of my back pocket and opened the picture of the Robin Hood sketch. "Because of the drawing and poem," I said. "It led us here."

In the land of Kirklees, you shall find a tomb,
Empty and barren, except for a clue.

We were at Kirklees. We'd found the tomb—a monument with low walls, a cracked stone, and a plaque. Now all we had to do was dig to find the clue.

There the first step, is where the arrow flies,
Dig where it lands, and you shall be wise.

I figured the *wise* part meant the clue. Simple enough. But I had no idea what the flying arrow and digging where it landed meant. Where was the arrow? Where should we dig if not inside the monument? I voiced my concerns to Jason and Zac.

"When we were on the plane," Jason said. "I researched

Kirklees and this grave."

"What'd you learn?" I asked.

"Robin Hood got sick," he explained, "and Little John brought him to Kirklees. At the time, this ruined building was a priory—kind of like a church. It was a place sick people would visit to get healing. But the prioress, the nun who ran the place, secretly hated Robin Hood for all of his thieving. Instead of healing him, she bled him to death."

"Bled him to death?" said Zac. "That's gross!"

"Not really," Jason said. "It was called bloodletting, and we talked about the medical practice already. Keep up." He took a deep breath. "Anyway, when Robin Hood realized he was about to die, he called for Little John by blowing three blasts on his hunting horn. Little John rushed to his aid, but he was too late. Robin was too far gone.

"Little John wanted to burn the priory to the ground and kill the nun, but Robin reminded him that their code was to never hurt women. He asked John to carry him to the window and to bring him his bow. Then he fired an arrow from the open window. He told Little John to bury him where the arrow landed."

My gaze darted to the drawing on my phone. There in the grass beneath the shade of the oak tree and kissing couple, was an arrow sticking out of the ground.

"Wait a minute," I said. "There's an arrow in the drawing. This really is like a pirate's treasure map. X marks the spot!"

I showed them the sketch. Then we all turned to stare at the monument and rundown priory building. A boarded-up window overlooked the cemetery. The grave of Robin Hood was about an arrow's flight from the window.

"Whoa," I said. "How cool is that?"

"I dunno," said Jason. "Something else I learned is that the Discovery Channel has a show called Expedition Unknown. Their host, Josh Gates, did an episode about Robin Hood. His team used ground penetrating radar on the grave inside the monument, and they discovered nothing is buried here."

"So it's a dead end?" I said. "But we came all this way."

Jason shrugged. "I guess we'll have to figure out where Robin Hood's arrow *really* landed."

"But it could've landed anywhere," Zac groaned. "This place is huge—and we don't have ground penetrating whatever you said."

Jason shook his head. "Look, I'm just sharing what I know. We'll need to conduct our own investigation to find the clue."

He marched closer to the ruined building and inspected the boarded-up window. "The position of the priory," he mumbled beneath his breath, "plus the velocity of the arrow and the arc of its flight. Consider Robin Hood's health at the time of firing the arrow, and you've got a range of about two hundred yards . . ." Jason paced away from the priory, counting as he went.

Oh, brother. Please don't tell me he was pretending to be an arrow.

"Seven. Eight. Nine."

Yep, that's exactly what he was doing. He walked farther and farther away, past the cemetery and beyond the oak tree. I didn't know the first thing about archery, but I was willing to bet arrows could fly pretty far if shot hard enough. Not only that, but the priory had windows on all sides. Who was to say Robin Hood didn't fire the arrow in a different direction?

I turned to stare at the grave inside the monument. Jason had said nothing was buried there, but why would a monument have been erected if the site wasn't important? Plus, the poem said the tomb was empty and barren, except for a clue. No wonder the host of Expedition Unknown didn't find anything. The grave was empty.

I stepped closer to the gravesite and set my hands on its low, rough wall. The stonework was probably hundreds of years old. The large, cracked stone inside of the monument rested on a bed of dead leaves and moss. It didn't appear to be a headstone—more like an honorary rock that must've been used to mark Robin Hood's grave. Save for the crack running through its center, the rock looked undisturbed. I glanced back at the rundown building. An arrow certainly could have landed here.

Figuring I had nothing to lose, I hopped over the stone wall and into the monument, landing on top of Robin Hood's supposed grave.

"What're you doing?" asked Zac.

"Searching this grave," I said. "There's gotta be something here."

"I'm telling you there's nothing there," Jason called from a distance.

I ignored him. "Come help me, Zac."

Zac hopped inside the monument with me. Together, we knelt and felt along the monument's rough walls for loose stones that might be hidden compartments. We scraped away dead leaves and moss and dug up dirt until we hit roots from the oak tree. We pressed each of the plaque's letters to see if one of them turned out to be a switch. But all of our attempts were a waste of time. There was nothing here.

Unless . . .

I turned my attention to the large, cracked stone. What if something was buried beneath it? I mean, why else would the stone be inside the monument if it wasn't important?

"Can you give me a hand with this?" I asked.

Zac and I crouched beside the rock. We dug fingers beneath its smooth edges and I felt moist dirt creep beneath my fingernails. We tried lifting the stone, but it was heavy. Even with my brother's athleticism, we struggled to flip the rock. My fingers scrabbled for purchase, trying to hoist it on one side.

"We've—all—most—got it—" I grunted.

The rock flipped over and landed with a hard *thump*. Earthworms wriggled in the dirt where the rock had been resting. And . . . holy crap, you're not going to believe this. A sentence had been etched into the underside of the stone.

Chapter 29

I STOOD AND SCANNED THE area for Jason. He was nowhere in sight. How far did he walk? Did he seriously think an arrow could fly that far? Deciding not to wait for him, I knelt beside the rock and brushed away soil from its underside. The sentence etched into the stone was faded and worn, but still legible.

In a churchyard where a little mountain lies,
Dig up his grave to uncover the lies.

"Ah, man, another grave?" Zac groaned. "What are we gonna have to do to find this treasure? Dig up a bunch of old people's bones?"

"Seems like it," I said.

Worried I might forget the new riddle's verses, I snapped a picture of it on my phone. Sunset crept across England as ruddy light darkened the cemetery in shades of pinkish red. My cell phone's light flashed and I glanced at the picture. The photograph wasn't the greatest, but I could still make out the words so it was good enough.

"Where's Jason?" asked Zac.

"No telling with that knucklehead," I said. "Let's find him and get out of here."

I set my hands on the monument's rough, stone wall to hop over—but my heart did a somersault. Jason stood near the old priory building.

He wasn't alone.

The fat guard held him hostage at gunpoint. His rifle was pointed at Jason's back.

"Hey, guys," Jason said sheepishly with his hands held high in the air. "I kind of got caught."

Chapter 30

HOW STUPID COULD YOU BE? Jason had probably been so immersed in his calculations that he'd forgotten we were on private property surrounded by guards with guns. My brother might be smart. But, wow, he lacked common sense.

"Hop out of that grave, girl," the fat guard wheezed in a British accent. "Show me your hands."

I realized two things at that moment. One, the guard was winded from catching Jason. And two, he hadn't seen Zac, since my brother was still crouched behind the monument's wall.

I did as instructed and slowly raised my hands into the air. I also made eye contact with Zac. *Pick up a rock*, I tried to tell him with my expression, my eyes darting back and forth between him and a rock on the ground. *Throw it at the guard.*

"You lied to me," the guard growled at Jason. "You said you were alone."

Jason lowered his hands slightly. "Look, bruh, we're just a couple of kids who wanted to see Robin Hood's grave. Let us go and we won't sneak in here again. Promise!"

The guard pointed his rifle at me. "You there," he wheezed. "Did you throw the rock that hit Mr. Hilton's car?"

I tensed. The gun made me nervous.

"It doesn't matter," he said. "The coppers will be here shortly. We'll get some answers."

He was lying. I was sure of it. "The cops aren't on their way," I said. "You wouldn't risk having your drug lord gala busted by the police."

"Drug lord gala?" he chuckled. "Kid, we're hosting a charity auction for children with Down syndrome."

"Wait," my shoulders slumped. "You're just guarding the manor and the artifacts on sale?"

He shrugged. "Yeah, what of it?"

"So the cops really are coming?"

"As we speak."

Fetch, this was bad. It appeared even in England I was going to end up with a criminal record. I glanced at Zac. His fist clenched around a rock the size of a golf ball.

"What are you looking at, girl?"

I tore my gaze away from Zac. "Nothing. Erm, nothing at all."

"Hop out of the grave," he demanded. "And no funny business—"

Zac suddenly reared up and threw the rock. It barreled through the air. The guard's squinty eyes widened—just as the rock smacked him square in the face.

"Arghh!" Blood squirted from his nose.

Jason turned and shoved the guard. The fat man tripped and fell on his butt.

BANG! The rifle fired into the air.

The gunshot startled me, but Jason ran past the Robin

Hood monument. "What are you waiting for?!" he shouted. "Run!"

Zac and I jumped over the monument's wall and ran after Jason.

"Hey!" the fat guard yelled. "Come back here!"

We didn't look back. We hopped over a squat wooden fence and tore across the grassy plain. In the distance, I could see the oak tree we climbed to sneak onto the property. It looked like its overhanging branches were low enough to climb back over.

"That was—close—" Jason panted as we ran.

"Too close," I agreed. "What the heck happened, Jason? Why'd you let him catch you like that?"

"I'm sorry—" he apologized. "He came out of nowhere to smoke a cigar."

"It's not the fat man we have to worry about." Zac lightly jogged beside us instead of racing ahead. "We need to worry about *them*."

I looked to where he motioned. Oh, no—guards were running from the mansion right toward us. And they were fast, sprinting at full speed with rifles gripped in their hands. Thankfully, none of them stopped to take aim and shoot.

We reached the oak tree before the guards did.

"Climb!" I yelled.

We scrambled up its gnarled and twisted branches. My brothers reached the top of the tree and hopped over the estate wall to the other side. I let go of a rough tree branch and braced a hand against the red brick wall—

BANG! A shot was fired. I flinched and stopped dead in my tracks, one foot on a branch, the other on top of the wall.

"Don't move," a guard said.

Holy crap, what kind of charity auction guards fired guns at kids? My heart thundered in my chest, but I forced myself to glance down at the guards. There were five of them. All breathing heavily from running so fast. All aiming their rifles right at me.

"Climb back down, slowly," the guard in front said, his knotted muscles too tight for his small uniform. His whole *look* gave off the impression of someone with a Superman complex.

I leaned my weight onto the wall, ready to jump over.

Superman pulled back the hammer of his rifle. "The next shot won't be a warning shot," he said, deadly serious.

"Meh," I said. "Your mamma's a warning shot." Then I leapt down from the wall, away from the guards, and raced for the Mini-Cooper with a British flag painted on its roof.

Chapter 31

"WHADDYA MEAN SHE WASN'T there?"

We now sat around in a hotel room. I lounged in one of the room's twin beds with pillows propped behind my back, idly fussing with the lion-head key around my neck. Jason and Zac were watching an older TV show called Game of Thrones—a big no-no in our house. Channels like HBO and Showtime were forbidden due to their "graphic content and questionable programming."

Dad's words, not mine.

Meanwhile, Kleopatra paced back and forth, furious that we hadn't met up with Aunt Heather yet. "Are you even listening to me, Maddie?"

I looked up from the lion-head key and stared into Kleopatra's eyes. They were painted two different colors. One was red, the other blue, both sparkling with glitter. After taking a shower, she'd spent an hour recording a makeup video for YouTube, saying it had been a couple of days since her last upload.

"It's like I said, she wasn't there," I told her. "I spoke to Aunt Heather on the phone and—"

"And she wants us to meet her in the morning at the local library," Kleopatra interrupted. "We've been through this already. But what I still don't understand is why she couldn't meet us this afternoon." She arched a sparkling, blue eye at me.

"Kleo," I said. "It's really hard to have a serious conversation with you when your eyes are painted like Bobo the Clown."

"I was showing my fans two different eye shadow colors."

"Well, you look weird."

She grabbed a cloth from her bag and started wiping the makeup from her eyes. "Explain something to me, Maddie," she said. "Why does your aunt want to meet at a library?"

"I dunno," I said. "Aunt Heather is a scholar. She's nerdy like Dad. Perhaps she wants to show us the history of this little town."

But the truth was, the boys and I wanted to research our latest clue. We'd found nothing on the internet while Kleopatra showered and filmed her YouTube video. The clue said to look for a churchyard where a little mountain lies, but no specific results popped up. As far as we could tell, there were numerous churches in the shades of mountains throughout the English countryside. A local library might help us narrow our search.

"Fine," Kleopatra said. She threw away her makeup wipe, then snatched up her cell phone from the top of the room's mini-fridge. "I'm gonna call my pops. You guys stay put." And she left the hotel room.

I sighed. As much as I hated it, we had to keep lying to Kleopatra . . . at least for a little while longer.

"Whoa!" said Zac.

"Oh, man, wicked!" said Jason.

I glanced at the TV. A dragon swooped down from the sky and breathed fire on an entire army of soldiers. Men in medieval outfits flailed and screamed as flames licked up their tunics. It was really violent. And the boys enjoyed every minute of it. Now I saw why Dad wouldn't let us watch the show.

I turned my attention to my phone. It had been almost forty-eight hours since I'd last heard from Amira. I typed out a quick text and hit send.

She didn't respond. I didn't know what time it was in Boston. Maybe she was asleep. I hoped her cancer treatments weren't making her sick again.

A little bored, I went back to idly fussing with the lion-head key. It was heavy, made of iron or some other metal from the time period it had been forged. The key was intricately carved. I could see every strand of hair in the lion's mane. The crown it wore included raised dots to represent jewels. The lion's head acted as the handle, so I gripped it and studied the key's teeth—the part that goes into the lock. The teeth were simple, just like any other skeleton key I'd seen. Upon closer inspection, though, I realized an engraving had been stamped into the metal.

Three worn letters: R.W.T.

Wait a minute, I'd seen these letters somewhere before. In the Robin Hood treasure map. I opened the picture app on my phone and zoomed in on the drawing of the man and woman carved into the oak tree.

Beside the man's foot, behind the woman's arched back, the letters R.W.T. were chiseled into the tree's trunk. Holy cow, the same letters in the drawing were also on the lion-head key. That seemed significant, but what did it mean?

"Another question to add to our ever-building mystery," I mumbled to myself.

Kleopatra suddenly burst into the hotel room. It made me jump. "You guys are *not* going to believe this," she said, slamming the door. "I just got a voicemail from Evansville PD, and your dad thinks I kidnapped you!"

Chapter 32

HOW THE TIDES HAD TURNED. One year ago, it had been me and my brothers who'd rescued Dad after he had been kidnapped. Now he thought his Egyptian intern had stolen his precious children.

Maybe we should've called him before flying to England. A courtesy heads-up, we're leaving the country, going to try and save the museum sort of thing. A little white lie could've gone a long way.

I'd even convinced Kleopatra to avoid his calls. She was still under the impression we were trying to surprise him with Aunt Heather's "generous museum donation." Man, things had gotten out of hand.

" 'Ey, you guys," Kleopatra said. "Did you hear me? Your dad thinks you've been *kidnapped!*"

I groaned. "Was it Detective Murphy?"

"What?" said Kleopatra.

"On the phone. The voicemail?"

"Yes, she sounded quite serious."

"She's a serious woman," I said. "What'd you tell her?"

"I haven't called her back *yet.* I'm still waiting on your big explanation of what's going on with your aunt. Because it's obvious you're not telling the truth, Maddie. You're a horrible liar."

"But I—I—"

"Aunt Heather doesn't know we're here," Jason said, turning off the TV. I gave him a murderous look.

Kleopatra glanced back and forth between the two of us, then her stern gaze settled on me. "Is this true, Maddie?"

Reluctant, I nodded.

She scoffed. "Oh, my God. So there's no money?"

"Well," I said slowly. "There's definitely money. It's just that the money is sort of, ah, locked up."

"Locked up?" she repeated.

Zac chuckled. "That's one way of putting it."

Kleopatra swore in rapid Arabic. She sat on the edge of my bed and fussed with her black hijab. I didn't know what to say, or what to do, so I scooted to the edge of the bed and sat beside her.

"Okay," Kleopatra looked up at the three of us. "Here's what we're going to do. You guys are gonna tell me everything. It's time to talk, kiddos. Starting with you, Maddie Jones."

Part of me didn't want to give up our secret so easily. If Kleopatra found out my crazy plan to save the museum involved finding treasure from the grave of Robin Hood, would she pack our bags and fly us home tonight? We'd just discovered the next clue. We couldn't turn back now.

"Well," Kleopatra demanded.

It appeared I had no choice but to tell her. So I powered on my cell phone and handed it to Kleopatra. She glanced down at the image on my phone's screen, the drawing of the kissing couple carved into an oak tree. She looked at me with a confused expression.

"It's a treasure map," I explained.

"Now you listen here, Maddie. I won't be lied to by a punk kid who thinks—"

"No, no, hear me out," I said. "The drawing is a map." I zoomed in on the image and pointed at the poem. "And that's its key. The poem led us here to Clifton. Today," I swiped my phone's screen to the picture of the cracked stone and secret words we discovered at Kirklees, "we found the next clue. Now all we have to do is visit a library to decipher it."

Kleopatra pinched the bridge of her nose. "Do you hear yourself, Maddie? You found a *treasure map*? And that's how you're going to save your father's museum? Kids—the police are *looking* for you!"

"Yeah, I know, but—"

"Do you realize how much trouble I'm in?!"

I winced.

"We'll explain everything," Zac said softly. "That way you won't get in trouble."

Kleopatra sighed. "The law doesn't work like that, kiddo."

None of us spoke for a minute. What could we say to fix the situation? *Nothing*, I realized. Empty words couldn't fix the mess I'd created. I set my hand on Kleopatra's shoulder and tried to comfort her.

She shrugged my touch away and stood. "They're going to arrest me," she said. "Your dad's going to fire me. I won't finish archaeology school. And without archaeology, I'll never find a historical artifact that'll make me filthy rich. The cosmetology school I've always dreamed about—I can kiss it goodbye. My papa won't loan me the money. He's going to make me move back home. Guys—I'm doomed!"

My inner self *dinged* with hope. There was still a chance Kleopatra would be on board with this trip—and maybe even with the treasure hunt. I just had to play my cards right.

"Well, it's too bad you feel that way," I said, really laying it on. "I mean, your cosmetology school sounds nice."

"It will be," Kleopatra said.

"But with no money," I said. "How will you afford to open one? There goes your dream. Poof."

She gave me an evil look. My brothers did, too, but I pressed on anyways.

"Team up with us, though," I said. "Help us find the treasure—which I promise is real—then, I dunno, maybe we'd be willing to split the loot with you. The question is, are you willing to team up with a couple of kids?"

Kleopatra didn't answer, but I could see the gears spinning behind her clear gray eyes.

"Please, Kleo," I pleaded. "We need you. Without your help, we won't have an adult to get us to places."

"Plus, we don't have any money," Jason said.

"And there's that," I said. "But soon," I added quickly, seeing Kleopatra's frown. "We'll have so much money it'll make the Queen of England look like a street beggar."

Kleopatra's frown turned into a smirk.

"We don't really want the money, anyways," said Zac.

"Just enough to save Dad's museum," Jason said.

I pointed at my cell phone and to the image of the Robin Hood treasure map. "*This* is our ticket to fulfilling our dreams, Kleo. It leads to a tomb filled with so much gold you could travel to all the places Prince Harry and Meghan visited on their honeymoon."

Kleopatra's eyes sparkled, and not from glitter makeup.

"Or you could buy, like, all the Egyptian rock music you wanted," Zac added.

I suddenly felt like we were little devils on Kleopatra's shoulder, but it was working.

"Okay," she said. "I'll help you guys, but only on two conditions."

"Name them," I said.

"One, no more lying. From here on out, you tell me everything."

"Deal," I said. "And your second request?"

"You're going to call your father and fix this mess with Detective Murphy, *right now.*"

Chapter 33

THE CONVERSATION WITH DAD wasn't pretty.

He yelled, swore, cussed, the whole nine yards. What is more, all of his anger was directed at me because he assumed I was the mastermind behind our grand scheme to flee the country.

He wasn't wrong.

After all, *I* came up with the idea to save the museum with Robin Hood's treasure. *I* convinced my brothers to skip school and travel to England. *I* recruited our babysitter to front the bill—who unknowingly became a wanted criminal in the process.

This was all my fault.

So.

As Dad laid into me, I held the phone a few inches from my ear and listened to everything he had to say. Occasionally, I mumbled, "Yes, Dad. It won't happen again, Dad. Geez, watch your language, Dad!" just to let him know I was listening.

Finally, when his voice was hoarse enough to pause for a moment, I attempted to explain my point of view. I told him about Aunt Heather and her "donation" to the museum. Look, I know I shouldn't have lied, but if Dad knew the truth, he would've made Kleopatra bring us back home immediately. And if that happened, we'd never find Robin Hood's treasure and we'd never save the museum. Dad would lose his job. We'd likely lose our home.

Dad didn't like us going behind his back to ask his sister for money, but since the museum was in ruins and would likely be closing its doors for good by the end of the year, he agreed it was worth a shot. He also agreed to call Detective Murphy to get the kidnapping charges against Kleopatra dropped.

Some lies are good, I told myself as I hung up the call.

Sleep didn't come easy.

I tossed and turned and forced my eyes shut, but my mind raced with everything that had happened so far. I thought about the mysterious package arriving at the museum. The museum blowing up. Rummaging through debris and finding the iron box. Robin Hood's letters. Flying to England. Finding another clue . . .

I don't remember drifting off, but I must've fallen asleep because now I was standing in a densely wooded area.

Sherwood Forest, I thought.

Overhead in the tree branches, high up in the canopy, tiny tree huts and rope bridges formed a village fifty feet off the ground. People dressed in medieval tunics and cloaks stood outside of the huts or walked across rope bridges as they gripped the handrails tightly so they wouldn't fall to the forest floor.

A man wearing a green tunic, trousers, and a medieval archer hat swung down from one of the trees using a rope.

He landed beside me in a crouch. As he stood, his gaze pierced right through me—but he didn't *see* me. It was as if I was invisible and he looked right *through* me. A longbow was slung across his shoulder. Shaggy blond hair stuck out beneath a pointy hat. He was handsome in a movie star kind of way.

The archer turned and marched away.

I followed him.

He stopped in a grassy area with three archery targets set in the distance—straw men dressed in iron helmets and breastplates. Spears and swords were tied to their straw hands. The archer unslung his bow and nocked an arrow. He aimed. The bowstring snapped.

Thwack! His arrow struck the mark, right between the eyes of the straw man on the left.

Thwack! Thwack! The next two arrows struck straw man two and three, one in the neck, the other in the sword hand. Wow, this guy was good.

"Robin," someone called the archer. The archer turned toward the person calling his name. A portly monk with a crown of brown hair around a bald scalp approached.

Hold up. Was the archer Robin Hood? He did kind of look like the actor who played him in the 1990s action flick my dad loved so much. The monk held out his hands and offered something metal and shiny to Robin Hood.

It was the lion-head key.

"Fresh from the blacksmith's forge," said the monk. "Is it to your liking, m'lord?"

I tried to get a better look at the key to see if it was the same as mine, but the scene suddenly changed.

Now I stood in a dank and darkened room. Dim torchlight flickered weakly in a sconce on the far wall, almost as though the torch had been burning for hours already. Strange contraptions came into focus as my eyes adjusted to the wane light.

A bed of metal spikes.

A table with leather straps to restrain someone.

Wooden gears and cranks to tighten the straps.

Knives, axes, and curved swords hung from hooks on the ceiling.

I shuddered. It was a torture chamber.

"Nggghhh! Nooooo!" a scream strangled the air. Whoever shouted sounded hurt, and terrified.

I whirled around and found a creature strapped down to a torture table in the corner of the room. I say *creature* because the figure didn't look entirely human. He wore nothing but a loincloth and his skin was translucent and gray. Thin hair formed a ring on his balding head. Wait, the creature looked a lot like the monk who had visited Robin Hood in Sherwood Forest, but frail and starved.

Crank! Crank! A shadowy figure stood over the monk, turning a set of gears. The monk screamed again.

"Aggghhh! Please—no more!"

The Shadow leaned in close so that he, or she, was face to face with the monk. I attempted to get a better look at the shade, but no matter how hard I tried its features remained cloaked in darkness.

"Where is the k-k-key?" the Shadow hissed, its stutter giving me an eerie feeling of déjà vu. Its voice reminded me of the decrepit old woman who was in charge of the Secret Service agents.

Crank! Crank!

"Nggghhh! Stop, it hurts."

"Of c-c-course, it hurts. It's sup-p-posed to hurt."

Crank!

"Nooooo!"

Cautiously, and with the hairs on my neck standing on end at the sound of torture, I crept closer hoping to get a better glimpse of the Shadow's face.

"I'll ask once m-m-more," the Shadow stammered. "Where is the key?"

"I don't know," the monk shouted. "Please, I don't know!"

Crank!

"Aaaaggghhh!"

"Where?"

Crank!

"The girl!" the monk yelled, giving in to the torture. "The girl has it!"

"What girl?"

The monk raised a shaky hand. He pointed a bony finger right at me.

What? No, I thought.

The Shadow turned to face me, and my breath caught in my throat upon seeing its face. Where its eyes should've been were hollowed-out sockets. Its nose had completely rotted away and its cheeks were filled with holes, so I could see a white skull underneath rotting flesh. The Shadow was ancient, a withering shade who should've died long ago.

Breath misted from its mouth. The torchlight snuffed out, thrusting me into darkness. My heart thundered. I turned to run away, but the Shadow whispered in my ear as if standing right behind me.

"I'm c-c-coming for you."

Chapter 34

I WOKE WITH A START, MY sweaty palm clutching the lion-head key.

The Shadow's words had sounded real—like they'd been spoken directly into my ear as I slept. It was clear what the shade was after. The key I now grasped. Had it been just a dream, or something more? After last year's experience with supernatural forces involving the ancient terracotta warriors of China, I wouldn't have been surprised if something more was going on.

My hands were quivering. I tucked the lion-head key into my shirt so the compass and key rested against my clammy skin. Then I swept my gaze around the room for the source of the voice that had sounded so real.

Kleopatra's nasally snores reverberated from her drooling mouth. The air conditioning unit installed beneath the window wheezed cold air and made a slight rattle. My brothers were sprawled on the floor on a pallet of blankets. But as far as I could tell, we were the only people here.

There was no Shadow with a rotting, skeletal face. No monk being tortured.

I blew out a breath. *It was just a dream,* I tried to convince myself.

Still feeling tired, I rolled over and attempted to go back to sleep, but the dream left me shaky and paranoid. The digital clock on the nightstand told me it was 5:28 AM in big, glowing numbers. Kleopatra had stressed the importance of waking early to get a head start on treasure hunting today, so I went ahead and got up.

The hotel shower felt like buckets of ice water being emptied onto my head. I turned the knob to warm the water, but no matter how many times I twisted the handle, the water remained blizzard-cold.

"G-g-geez," I said through chattering teeth as I hopped out of the shower. Goosebumps covered my skin.

I toweled off and brushed my teeth. Then I dressed in blue jeans, a black long-sleeve Tee with a graphic of a punk rock unicorn, a leather jacket, and black combat boots. By the time I was completely dressed, warmed up, and ready to go, the boys began to stir.

"Mmm, what time is it?" Zac mumbled, rubbing bleary eyes with the palm of his hand.

"Almost six," I said.

Jason yawned, his hair sticking up in the back like a cow had licked the top of his head. "Is Kleopatra awake?"

"Squo-ha-ha-honk, she-hee-hee-ooo!"

"What'd you think?" I said.

Jason shook his head.

My brothers got dressed. Jason spiked his hair with gel. Zac took forever in the bathroom (and stunk it up. Boys are gross). All the while, Kleopatra snoozed like a teenager who had stayed up all night. She even ignored her cell phone's blaring alarm clock and groaned complaints every time I tried to nudge her awake. When she finally did wake up (which was close to eight), and finally got ready (which took two hours for her to shower, blow dry her hair, wrap it in a hijab, and apply makeup) it was after ten o'clock.

So much for getting an early start, I thought.

"What're you kids sitting around for?" Kleopatra said, grabbing her purse and car keys and heading for the door. "Let's get to the library already. Robin Hood's treasure isn't going to find itself, you know."

Chapter 35

THE LOCAL LIBRARY WAS A RED brick building in the middle of downtown Clifton. We asked Kleopatra to wait in the car again, and she only agreed because her father had texted saying he needed to speak to her about the credit card ASAP.

As we walked up the library's front steps, Jason glanced back at Kleopatra sitting in the Mini-Cooper as she spoke to her father on the phone. "I hope he doesn't cut her off. It would suck to get stranded in England with no money."

I pushed open the library's glass doors and walked inside. It must've been a slow book reading day because the place was empty of visitors save an elderly lady who sat at a corner table with a stack of books. A walking cane rested against her leg. The librarian, a woman in her mid-forties with streaks of gray in her frizzy brown hair, seemed excited to see us as we approached the front desk.

"Visitors," she said breathlessly, adjusting the bifocal glasses perched on her nose. "We don't get many these days, and I rarely see children anymore. Blasts those video games. What can I do for you?"

"Well . . ." I glanced at Jason for help. He was the expert when it came to library research.

He cleared his throat. "We're, ah, doing research for a

history project at school," he lied. "We have to use primary sources, but we're not very good at finding them. We need to see anything you have on Robin Hood."

Jason had her hooked at *primary sources*. The librarian was so eager to help—or maybe she was simply bored and wanted something to do—that she nearly fell over herself to assist in our "history project." She led us to a climate-controlled reading room, provided us with latex gloves to wear, and proceeded to stack books, journals, and newspapers onto our tiny desk.

"The original stories about Robin Hood were ballads sung by troubadours traveling from town to town," the librarian said, setting a book titled *A Gest of Robyn Hode* in front of Jason. "Troubadours were medieval entertainers much like today's pop stars. Eventually, their songs were written down. You'll find them all here." She tapped the book's brown cover. "Is there anything else I can get for you?"

Jason looked at the spread of materials laid out on the desk before us. "I don't think so."

"In that case, I'll be at my desk. Don't damage the documents, please."

"Yes, ma'am."

The librarian exited the reading room.

I snatched up a pencil and a blank sheet of paper, then I wrote down the clue we found at the Kirklees Estate cemetery. We read it over one more time.

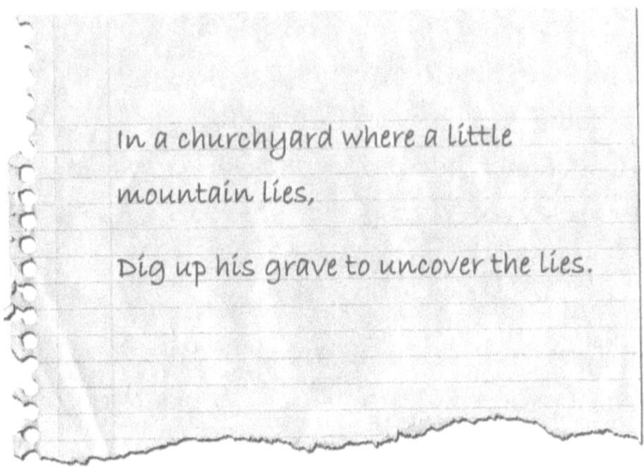

Then we each grabbed something to read and began searching through countless pages of text. The book I grabbed was called *The Merry Adventures of Robin Hood*. It was a novel written by Howard Pyle in 1883. Since the clue alluded to a churchyard in the shadow of a mountain, I skimmed the book's pages for words like *church* and *mountain*. But I didn't have any luck. Nothing screamed *clue*. Interspersed throughout the novel were illustrations, so I studied each drawing for tiny details.

"Okay, so legend says Robin Hood was an outlaw living in Sherwood Forest with his Merry Men," said Jason, looking up from *The Gest of Robyn Hode*. "But did he really exist? I mean, there are several versions of Robin Hood mentioned in this book. In one of the songs, Robin Hood robs from the rich and gives to the poor. But in another song, Robin Hood is a villain who mutilates an enemy's corpse and kills a child. In one version, he's a peasant. In another, he's a nobleman." He set the book down. "Plus, there's all the Hollywood movies starting with Errol Flynn."

"Who's he?" asked Zac.

"An incredibly handsome actor from the 1930s," I said, having watched a couple of his black and white movies with Dad. "Hubba hubba."

"Ew, gross, Maddie's not supposed to like boys."

"Hey, I like boys."

"The point is," Jason went on, "there are so many versions of Robin Hood that it's easy to believe the guy wasn't real. What if Robin Hood was simply a myth—a medieval hero equivalent to today's comic book characters? Which means, the treasure map we found is likely a load of hubbub, too—a wild goose chase."

"Whoa, slow down, Mr. Pessimistic," I said. "We found clues so the treasure has to be real."

Jason shook his head. "I'm not convinced."

"Hey, check this out," Zac said. He pointed our attention to the journal he was reading. "This says Robin Hood was a *hooder,* a maker of hoods for cloaks. That's kinda funny."

"Is it?" I asked.

"Of course it is. Robin Hood was basically a medieval thug with a hoodie."

"I guess it's funny when you put it like that."

Jason sighed. He picked up *The Gest of Robyn Hode.* "I guess I'll keep researching, but until we stumble upon concrete evidence, I will continue to believe Robin Hood is alive and living with Bigfoot in upper Montana."

We got back to work. I turned my attention to the novel in my hands and flipped a few more pages until I found a new drawing to study. The image depicted a towering man with a quarterstaff, standing on a log while another man floundered in the water beneath him. A caption under the illustration read: ROBIN HOOD MEETETH THE TALL STRANGER ON THE BRIDGE.

I knew who the tall stranger was right away: Little John. I'd seen this confrontation play out between him and Robin Hood in the 1990s movie my dad loved so much. The two men fought each other with quarterstaffs, and after a brutal battle, Robin Hood lost. He fell into the river, but Little John was so impressed with Robin's bravery and strength the two men became fast friends.

Wait a minute. What if we weren't looking for a literal mountain?

"Holy crap, I think I just figured it out," I said.

My brothers glanced up from the documents they were reading.

"The mountain isn't a mountain at all," I explained. "We're looking for Little John—a man who many thought was a *giant*."

"What?" asked Zac.

"In a churchyard where a little mountain lies," I recited the clue. "Dig up his grave to uncover the lies. Do you realize what this means? Our next clue is inside the grave of Little John!"

Chapter 36

"BUT I DON'T WANNNA DIG UP the graves of all these old people," Zac groaned. "It's gross!"

"Better get used to the idea," I said. "Because that's how we're going to save the museum."

"*If* there's a treasure," Jason mumbled.

"Oh, will you shut up?"

The librarian entered the climate-controlled reading room at the exact moment I barked at Jason to *shut up*. She looked at us with a concerned expression. "Is everything all right, dears?"

"Yes," I said. "Sorry. We were just . . ." I couldn't think of a lie to offer.

"We were arguing about our project," Jason chimed in. "I thought it might be a cool angle to research Little John instead of Robin Hood, but my sister disagreed."

The librarian smiled. "Oh, I love unique research interests. And I think I might have just what you're looking for—a publication from the 1800s called *The Merry Men of Sherwood Forest.*"

"That's great and all," I blurted out, "but all we really want to know is where the dude is buried."

The librarian scowled.

Jason intervened. "Please excuse my sister," he said.

"She's recovering from jet lag and needs a nap, but it *would* be helpful if you know where Little John is buried."

"I suppose I can forgive your sister's brusqueness this once," she finished her sentence with a wink at Jason. Usually, I found my brother's ability to schmooze teachers and librarians annoying, but today I was thankful. "Every good Englishmen knows where Little John is buried. His grave is in the village of Hathersage in St. Michael's churchyard. It's a three-hour drive from here."

My brothers and I shared a look. Now we had a destination.

"Back in a jiffy," the librarian said. She left the reading room with a spring in her step at the prospect of finding us a new book.

My gaze flitted to Jason.

"Nuh-uh," he said, cutting me off before I could speak. "No way. We're not driving three hours for something that may or may not be real."

"But we're getting closer to the treasure," I said.

"Or we're just wasting time. What if there isn't treasure at the end of the rainbow?"

"We won't know unless we keep going."

"What the fetch?" Zac picked up a newspaper clipping protected inside a clear plastic sheet. "Look at this . . ."

I glanced at the newspaper. It was an American paper called *The Wyoming Weird*. The date in the upper right corner read August 23, 1887. The newspaper's cover included an article about a woman giving birth to a bat baby, and another strange story about a river monster terrorizing a settlement of villagers. The main story included a large black and white photograph of a sleepy Western town with old-fashioned buildings and horses hitched to posts. A cowboy wearing a black hat and duster with a sheriff's badge pinned to his breast stood in the foreground. He was close enough to the photographer that his features were clear and unmistakable. And now that I studied the cowboy in more detail, I realized he was actually a *she*—with white hair, a stooped back, and grizzled, leathery skin.

"Doesn't she look a lot like that old woman you snapped a picture of?" asked Zac.

"Who, the one from the shootout?"

"Yeah, the walking corpse you thought was a cop."

I glanced at the newspaper again, and the hairs on my neck stood on end. Zac was right. The sheriff in the photograph looked like the same person I saw in Evansville. I snatched the paper out of his hand and read the article.

SHERIFF OF NOTTINGHAM
DEAD OR ALIVE?

As the bitter archrival of Robin Hood, the Sheriff of Nottingham has fascinated readers for centuries. A notoriously unjust tyrant who mistreated the local people of Nottinghamshire, he was infamous for his abuse of the badge and his eternal struggle to capture the noble thief, Robin of Loxley. But who was the Sheriff of Nottingham?

In a recent investigation, author Bill Anderson has uncovered new clues regarding the Sheriff's true identity—and the results are shocking. Anderson suggests that the Sheriff of Nottingham has cropped up in places throughout history, and not just in the stories involving Robin Hood. What is more, Anderson claims the sheriff isn't even a man—but a woman.

"Again and again, a female Sheriff of Nottingham has surfaced to terrorize innocent townsfolk," says Anderson, brandishing his book like a Bible-thumping preacher. "But the question remains: Are these 'sheriffs' different policewomen, or the same person weaving in and out of history as an immortal soul?"

As outlandish as it may sound, Anderson believes the Sheriff of Nottingham is still alive and very much immortal. "I'm telling you she's been around for hundreds of years—maybe longer—and she's just as dangerous as the Robin Hood tales suggest."

I stopped reading and glanced at the newspaper's

photograph. The female sheriff had deep, sunken eyes and pockmarked skin. Wrinkles lined her face. Thin lips framed a mouth of jagged teeth. She leaned against a wooden cane, almost as though one of her legs was injured.

I shuddered. The resemblance was striking.

"Erm, Maddie—" said Zac. "What's wrong? You've got that look."

"The old woman. The sheriff in this photo," I breathed. "They're the same person."

"What? No way," said Jason "This newspaper is old. Plus, it's a paranormal magazine. Nothing in these things is ever real."

I couldn't stop staring at the photograph. The sheriff's eyes were piercing, as though her gaze could cross through time and stop me dead with corrupt authority.

Click. CLACK!

I glanced up toward the sound. The old woman who had been researching in the library when we first arrived stood at the end of the hallway. She leaned against elbow crutches to support her weight, and she stared right at us.

Click. CLACK! Her elbow crutches rattled as she limped closer.

She wore a black leather duster. A star-shaped badge was pinned to her breast. Beneath a crown of thin, white hair her eyes shone in the gloom—piercing. Her wrinkled face reminded me of a half-rotting corpse. Goosebumps crawled up my spine.

"Sh-sheriff," I stammered.

Then all the lights went out and we were thrust into darkness.

Chapter 37

BOOOM!

An explosion rocked the library. Glass windows shattered. The whole building shuddered. The force of the blast threw me into Zac, and we crumpled to the floor in a heap of arms and legs. A cloud of debris swept over us. I kept my head low and shielded my neck with my hands, feeling pellets of debris striking them.

What the heck was happening?!

When the dust settled, I stumbled to my feet with my head feeling fuzzy and my ears ringing like they do in movies when bombs go off.

Fire alarms flashed. The sprinkler system kicked on. Water rained down from the ceiling, wetting my hair and soaking my clothes. My survival instincts screamed *danger*— that I needed to run.

There was a predator inside the library!

I whirled around to find the old woman, but I couldn't see her through the haze of smoke. Flames licked up the walls.

I tugged at Zac's hand. "Let's go!" I shouted, but I couldn't hear my voice.

"What?" he mouthed. His face was covered in black soot.

I hauled him to his feet and noticed that my skin was coated in grime. I looked around for Jason, and sheer panic threatened to paralyze me. His shoes were sticking out from a pile of rubble and blown-apart books. Zac threw himself at the rubble and dug to free our brother. His reaction kicked my brain into gear. I dropped to my knees and helped.

We freed Jason and he coughed, his face covered in ash. "Wh–what happened?"

I breathed a sigh of relief. "I don't know, but we have to get out of here!"

Sounds began to reach my ears and I heard the crackling of fire. Heat from the flames made it feel like we were inside a pizza oven. Black smoke billowed on the ceiling and spread out, choking the air.

The three of us staggered out of the climate-controlled reading room. The smoke stung my eyes and made it hard to see. We tried heading for the library's entrance, but a wall of fire blocked our path. We turned around and stumbled down the hallway, looking for an exit.

"Do you guys—" I began coughing. "Do you guys see a way out?"

"No," Jason coughed, too. "I can't see anything. There's so much smoke."

"Over here!" Zac yelled.

We followed Zac's voice, and he led us through a door with an EXIT sign and down another hallway. We rushed past open doors leading into office spaces and turned a corner—only to find a pile of rubble blocking our escape. The ceiling had collapsed. Overhead, a bright blue sky loomed beyond the gaping hole in the roof.

"Climb the debris," I said. "It leads outside."

Jason pointed. "Oh, my God," he gasped.

I turned my attention to where he pointed. "On, no . . ."

The librarian's pale, white hand stuck out from heavy blocks of stone. A book was still locked in her lifeless grip: *The Merry Men of Sherwood Forest.*

"The poor lady," Zac whimpered. "She died while getting us our book."

Click. CLACK! The sound jolted me like an electric shock.

The hair on my skin raised like an animal scared for its life. Slowly, I turned around to find the source of the noise—and found the sheriff standing right behind us with a six-shooting revolver aimed directly at my head.

"G-g-give it to me," she stuttered, her voice gravely like she hadn't spoken in a really long time. "*NOW!*"

I winced. Her voice promised death if we didn't comply. "Look, whoever you are," I said, straightening my posture to try and appear brave. "We don't have whatever it is you're looking for."

"D-don't toy with me. Hand over the k-k-key."

I swallowed. She meant the lion-head key we found inside the iron box. The old woman had stolen the letters from the Abercrombie model—I mean, archer—and after reading through the documents, she must've realized an important part of the treasure map was missing.

The key now attached to my necklace, hiding beneath my shirt.

The sheriff pulled back the revolver's hammer and a

bullet rotated into the chamber. "Fine. I'll k-k-kill you and pry it from your c-corpse." Her lips spread into a sneer, revealing yellow, jagged teeth as she aimed. I think she was smiling, but it was hard to tell because her expression reminded me of a jackal—deadly and feral.

Her finger squeezed pressure on the trigger—

—but an aftershock from the explosion rumbled in the distance. Debris rained down from the section of ceiling still intact over the old woman's head. It dusted her balding scalp and shoulders. She glanced up at the unstable ceiling—just as it came crashing down on top of her.

BOOOM! The collapse vibrated my teeth.

"Whoa!" Jason yelled. "The library literally just killed that chick."

"She must've had outrageous late fees," I said. "C'mon!"

The three of us climbed up the rubble and out the gaping hole. We scrambled across the rooftop and climbed down a water drain to reach the ground. Then we found Kleopatra and the British flag Mini-Cooper—and sped away from the library as fire trucks were pulling in to extinguish the blaze.

Chapter 38

I DECIDED THAT EXPLOSIONS sucked.

They looked cool in movies, especially when heroes walked away from them in slow motion, but after surviving two bomb blasts in less than a week, I realized there was nothing cool about them. The explosion rattled teeth. Soot covered everything in grime. And they caused serious hearing loss. For the next several hours, everyone sounded like they spoke from a distant tin can connected to a long wire.

"I can't believe this," Kleopatra said as she drove the M-5 Motorway, a highway leading north to the town of Hathersage—and to the churchyard where Little John was buried. "A bomb? You're saying a *real bomb* blew up the library?"

Zac wiped his bleary eyes. "The librarian. She just . . ."

"Maybe she's okay," I said, but even as the words left my mouth I knew it sounded lame. How could the librarian have survived a roof falling on top of her?

Kleopatra yanked the wheel, and we swerved around a mini-van going the speed limit. "You guys, this is serious. Somebody tried to kill you."

"On the bright side," I said. "The person who tried to kill us is dead."

"This isn't something to laugh about, Maddie."

"Trust me, I'm not laughing."

"Then stop being sarcastic. If you can't see how dangerous this situation is, then I'm done playing chaperone. I'll take you kids back to the States and explain everything to your dad."

"Kleo—you can't!"

"Oh, I can," she said. "Whatever trouble you've gotten into is way too dangerous for a couple of kids. Why would somebody attack you?"

Jason leaned forward from the backseat. "I think you need to show her."

Kleopatra eyed him through the rearview mirror. "Show me what?"

I reached into my shirt and pulled out the lion-head key dangling from my necklace. "This is what the old woman was after."

Kleopatra took her eyes off the road long enough to stare at the key. "What does it open?"

"We don't know."

"We found letters addressed to King Richard the Lionheart," Jason said. "One of them was written by Little John. In the letter, he told the king that this key belonged to Robin Hood—and described how it unlocks a tomb filled with treasure collected from the Crusades."

"Treasure?" Kleopatra repeated. "Crusades?"

Jason shrugged. "If you believe the treasure map is real, then, yeah. But I'm not convinced."

"And this is the same Little John whose grave we're driving to now?"

I nodded, then tucked the lion-head key back inside my shirt to keep it hidden.

"Then why are we driving slow?" Kleopatra demanded.

She floored the gas pedal and the Mini-Cooper lurched forward even faster. My stomach did a somersault from the sudden change in speed. I squeezed my seatbelt in a white-knuckle grip as we raced toward the grave of Little John.

Chapter 39

A BRITISH POLICE OFFICER WITH a bushy mustache pulled us over.

"Do you know how fast you were going, Ma'am?"

"Erm, fifty, maybe sixty miles an hour," Kleopatra said in a falsely innocent voice. She batted glittery eyes and smiled brightly at the officer as she ran fingers through her silken, black hijab. Oh, good God—was she flirting?

The police officer stared at his clipboard. "I clocked you at one hundred and twelve, Ma'am. Where are we heading in such a hurry?"

Kleopatra laughed as though the police officer had told a joke. "Why, are you asking me out on a date?"

"Can I see your license and registration, please?"

"You have the cutest butt," Kleopatra blurted out. I palmed my face and stifled a laugh. She grabbed her purse and found the necessary documentation. She leaned out of the window and held her documentation in one hand while the other traced newly painted nails along the edge of the officer's brown clipboard. "Do you work out? Oh, don't answer that—it's obvious."

The officer took her ID and passport, then clicked his pen and began to write.

"C'mon, Mr. Police Man. You wouldn't give a gorgeous

girl like me a ticket, would you?"

One hour later, and with a yellow traffic ticket now resting on the dash, the Mini-Cooper's tires crunched into the gravel parking lot of the St. Michael's church in Hathersage. The church was a beautifully constructed building with a steeple and arched windows. A small cemetery rested in the shade of the building. Oak trees and bushes were interspersed between the tombstones.

As soon as I spotted the church and graveyard, I knew I'd seen the place before—in the Robin Hood treasure map. I pulled up the image on my phone to confirm it was the same place. Although the real-life location was bigger and grander in decor, the church and graveyard in the drawing shared similar characteristics—such as the stained glass window, steeple, and the shapes of the tombstones.

I also noticed in the image that the tree behind the church looked like a roaring lion, which could've been a reference to King Richard the Lionheart.

This has to be the place, I thought.

We got out of the car. Gray storm clouds had rolled in creating a blustery afternoon. Chill winds whipped my hair and the flaps of my leather jacket. I followed Kleopatra and my brothers toward the cemetery, rubbing my arms to try and stay warm.

"The story goes," Jason said, reading facts from his phone as we walked past the church, "that Little John died in a nearby cottage. There's a headstone here under a yew tree that allegedly marks his grave."

"Allegedly?" said Zac. "What does that mean?"

"It means there's no proof," Jason answered. "Nobody knows for sure if the person buried here is Little John."

"Then why are we here, kiddo?" asked Kleopatra.

"Because in 1784, the grave was dug up and they found the bones of a man over seven feet tall."

"Little mountain," I mumbled. "Just like the clue."

We reached a tree at the end of the cemetery different from the rest. The others were oak trees, but this one must've been yew. A worn, chipped tombstone beneath the tree marked a grave. An inscription on the tombstone read:

HERE LIES BURIED LITTLE JOHN
THE FRIEND AND LIEUTENANT
OF ROBIN HOOD

There was movement near the church. Someone had

exited the building and was now watching us from a distance. The person wore all black save a white strip of cloth over the neck—a Catholic priest.

"We're not alone," I said, nodding toward the priest.

Kleopatra and the boys turned to stare at the priest. When he saw the four of us looking at him, he rushed back inside.

"I don't think we have much time," Kleopatra said.

"You're right," I said. "Let's dig up this grave and get the heck outta here."

Chapter 40

WE SPENT THE NEXT SEVERAL minutes trying to find a shovel.

You'd think we would've planned for something like this. I mean, we did travel all this way to dig up a grave for crying out loud. But no, not one of us thought to include one in our treasure-hunting toolbox. Talk about being a complete bunch of noobs.

But Lady Luck must've been on our side. We found two shovels in another part of the cemetery near a freshly dug-up grave. It looked like the church was preparing for a funeral.

Zac picked up one of the shovels. "What are the odds?"

"Pretty high," I said, snatching up the extra shovel. "We *are* in a cemetery."

We rushed back to Little John's grave and broke ground with our spades. I jabbed my shovel into the grass and pulled up a small mound of dark soil. Earthworms wriggled to get away. I tossed the dirt aside, and Zac stabbed his shovel into the earth, pulling up dirt. We quickly found a rhythm as we dug. I jabbed and tossed dirt, then Zac dug while my shovel was out of the way.

Half an hour later, our hole was three feet deep, and my arms and shoulders felt like they were on fire.

I tossed my shovel aside and climbed out of the hole. Despite the chill English air, the exertion of digging had given me quite a sweat. "All right, somebody else's turn," I said.

Kleopatra stopped reapplying lipstick—it was a new lavender color today—and she snapped her tiny makeup mirror shut. "I'm not getting my nails dirty. Do you know how much these things cost?"

"I don't care." I wiped sweat from my brow. "If you want the treasure, you gotta help."

"And I am helping," she said. "With my papa's money."

I gave her a disgruntled look. "Aren't you an archaeologist?"

"An archaeologist in training," she corrected. "There's a difference. And besides, it's not like I want to *be* an archaeologist. I'm only doing this stupid profession because my papa won't pay for cosmetology school."

"Everything okay with your papa?" I asked, remembering she spoke to him this morning about her credit card situation.

"No. He got a bill in the mail today and he's ticked." She eyed the grave we were digging up. "Are you sure we should be doing this? It seems wrong."

"Treasure," I said.

"Prince Harry," Jason said.

"Egyptian rock music," Zac finished.

"Okay, okay, but let's make this quick." Kleopatra glanced toward the church. "I'm worried the priest might catch us."

I hopped back into the hole. Jason took the shovel from

Zac so he could have a break, and he joined me in the pit. We continued digging.

Then it started raining.

It was a drizzle at first, but soon it became a shower that turned the soil to mud. My clothes were soaked and covered in grime. My hair was sopping wet and flat on my forehead. Rainwater dripped down my face and blurred my vision. The air felt colder down in the hole.

"Ugh, you guys," Kleopatra's voice sounded shrill. "Hurry it up already. The rain is ruining my makeup!"

Oh, brother, I thought.

We kept digging, five feet, six feet, each shovel of mud feeling like it weighed twenty pounds. My arms hurt so badly I feared I'd never be able to use them again.

Thump! Thump!

"What was that?" I said.

"I hit something!" Jason yelled, thumping his shovel against the ground.

I knelt in the mud and brushed away wet soil to see what he'd struck. As my hands scraped through the muck, I felt them brush up against a hard surface. I cleared away mud to uncover a stone lid. Weathered initials had been carved into the stone:

L. I.

The 'I' could've been a 'J'. If so, the letters could only stand for one thing: Little John.

"It's a coffin," I gasped.

"It's about time," said Jason.

Together, we dug until the coffin was fully exposed. Then we tried prying open the lid—but the hole we'd dug was too confined for both of us to work. Jason climbed out of the grave. Now I had more room. I scraped away dirt around the coffin's edges, and after a few minutes of labor, I had a small space wide enough to stand beside the coffin. I wedged my fingers between the seam of the coffin and its lid, then lifted with all my strength.

"Ngghhh!" I grunted. The stone lid felt like it weighed a ton, but I managed to crack it open enough to peer inside.

The coffin was empty. What the fetch?

"Guys," I shouted up to the surface. "We've got a problem!"

Nobody answered. I glanced up, but this deep in the earth I could only see gray sky overhead and raindrops pattering into my eyes. I wiped water from my lashes with a dirty hand, then turned my attention back to the coffin.

There had to be *something* here. Robin Hood's clue led us to this place after all. I grasped the lid once more and pushed until the corner of the coffin was propped open enough for me to investigate. It was too dark to see much inside the coffin, so I took my cell phone out of my jacket pocket and shined its light.

Cobwebs and bugs. That's all I found. Nothing else.

What had we missed? What part of the clue did we get wrong?

> *In a churchyard where a little mountain lies,*
> *Dig up his grave to uncover the lies.*

We'd found the churchyard where Little John had been laid to rest. We'd busted our butts over the last hour to dig up his grave. I was literally standing next to his coffin. Yet I had no idea what the poem meant by, *Dig up his grave to uncover the lies.*

Wait, hold up! The coffin was empty. The *grave* was a *lie.* Even Jason had said Little John was allegedly buried here. This whole scenario screamed misdirection. Robin Hood must've meant for this discovery to be a stumbling block for any would-be treasure hunters.

"Which means something is here," I said to myself.

I poked my head into the coffin, shining my light. It smelled earthy. A spider skittered from the sudden illumination. I felt along the coffin's walls for a hidden compartment or secret switch, but I found nothing unusual. I looked upside down at the bottom of the lid. Again, nothing stood out. I was beginning to feel frustrated at not finding anything. Plus, my neck was cramping and I needed a breath of fresh air, so I pushed off the base of the coffin to climb out.

My hand punched a hole in the bottom of the coffin. I fell inside and landed with all my weight on my shoulder. Dust shot up. I coughed and waved it away to clear the air. It took a few seconds for the dust to settle. As it did, I saw an object my clumsiness had inadvertently exposed.

A small container made of pure gold.

Chapter 41

THE GOLDEN CONTAINER WAS the size of a coffee mug and as heavy as a bar of lead.

Intricate carvings were etched into the tarnished gold. They appeared to be scenes depicting different eras from Robin Hood's life. In one image, Robin Hood looked like a nobleman in front of a castle. In another, he appeared as an outlaw robbing a stagecoach with a bow and arrow. I turned the container over, and discovered a final image of him kissing a woman beneath a grand oak tree, just like in the treasure map drawing we'd found.

Although the golden container was likely a valuable artifact, I didn't think it was the treasure we sought. The reason I thought this was simple—there were eleven buttons along the edge of the container. They twisted and turned, revealing different letters of the English alphabet. It reminded me of a bicycle lock, but instead of numbers, there were eleven combinations of twenty-six letters.

I groaned. It was another puzzle box. The last one had been extremely difficult to crack.

I placed the golden container into one of my leather jacket's deep pockets. Then I climbed out of the grave and into the downpour.

"You guys won't believe what I found—"

My heart did a somersault. Kleopatra and the boys weren't alone, and now I realized why they hadn't responded to my calls when I was deep inside the grave.

Duct tape had been placed over their mouths.

"Mm-mmm," Kleopatra said, lying on the wet grass with her hands cuffed behind her back. The boys lay beside her in a similar predicament, blinking stupidly at me behind their taped-up mouths.

A Secret Service agent with dark skin and a braided ponytail stepped in front of me. I recognized her. It was the same woman who ran over the boy-archer with an SUV back in Evansville. Raindrops pattered against an umbrella gripped in her hand. She wore pinstriped pants, dress shoes, and a neatly pressed white button-up shirt with the sleeves rolled up to her elbows. She no longer wore a suit jacket and tie, instead choosing to don a Glock pistol strapped into a shoulder holster.

"What'd you find, dear?" Ponytail asked, her tone soft and calm like an elementary school teacher.

Her demeanor unnerved me. Mainly because two more agents stood behind her: a blonde woman who looked like a supermodel, and a curly redhead who reminded me of an older Merida from Disney's movie *Brave*. Both women loomed over my brothers and babysitter with pistols drawn.

I also noticed the priest. He stood huddled beneath an umbrella of his own, his expression horrified as he stared at the desecrated grave. Lightning flashed. "I had to call the cops," he said, his turkey neck quivering beneath a strip of white cloth as thunder rumbled in the distance. "What you people are doing—it's terrible. Sinful!"

The cops? I thought. *These Secret Service chicks don't look like police officers.*

Click. CLACK! The noise made my lunch curdle. I turned toward the sound—

—and came face to face with the decrepit old woman. "What?" she croaked. "Did you think I was d-d-dead?"

The last thing I saw was one of her crutches hurtling toward my face.

Chapter 42

MY NIGHTMARE WAS strange.

I was flying through the sky, soaring high above the clouds with brisk winds whipping through my hair. I glanced down at my body and realized I was costumed like a superhero.

Wonder Woman.

I wore a red cape and everything.

Flying was an otherworldly sensation. Honestly, it felt pretty awesome. I flew lightning fast and my cape snapped like a whip. Wind made my eyes water. As I shot up over a billowy cloud, a city came into view far below looking like a miniature model. The city's skyline reminded me of my hometown, Evansville. I scanned the buildings for my dad's museum, wanting to see if the place was still destroyed or if it had been rebuilt . . .

A vulture flew in front of my path. We collided in midair, and the huge bird smacked me straight in the face. Pain lanced through my forehead. The bird lashed out with its talons and scratched my arms. Its massive wings flapped wildly as the two of us plummeted down to earth in a tangled heap.

I kicked and scrabbled to break free from the vulture, but no matter how hard I fought I couldn't get away. We fell one hundred feet, two hundred, five hundred—the ground rapidly approaching as we flipped end over end like a plane in free fall. The vulture must've sensed our doom because it let out an ear-splitting shriek. I glanced at the ground and realized we were seconds from death.

I shut my eyes and screamed—

—but the impact never came.

Confused, I opened my eyes and saw that the dream had changed. Now, I lay on a table, strapped down by my ankles and wrists. I wriggled the constraints, but they wouldn't give. Flickering torchlight crackled and spit, illuminating a stone chamber with sharpened blades hanging from the ceiling. All manner of torture contraptions filled the room, from tables that stretched your limbs to coffins lined with spikes.

What the fetch?

I was in the dungeon from my dream last night. It was bad enough my dreams had been super weird as of late, but now my subconscious was recycling old content like reruns of cheesy sitcoms.

Click. CLACK! The noise echoed off the wet, moldy walls.

I sucked in a quick breath and craned my neck to find the source of the sound. The old woman's silhouette loomed at the end of a dark corridor. She limped closer, her elbow crutches *clicking* and *clacking* as she approached.

"I've b-been looking for you," she hissed.

I struggled against my restraints, desperate to escape, but they wouldn't relent.

"You have something that belongs to m-me."

"Don't come closer," I said, but my voice came out as

barely a whisper. "You're supposed to be dead."

She stepped into the torchlight. Her silhouette's darkened features gave way to a withering face and gnarled fingers. The woman was ancient and I could see blue veins beneath her wrinkly skin. Part of her cheek looked half-rotted off.

"Stay back," I breathed.

She cackled, her raspy voice sounding like a person's last breath as death took them. Then she raised an elbow crutch and swung it down, but I couldn't cover my face.

Chapter 43

I WOKE UP, WHITE HOT PAIN throbbing across my nose. An excruciating headache pounded in my temples. Spots blurred my vision, and when I rubbed my eyes to clear the fuzziness, a stinging pain made me flinch.

Ouch, the old woman's crutch had given me a black eye.

"She's awake," I heard a familiar voice say. It sounded like Zac.

I sat up and instantly regretted it. All the pain I felt in my face exploded in intensity. A groan escaped my lips.

"Easy, kiddo," said Kleopatra. "You've been out for a couple of hours."

I tried to blink away the pain, but with no luck, so I opened my eyes to study my surroundings. I was on the lower bed of a bunk bed. There weren't any sheets or blankets on the bed, just a stained pillow without a case. The mattress was faded blue with off-white stripes.

Jason stopped pacing and looked at me. "We were worried about you. Thank God you're awake."

"We're in a lot of trouble," Kleopatra added. She leaned against a set of metal bars that reminded me of a jail cell.

"Where are we?" I croaked, sounding half-dead.

"Prison," Zac replied. He sat on the floor beside my bed. His eyes were swollen red like he'd been crying.

"How many times have I told you, Zac? We're not in prison," Jason said. "We're in a cage inside of a warehouse."

"What?" I asked.

"Look around."

I scooted off the edge of my bed and glanced around. Sure enough, we were locked inside a thirty-foot by thirty-foot cage. It was centered in the middle of a vast warehouse. The cage was stocked with a single set of bunk beds and a solitary toilet—which had no walls for privacy. Talk about embarrassing if you had to, you know, really go. I squirmed because I kind of had to pee.

Beyond the cage, the warehouse didn't have any windows as far as I could tell, but yellow lights gleamed from a ceiling forty feet high. Massive shipping containers were stacked throughout the room. Distantly, I heard the faint blare of a fog horn . . . which meant we were somewhere near the coast, possibly a port.

"How long did it take us to get here?" I asked, knowing the church where we dug up Little John's grave had been located inland.

"Not sure," Kleopatra said.

"They blindfolded us," Jason explained. "The trip might've taken an hour, maybe more. It was hard to tell in the dark. When they removed the blindfolds and duct tape covering our mouths, we were already inside the cage." He shrugged. "Kleo is right—we're in a lot of trouble. There's no way out."

"Has someone come by to check on us?" I asked.

"Nope," Zac said, wiping away tears. "They just tossed us in here and left. The only person we've seen since is the guy locked in here with us."

I glanced at the three of them and then around the cage. "I don't see anyone else."

Zac pointed toward the top bunk.

Oh, someone was lying on the bed right above me. I stood, feeling wobbly in the knees. My head pounded like a construction worker used a jackhammer on my skull. I peeked at who rested on top.

A black boy lounged with his legs crossed and his arms casually resting behind his head. His hair had mini-dreadlocks and a gash was cut through one of his eyebrows. He wore a green cloak that reminded me of those stylish outfits characters wore in Assassin's Creed video games. He looked over at me with dark ebony eyes, and smirked.

"Yo," he said, giving me a mock salute.

Oh, my God! It was the seriously gorgeous archer I chased through the streets of Evansville after he stole our letters. The same boy who was struck by an SUV and then kidnapped in broad daylight by the sheriff and her goons.

Chapter 44

"WHO THE HECK ARE YOU?" I asked the black boy. "And why'd you try and steal our letters?"

The archer hopped off the top bunk, his black boots with buckle straps not making a sound when he landed. "Dang, girl," he said, turning to face me. "Why you actin' all hard like you gonna do something? Don't be steppin' on my swag when we haven't even met." He stuck out a closed fist. "Name's Jamari."

I stared at his outstretched fist.

"You s'posed to pound it, girl."

"I know that," I said, then I bumped his knuckles. "Maddie."

"There ya go, Maddie." He threw his cloak's hoodie up over his head. "Now where were we? Oh yeah, you were just layin' into a brotha over letters that don't belong to you."

"Hey, those letters are mine."

"No, they ain't. You stole them from the Evansville History Museum."

"Yeah, and that's my Dad's museum."

"Don't mean those letters be yours," he said. "Way I see it, those letters belong to the Merry Men of Sherwood Lumber."

"Erm, don't you mean Sherwood Forest?" asked Jason.

"Nah, fool," the archer said. "Sherwood Lumber. But not like it matters, anyway. The sheriff and her cronies got those letters now. They useless to you and me." He paused to look Kleopatra up and down. "Mm-mmm, you fine. What's a brotha gotta do to get a girl's number?"

Kleopatra blushed, but her tone was stern. "How old are you, kid?"

"Sixteen," he said, pretending to brush imaginary dust from his shoulder, "but I'm mature for my age."

Kleopatra rolled her glitter-painted eyes.

"And you," the archer whirled on me. "You fine, too, even with your black eye and snippy attitude." My breath caught in my throat. I'd never had a boy tell me I was beautiful before, especially not one so handsome. "But you dirty and stanky," he said, "like you've been diggin' up a grave all morning."

"We have," Zac said, his face lighting up. "We dug up Little John's grave."

"Is that right?" the archer said, eyeing me. "Little John? The right-hand man of Robin Hood? And is that where you found the golden container?"

My eyes narrowed. "How'd you know about that?"

Jason cleared his throat. "We all saw it. Ponytail found it inside your jacket pocket after lying you down on the bed. She also took your necklace."

"W-what?" I stammered.

I patted my jacket pockets and felt around for my necklace, but both items were missing. A pang ached in my chest. They'd taken my mini-compass—the one thing I still owned which represented my late mom's love. Losing the compass hurt more than having the lion-head key and golden container stolen.

"What total *jerks!*" I groaned.

"Oh, they more than jerks," Jamari said. "They killers."

Zac's face turned pale. "What I still don't understand is how the old woman is still alive. Didn't we see her die?"

"Yeah," said Jason. "I was wondering the same thing."

Jamari chuckled.

"What's so funny, kid?" asked Kleopatra.

Jamari's lighthearted tone suddenly became serious. "The Sheriff of Nottingham can't be killed. I seen her struck by a dozen arrows—enough to bring down an African elephant—yet she walked away like a zombie on steroids." He shrugged. "The hag doesn't bleed. Nothing seems to hurt her. The sheriff's immortality is a mystery."

Jason scoffed. "No one can live forever."

"Yet we've been fightin' her for centuries," Jamari said.

"Wait—so you're immortal, too?"

"Nah, bruh, I'm sixteen—haven't you been listening?" Jamari winked at me, then he leapt off the cage's bars and back onto the top bunk like a parkour master. The leap must've been taller than my dad—and he's over six feet. "My company has been fightin' that witch for hundreds of years. Me—not so much. My dad yells at me every time I engage her in battle."

"Wait a minute," I said. "Your dad yells at you for fighting the immortal Sheriff of Nottingham?"

"Yeah, he sucks like that." Jamari propped his hands behind his head and reclined on his bed. "Heck, I'm probably grounded for getting kidnapped."

"Grounded for getting kidnapped," Zac snickered. "And I thought our dad was strict."

"No joke," Jason said.

I tried to process everything Jamari had told us about the Sheriff of Nottingham. How could she be immortal? I mean, sure, she looked like death and I witnessed a building fall on top of her—but somehow the old woman survived. If she couldn't die, how old was she?

Not important, I told myself. *We need to figure out how to escape this cage.*

I studied the cage in more detail. The bars were too narrow to squeeze through, and the door to enter and exit was secured with a fat padlock. Maybe there was a pipe beneath the toilet big enough to fit inside. I knelt beside the ivory commode. The inside of the bowl was stained yellow and brown. It reeked of urine. I held my breath and began inspecting its base.

"Girl—you relentless," Jamari said. "But you can give up already. I've checked every nook and cranny of this trap, and there's no way out. We'll just have to wait until my company arrives."

Jamari's attitude was starting to get on my nerves, the way he talked, and how overconfident he appeared. "Well, when will that be?" I asked, my frustration at our predicament spilling over onto him. "Because you were kidnapped last week, weren't you? Yet you're still being held prisoner."

He waved my comment away.

"Ugh," I groaned. "Has anybody ever told you you're a showoff? I mean, c'mon, who leaps off barred walls to climb onto a bunk bed?"

"Nobody's called me a showoff before, but my sister says I'm bigheaded."

"They're the same thing!"

Click. CLACK!

The noise sent a shock through my nerves. I whirled toward the sound. From behind a pair of shipping containers stacked three stories high, the old woman's crutches echoed inside the warehouse. Our time was up.

The sheriff was coming.

Chapter 45

THE SHERIFF APPEARED FROM the gloom.

Her elbow crutches *clicked* and *clacked,* sending chills down my spine as she approached our cage. She now wore a wide-brimmed hat along with a black, leather duster. A golden star-shaped badge was pinned to her breast. The revolver she threatened to shoot me with before now hung from a gun belt on her hip. The sheriff looked as if she'd been taken straight out of a clichéd western movie. Although, in the movies, villains never looked like the walking dead unless it was a horror flick.

I shuddered.

Three Secret Service women followed in her wake: Ponytail, Blondie, and red-haired Merida. They all wore neatly pressed suits, and as they walked, I caught glimpses of shoulder-holstered pistols beneath their jacket flaps. Each of them also donned silver star-shaped badges pinned to their jackets over their hearts.

Of course, it made sense now. The agents were deputies.

The sheriff banged a crutch against the cage, her metal cane *clanging* against the metal bars. "Wake up," she croaked, spittle flying from her cracked lips. "Time to answer some q-q-questions."

Ponytail stepped forward. "You there, dear," her tone was soft as she looked at me. "Do you know how to open the golden container?"

Ah, so that's why we were still alive. They hadn't figured out how to unlock the new puzzle box. I recalled the golden container and remembered how it had eleven buttons that twisted to one of twenty-six letters of the English alphabet. I had no clue how to open it.

"Yeah, I know how to open it," I lied.

"G-good," the sheriff said. "Bring her. Leave the others."

A pair of keys appeared in Ponytail's hand. She unlocked the cage's door, then stepped inside. "Come along, sweetie," she purred. "This will all be over soon."

I backed away. Her tone might've been soft, but I'd witnessed these people shoot a stranger in the leg last week in Evansville. My back bumped into the cage's metal bars— I had nowhere else to go. Ponytail grabbed me by the arm, squeezing so tight I cried out in pain.

"Maddie!" my brothers rose to protect me.

But my babysitter reached Ponytail first.

Kleopatra slapped the agent in the face. I'm talking about an open-handed, right across the cheek—*SMACK!* "Keep your grubby hands off her!" Kleopatra said through gritted teeth. "I—am—her—babysitter! And if you harm one hair on that girl's head—"

Ponytail grabbed a fistful of my brown locks. She pulled roughly, forcing me to my knees. "Ow, ow, ow," I said.

"What will you do, dear?" Ponytail said. She didn't flinch as I clawed at her hand, nor did the softness of her voice break. She acted and sounded just as casual as if she spoke to a close friend on the phone.

Kleopatra yelled a war cry and flung herself at Ponytail. Her manicured nails raked at the deputy's face, but before she could sink her claws, Blondie and Merida tackled her to the ground. My babysitter fought to break free, but she wasn't strong enough to escape two deputies.

Ponytail dragged me out of the cage by my hair, which really frigging hurt.

The sheriff addressed the deputies restraining Kleopatra as they handcuffed her to the cage's bars. "Watch over the p-p-prisoners."

The deputies inclined their heads.

Click. CLACK! The old woman turned to depart. Ponytail yanked my hair and urged me forward.

"Maddie," pleaded Kleopatra, her cuffs clinking as she struggled against the restraints.

The sheriff and my captor stopped, which gave me a chance to glance at my babysitter. Her face was covered in grime. Tears streaked down her cheeks, ruining her makeup. "I'm sorry," she said.

"Hey, don't worry about it." I tried to sound brave despite my fear. "I'll think of something." Then I looked at Jamari, who casually lounged in bed even though dangerous people held us prisoner. "Yo, archer boy—" he glanced at me out the corner of his eye. "Keep my family safe, will ya?"

He gave me a lazy thumbs-up.

The sheriff smiled, revealing jagged teeth. "Oh, and one more thing," she hissed at the deputies staying behind. "If the girl hasn't opened the puzzle box within the hour . . . k-k-kill one of the hostages."

"What? No," I said.

"And if she still hasn't opened it after another hour. K-k-kill another one."

"NO!"

The sheriff cackled. I was ushered away, with the fate of Kleopatra and my brothers now hanging on my ability to unlock a puzzle box I knew absolutely nothing about.

Chapter 46

I WAS LED DOWN A DARK HALLWAY, up a set of
stairs, and into a small office. Florescent bulbs illuminated
the room in harsh, white light. The office was filled with
rusting filing cabinets, cheap carpet, and a wooden desk with
its veneer peeling. A round clock hung on a wood-paneled
wall. The clock's second hand *ticked, ticked, ticked*—a not so
subtle reminder of the lives at stake if I failed to open the
puzzle box.

Ponytail shoved me roughly into a rolling chair. She
handcuffed my left wrist to its armrest.

I shook the cold metal to try and loosen the cuff, but
with no luck. "Don't you think handcuffing me is a bit
extreme?" I asked. "I'm just a teenager!"

"Just do as the sheriff says," Ponytail said. "Please. I
don't want anyone to get hurt."

"You could've fooled me when you grabbed my hair
downstairs."

Ponytail exited the room.

"Hey!" I shouted, but I was left alone.

Immediately, I tried pulling the armrest loose from the
chair so I could slip the handcuff free—but it wouldn't
budge. I rolled to the filing cabinets and tried opening
drawers to find a key, but they were all locked. A large

window overlooked the warehouse. I rolled closer and peered through the glass. Downstairs, I could see the topmost portion of the cage—with Kleopatra handcuffed to the bars while my brothers paced around the cage's perimeter. Jamari was still lying in bed. Shipping containers blocked some of my view so I couldn't see the deputies, but I knew they were down there with loaded guns, ready to kill when the hour was up.

Click. CLACK! The sheriff limped into the office. She staggered behind the desk, opened a drawer, and tossed the golden container into my lap.

"Oomph!" I said, catching it.

"Fifty minutes," she croaked.

"Fifty minutes?" I repeated. "But you said one hour."

"Your t-time started downstairs."

"That's not fair!"

The sheriff grabbed her revolver, cocked its hammer, and set the gun down on the desk with a thud. Its barrel pointed right at me. I swallowed and glanced at the clock on the wall. Fifty minutes . . .

No time for mistakes, I told myself. *Kleopatra and my brothers are depending on me.*

I lifted the golden container and studied the intricate carvings etched into the gold. Scenes depicted Robin Hood standing in front of a rich castle, robbing a stagecoach, and getting married beneath a grand oak tree. I turned the puzzle box over—my handcuffs clinking with each little movement—and I analyzed its eleven rotating buttons. I rolled the first button. It clicked with each change of the letter.

A quivering sigh escaped my lips. How the heck was I supposed to solve this thing? I had no clue what combination of letters to use. I set the golden container down in my lap and wiped clammy palms on the sleeves of my jacket. My hands were trembling. I glanced over at the sheriff to see if she noticed how scared I was—but the hag just watched me with her bony fingers pressed together in a steeple.

She didn't blink.

She didn't appear to be breathing.

Creepy.

I turned my attention back to the puzzle box. There were eleven buttons, which meant I needed to find the correct combination of eleven letters. *The answer must be a secret word or phrase*, I thought.

I tried recalling everything I'd learned about Robin Hood. Jason said he was possibly a nobleman who became an outlaw after King Richard left on a crusade. England's government grew corrupt while the king was away. During this time, Robin Hood became a noble outlaw.

Noble outlaw.

I counted the letters. Eleven. Worth a try. I twisted each button until the puzzle box's letters spelled out the words: *Noble outlaw*. But nothing happened.

Something else, then?

How about Little John? He was Robin Hood's lieutenant and friend. Plus, we found the puzzle box inside his grave. I counted the number of letters in his name, but there were only ten. Not enough.

Robin of Loxley? Thirteen letters. Too many.

What about . . . Robin's grave?

The phrase had eleven letters. Could it be the right answer? The map we found alluded to a vast treasure hidden inside of Robin's grave, so it seemed like a promising lead. I manipulated the golden container's buttons—but again nothing happened.

Fetch!

I glanced at the time. Twenty minutes had already flown by. Holy cow, it felt like time was moving in fast forward. With a flutter of nervousness in my belly, I busied myself inputting random names, places, and phrases related to Robin Hood into the golden container—but I didn't have any luck. None of my words seemed to work.

"Ten more minutes," the sheriff croaked.

"W-what?" I stammered, glancing at the time. "But I still have half an hour."

"I've grown impatient."

"But that's cheating!"

The sheriff didn't say another word. She just stared at me with an expressionless face. The clock on the wall continued *ticking* seconds, each tick sounding like the chop from an executioner's axe. If I couldn't solve this puzzle box, right now, then someone I cared about was going to die.

C'mon, Maddie. Get it together!

But I had no clue what the answer could be. If only there was a hint like in the crossword puzzles Dad liked to do in the Sunday newspapers. Wait! What if a hint had already been given and I'd just overlooked it? Up until this point, we'd been given hints for each discovery—in the

Robin Hood sketch.

The boughs of an oak tree formed the shape of Great Britain, I thought, retracing our clues. *We ended up in Kirklees, where Robin Hood died of treachery and shot a final arrow to mark his grave. A discovery there led us to the grave of Little John. The treasure map sketch depicted Little John's grave in the shade of a church. Something had been written on his tombstone, but what was it?*

"One m-minute," the hag said, her voice as cold as the grave. Ten minutes hadn't passed on the clock, but the sheriff didn't seem to care.

I reached into my pocket and found my cell phone. I wasn't sure why they hadn't confiscated it, but maybe they weren't concerned about me calling for help since they were, technically, the police. I opened my camera app and found the photograph of the Robin Hood sketch, then I zoomed in on the church and graveyard where we found the golden container.

And there it was! The answer had been written on Little John's tombstone.

R.I.P.

Rest in peace. Eleven letters. Bingo!

My fingers scrabbled to set the buttons into the correct sequence. The sheriff stood and grabbed her revolver. "Please, just another second," I mumbled as I started on the final letter. But right when I was about to slide the E into place—gunshots rang out from inside the warehouse.

Chapter 47

I FLINCHED AT THE SOUND of gunshots.

At first, I feared one of my loved ones had been executed, but then more gunfire erupted from the warehouse and I realized the deputies were shooting at *something*. I whirled around in my chair to peer out the window, but all the lights blacked out. Red emergency lights blinked on. For a fraction of a second, I thought I saw a green-cloaked archer leaping between shipping containers with a bow and quiver of arrows.

Then the emergency lights flashed and the figure was gone.

"What is all that—" the sheriff began coughing, "—r-r-ruckus?!"

"It's the Merry Men!" shouted Ponytail from the hall, which was followed by a *pop, pop, pop* of her pistol. "We're under attack!"

The Merry Men? I thought, but I didn't have time to process what Ponytail could've meant because the window suddenly shattered as bullets sprayed into the glass. I dove to the ground. The rolling chair I was cuffed to fell over with me. Glass rained down and I covered my head to keep from getting cut.

Click. CLACK! Click. CLACK! The sheriff limped out

of the small office faster than I'd seen her move. A second later, her revolver fired—its gun blasting a high-pitched metallic sound. I glanced around and realized in the chaos they'd left me alone.

Now was my chance to escape.

I crawled to the desk, dragging the rolling chair with me as it crunched across broken glass. The golden container was still gripped in my hand. I set it down on the stained carpet, reached into the bottom desk drawer, and rummaged through its contents in search of a handcuff key. I pushed aside clipboards, staplers, a box of bullets, and a bottle of whiskey—but I didn't find any keys. I moved to the next drawer and searched inside.

More gunfire ripped into the office through the shattered window. Bullets walloped the foam ceiling tiles and shredded them to bits. An arrow soared into the room and *thunked* into a wall.

I ducked behind the desk. When the gunfire stopped, I continued searching. I found a set of keys attached to a bottle opener. One of the keys was small enough to fit inside a handcuff lock—so I quickly got to work trying to get the cuffs off my wrist.

The handcuffs came loose and fell to the ground.

Yes!

I rubbed my wrist where the metal cuff had chafed me. Then I picked up the golden container and input the last letter of the puzzle to spell out *rest in peace*. The top twisted open. Inside, there was a pair of rings—one gold, the other silver, both tarnished and worn. I poured them out of the container into my hand. They felt cold and were made of heavier metal than the rings I wore. Several lines of verse had been etched onto the insides of both rings, but with the battle waging in the warehouse, I didn't have time to read the sprawling script. I shoved the rings deep into my pocket and started to rise—

—but something metallic gleamed from inside the drawer, catching my attention. It was a silver, star-shaped badge just like the ones the deputies wore. I snatched it up. There was an engraving on the front.

DEPUTY SHERIFF OF NOTTINGHAM

I flipped the badge over and found another engraving in a smaller print.

WHOMSOEVER WEARS THIS BADGE,
SHALL BE BOUND TO WELMA DE WENDEVAL.

AND SHOULD HE FAIL TO OBEY ORDERS,
HE SHALL DIE IN THE PITFIRES OF HELL.

Geez, if the engraving wasn't ominous enough, the pin on the back was a sharp metal spike the size of a golf pencil. A thin piece of gray fabric was glued to the spike. What the heck did deputies do with the badge? Stab it into their hearts? The thing gave me an eerie feeling, so I tossed it back inside the drawer and slammed it shut. Then I pocketed the keys and rushed out of the small office with the golden container gripped in my hand.

I crashed into Ponytail in the hall.

We fell to the floor. Her Glock went tumbling from her grasp. When she saw that I was attempting to escape, she scrambled for her pistol.

I noted the heavy weight of the golden container. Ponytail struck me as a formidable, professional killer—but I doubted she'd be immune to blunt force being struck against her temple.

So.

While she reached for the gun, I smacked her on the side of the head with the golden container. Adrenaline must've been coursing through my veins, making me stronger than normal, because the impact struck Ponytail like a truck. Her eyes rolled into the back of her head, blood squirted, and she collapsed violently to the ground.

Whoa, I knocked her out.

Gunshots sounded from the warehouse.

Kleo and the boys, I thought.

I raced for the stairwell at the end of the hall, hoping the set of keys I found would unlock the padlock keeping them locked inside the cage.

Chapter 48

THE WAREHOUSE WAS A warzone.

Emergency lights flashed. The sounds of gunshots echoed off the walls. A haze of gunpowder dust lingered in the air, filling the space with the stench of sulfur. I made my way through the maze of shipping containers in search of the cage, and stumbled across countless arrows littering the floor. A few arrows were sticking out of metal shipping containers and still quivering on the spot.

I feared ricocheting bullets so I kept low and moved quickly. Every once in a while, the lights flickered and I got brief glimpses of archers in the rafters or archers atop shipping containers shooting arrows. Then the lights blinked off and the archers disappeared.

It was hard to tell how many archers there were. They all wore the same green cloak, hoody, and mask. Some looked masculine with muscles bulging through their cloaks. Others appeared slender or feminine. There might've been a dozen archers inside the warehouse, maybe more, but if that was true, why couldn't they defeat the sheriff and her deputies? They clearly outnumbered the enemy.

The hag cannot die, I reminded myself.

A bullet pinged into the metallic shipping container beside me, creating a burst of sparks. I screamed and ducked to avoid the ricochet. Lights flickered on, and the red-haired deputy appeared with a Glock pistol aimed right at me. She was wounded. An arrow stuck out of her shoulder. Blood seeped through her white dress shirt and dripped onto the floor.

I put my hands up. "Whoa, whoa, don't shoot!"

"But I've been commanded—*nggh!*—to kill on sight. If I disobey the sheriff's orders—"

The lights flickered, causing what I saw next to look like it happened beneath a strobe light. A cloaked archer dropped down from the ceiling. His bow smacked the deputy's hand, slapping the gun from her grasp and sending it skittering across the floor. The lights flashed, and when they came back on, the next image I saw was the deputy stumbling back while gripping the arrow sticking out of her shoulder. The archer now stood between us, aiming his bow and arrow at the deputy.

"No, please," the deputy said, as the archer pulled his bowstring taut. "I have a husband. A daughter . . ."

The archer slacked his aim, but only slightly. In that brief moment of hesitation, the deputy turned and sprinted away—but the strangest thing happened.

Her legs caught fire.

Red flames licked up her dress pants, catching her suit jacket ablaze.

"NO!" the deputy screamed, stumbling to the floor. She slapped at the fire consuming her flesh and attempted to roll to quiet the blaze, but flailing proved useless. Her curly red hair caught flame.

The archer turned to face me. His dark ebony eyes

seemed familiar. "Don't look," he said, and he threw his cloak up and embraced me in a protective hug. His breath smelled of peppermint.

Agonizing screams rent the air. Fire crackled and spit. The stench of burnt hair wafted beneath my nostrils, causing my cheeks to puff as I fought my heaving stomach. The sound of flames died down, and as the red-haired deputy's horrifying yells of pain turned to strangled gasps, the archer let go of me so we could see what had become of her.

Ash and scorch marks. That's all that remained, and the sickening odor of charred meat.

"What the *freak*?" I shouted. "Why'd she catch fire like that?!"

"She disobeyed the sheriff's orders," the archer said. He approached the deputy's charred remains, knelt beside the heap, and sifted through the ashes. "When a deputy doesn't follow a command, or if their badge is removed by anyone other than the sheriff, they burn in hellfire."

"Hellfire?" I repeated, remembering the badge I found upstairs inside the office desk. An engraving on its back had alluded to obeying orders and dying by hellfire if a command wasn't followed.

The archer lifted a silver deputy badge from the charred remains. Its sharp spike was still bloody. The metal should've been hot to touch and steaming from the fire, but the archer held the badge as if it were cooled.

"So that craps real?" I said, my voice rising. "They stab those things into their hearts and die if they disobey the old hag?"

"Yeah." The archer pocketed the badge. "It's some kind

of cursed metal. We destroy the ones we can."

"And the ones you can't?"

A gloom darkened his expression. "The sheriff chooses strong, capable women and forces them into servitude. The deputies are all victims. If we can save them, we do, but sometimes we're forced to kill. The woman who just caught fire—we've been trying to rescue her for a few months now. She was a stay-at-home mom."

"Oh, my gosh."

"I know, the sheriff is pure evil."

"And the other deputies? Who are they?"

Gunshots sounded from the other side of the warehouse. The archer turned his head toward the noise. "We'll talk about this later," he said. "For now, let's worry about getting outta here."

"But Kleo and my brothers—"

"—have already escaped. Come with me and we'll join with the others." He looked me in the eyes, and I noticed his brown skin and a gash cut into his eyebrow.

"Jamari?" I said.

He winked. "Whad'up?"

"Hey—they're over here!" a deputy shouted.

I turned to see Blondie charging straight at us, reloading her pistol as she ran. Jamari grabbed me by the back of my jacket and pulled me down an aisle of shipping containers. Gunshots rang out—bullets pinged into metal—and as Jamari and I raced to escape the warehouse, the sheriff and her deputies closed in on our position.

Chapter 49

JAMARI RAN FAST. THE BOY was fit. I tried my best to keep up with him, but the only reason I was able to stay close was because he occasionally stopped to fire arrows at Blondie. The deputy chased us as if her life depended on it.

Her life does depend on it, I realized.

The thought both saddened and scared me. The deputies would stop at nothing to obey the sheriff's commands. The slightest hesitation could end in their death just like it had for the stay-at-home mom.

The women are victims.

"Fetch—this way!" Jamari said.

Ponytail ran at us from the opposite direction, her braided ponytail swishing from side to side. She raised her Glock pistol and aimed, but Jamari and I raced down a new aisle of shipping containers before she could fire her gun. He turned while in mid-run, nocked two arrows in his bow, and when Blondie and Ponytail appeared from around the corner, he let the arrows fly.

TWANG! The arrows soared like homing missiles.

One struck Ponytail's gun hand, forcing her to drop the weapon. The other pinged into Blondie's silver badge, causing her to stumble and grab her chest like she suffered a heart attack.

"Whoa!" I breathed. "You're really frigging good."

"Yeah, I got hella swag," he said.

I shook my head. Even in danger, he was a showoff. Jamari bolted down another aisle of shipping containers, and I raced after him before the deputies could recover. My breath wheezed and my lungs screamed for air. I wasn't sure how much longer I could run. Zac exercised daily, but I avoided it like a sickness. Now I seriously regretted my laziness.

"This place is a maze!" I panted heavily. "How do we get outta here?!"

"Dang, girl, can't you see I'm working on it?"

"Are you? Kinda seems like we're running in circles."

"Well, if you're unhappy with my methods, feel free to stay behind. I'm sure the sheriff would love to restore her deputy ranks to full strength. Heck, she probably has a badge with your name on it."

The idea of having a spike stabbed into my heart made me shudder. "All I'm saying is, maybe we need a plan."

"If you've got one, I'm all ears."

Whenever one of my pranks got out of hand and I was forced to run from the law, I usually escaped by causing a distraction. Sometimes, I dressed up as a cavewoman and hid inside my dad's museum amongst the exhibits. Other times, I snuck into zoos and let the animals loose—the harmless ones, not the man-eaters. I'm not a murderer for crying out loud. The point is, distractions create misdirection which provides opportunities to escape.

I reached into my jacket pocket and pulled out my cell phone.

"What're you doing?" Jamari asked as we darted past the empty cage, now unlocked with its door wide open. Kleopatra's handcuffs were still clasped around the bars, but she was missing along with my brothers. "B'cuz calling your pops won't get us out of this mess."

"Do you ever stop talking?" I asked.

"Sure," he said. "When I'm sleeping."

I rolled my eyes, then found the number I wanted to call and hit dial. The phone rang a couple of times before someone picked up on the other end.

"Hello?"

"Amira!" I said, now staring at her face as we spoke through FaceTime. She appeared to be propped up in a hospital bed with pillows fluffed behind her back. Her complexion looked paler than usual. Her treatments must have been difficult lately.

"Maddie?" she said. "Why haven't you called? I was starting to get worried—"

"Yeah, look," I interrupted. "I'm in trouble, Amira. We need your help."

"We?"

I angled the phone so she could glimpse Jamari, who ran beside me with a fresh arrow nocked in his bow.

"Wait, is that the gorgeous hunk?" she asked. "The archer we thought was a model?"

Jamari overheard. His eyes glimmered as he glanced my way. "Hunk, huh?"

"Amira," I said through gritted teeth. "Now's not the time."

"Oh, okay," she said. "So what's new with you?"

I palmed my face.

"This is a great plan," Jamari said.

"Shut up!"

Gunfire erupted in the distance. I didn't see any deputies nearby so they were either shooting at another archer or trying to lure us out.

"What was that noise?" asked Amira.

"Bad guys," I said. "That's why we need your help. Can you cause a distraction?"

"Erm, I guess. Not sure what I can do from here."

I turned my phone's volume all the way up, skidded to a stop, and set it down on the floor. "Just be loud and draw their attention. Don't stop until they hang up on you."

"They? Who's *they*? Maddie—wait!"

We were already gone. Jamari and I bolted down another row of shipping containers with the speed of loosed arrows. Behind us, Amira's voice sounded from my phone: "Hey, bad guys! Over here. Come and catch me, ya sketchy pieces of garbage!"

Atta girl, I smiled.

"I can't believe you did that," Jamari said.

"What?"

"Threw away your phone like it was nothing. Don't you care about keeping up with your Insta followers?"

"You're kidding, right?"

"Nah, bruh, I've got an online image to maintain."

I snorted.

The sound of footsteps made us stop dead in our tracks. They sounded close. Jamari grabbed my arm and pulled me into the shadows between two narrow shipping containers.

It was a tight fit and the closeness forced us to press together. This close, I could smell the peppermint on his breath and feel the tightness of a muscled arm through his cloak.

My heart fluttered, pounding so hard I could hear it in my ears. I wasn't sure if my sudden nervousness was from the near-death encounter with the sheriff's deputies, or from being so intimately close to Jamari.

Ponytail and Blondie darted by. It looked like they were heading in the direction of my cell phone. The distraction was working.

"It's clear," Jamari's breath felt warm on my cheeks.

"Okay," I whispered.

"You ready to escape this death trap?"

Part of me wanted to stay here with Jamari, but I said, "Abso-frigging-lutely."

We exited the confined space and looked around. Nobody in sight. Jamari reached into his quiver of arrows and pulled out one with a rope attached to it. He nocked the arrow into his bow and shot it at the ceiling. The arrow pierced a rafter and stuck. He pulled on the rope to make sure it was secure, and looked at me.

"Let's go."

"On that?"

"Yeah, just hop onto my back."

"Promise not to drop me?"

"Not if you keep asking stupid questions."

"Watch it, jerkweed," I said. He bent low and I climbed onto his back. It felt awkward to be piggyback carried by a boy only a year older than me.

"You ready, girl?" he asked.

I made sure my grip was tight around his neck, and nodded.

"Hang on!"

He leapt into the air and scaled the rope while kicking off shipping containers to help our ascent. I clung on, surprised at how strong Jamari was. He carried me like I weighed no more than a newborn baby.

Click. CLACK! The noise forced me to look down. Below, the Sheriff of Nottingham appeared from the gloom. She glanced up to see us scaling the rope toward the rafters.

"They're g-g-getting away!" she hissed.

Her revolver gleamed. I shouted at Jamari just as the sheriff fired. He kicked off a shipping container, shifting our momentum, and the bullet missed. She fired again, but he kicked off another container and we dodged the gunfire again. I held on tightly as we swung wildly in the air, ascending higher and higher as Jamari reached hand over hand to climb the rope. Gunshots continued to blare, but before I knew it, we were climbing through a hole in the ceiling and onto the rooftop . . .

Chapter 50

MUSTY SALT AIR FILLED MY nostrils. The air felt chill and a nighttime sky blanketed the cityscape with a million stars. I looked out beyond the rooftop's edge and discovered a harbor. Lamplights illuminated boats, yachts, and a massive cargo ship anchored in the distance. I turned around, and found a downtown district across the street with four- and five-story buildings dotting the horizon.

We were in a port city.

Jamari stood on a ledge overlooking the downtown district. "My company's hideout isn't far." He held a coiled rope with a grappling hook fastened to its end. "We'll travel the rooftops to get there."

I walked closer. "Is that where my family is? Are they safe?"

He twirled the grappling hook and let it fly. It flew across the street and latched onto a tall light post halfway between the buildings. "They should be. The Merry Men leave no one behind."

"The Merry Men?" I scoffed. "You can't be serious?"

Jamari looked at me and smiled. Well, beneath his mask he smiled. I could only tell because his beautiful eyes glinted at the corners.

I wiped the smirk off my face. "Oh, you *are* serious."

He offered me his hand. "Will you travel with a brotha' tonight?"

I eyed the rope and the three-story drop to the street below. I gulped. If the rope snapped, we'd go splat against the concrete. "On that flimsy thing? Will it support the two of us?"

"It's a strong rope." Jamari yanked on the rope to prove his point. It held. "We'll swing to that building over there, hop a few more rooftops, and rejoin with my comrades. There will be a feast tonight to celebrate our victory. Your family will join us. What'd you say?"

I thought the English language never sounded more beautiful. Jamari's gorgeous eyes studied my reaction, and my heart thundered in my chest . . . and not because he wanted me to leap buildings with him from dizzying heights.

No.

Jamari was strong. Athletic. Confident. Pretty much everything I hated about football jocks back home. So why was I so smitten by him?

"I can leave you here if you'd like," he said. "I'm sure the sheriff wouldn't mind keeping you around a bit longer."

Hearing the word *sheriff* brought me back to my senses. I did *not* want to be captured by her again. I accepted Jamari's outstretched hand. His touch was firm and warm, yet gentle.

He set my hand on the rope alongside his. "Squeeze tight and kick off with your legs," he instructed. Then he pulled me close and wrapped an arm around my waist. Even through his mask, I could smell the peppermint on his breath. "On the count of three, we'll jump. Ready?"

I nodded.

"One. Two."

We kicked off on three and soared high over the street. Brisk winds whipped through my hair. My stomach did a somersault from the sudden drop, then fluttered again when the rope leveled out and swung us over to the other side. It felt amazing hurtling through the air. We landed smoothly on the building's rooftop. Jamari set me gently down. Then he ran to retrieve his grappling hook and we prepared to swing over to the next building.

Each time we leapt from building to building, I couldn't help but think I was living in a fairy tale. The sensation was unlike anything I'd ever felt before. My emotions were heightened by Jamari's strong, capable demeanor—and, I'll admit, his charming "swag." Traveling by starlight with a gorgeous archer to a hideout far in the distance seemed like a scene taken straight from a fantasy novel.

If only the trip could've lasted longer.

Chapter 51

"OVER HERE," JAMARI whispered.

We arrived at a limestone building in the middle of downtown. The clear, nighttime air felt crisp and cool after our magical trip. From my vantage point on the building's rooftop, I could make out quaint shops and restaurants down on the street level, even a Starbucks on the corner. All of the businesses were currently closed. The street was quiet and deserted. It must have been early in the AM, but I wasn't sure of the time.

Jamari led me to a door with a bronze plaque hanging on the wall beside it. The plaque read: SHERWOOD LUMBER.

I pointed at the sign. "Hold up, your band of Merry Men hide out in a building named after Sherwood Forest. The infamous hideout of Robin Hood?"

"We do," Jamari said. "But Sherwood Lumber isn't only a hideout—it's a lumber store. We sell all kinds of hardwood flooring, drywall, tiles, and carpets. Pretty much anything you might need for a construction job, we supply it."

"The Merry Men are construction workers?" I scoffed.

"Not all of us. Some of the guys are accountants or receptionists." He leaned in close and whispered, "Actually, our store manager is a short dude named John."

I stared at him with a blank face.

"You don't get it? The manager is short and his name's John—like Little John, duh."

I rolled my eyes.

"Well, the rest of us think it's hilarious."

"Yeah, and I bet you're all a blast to hang with at your Magic the Gathering tournaments," I teased.

"Nah, not Magic. A few of us are hella good at Dungeons and Dragons, though."

"Nerd," I mumbled.

"What'd you say?"

"Nothing," I smirked.

He removed his mask and smiled—a gorgeous, perfect teeth smile with dimples in his cheeks. I suddenly felt wobbly in the knees.

"C'mon," he said. "I'll show you inside."

Jamari started to open the door, but a loud *thump* sounded behind us. We turned around to see what caused the noise. A cloaked archer knelt with one hand planted against the ground as though he had just landed there. A long stick was strapped to his back, which I think was a bo staff—like Donatello's from Teenaged Mutant Ninja Turtles.

The archer stood. He took off his hood and lowered his mask, revealing a long mane of braided hair, dark ebony skin, and a long face. A woman's face. "Jamari!" the archer said. "You know the rules. No newcomers unless they pass the test."

Jamari groaned. "C'mon, sis. She's just a kid. You can't expect her to complete the ritual."

I felt a sharp pang in the pit of my stomach as if

somebody had stabbed me with a knife. Jamari thought of me as a *kid?*

"Don't call me *sis*," the archer said. "Brother and sister we may be, but when we wear our warrior cloaks, you must address me by name. Treat me as you would treat the others—as equals."

Jamari bit his lip, seeming frustrated by his sister's reprimand. His scowl looked just like hers, now that I thought about it, with dimples and fierce eyes. As the siblings glared at one another, others began to emerge from shadows all across the rooftop. Archers of all shapes and sizes, guys and girls, materialized to watch the exchange between brother and sister.

"Oh, good, everyone's here," Jamari said. "All we need now is Dad and the dysfunctional family is complete."

"Don't be this way—" his sister began.

"Shut up, Kamari. You're breaking the Order's rules, too. You let the girl's family inside, didn't you?"

Kamari hesitated before answering. "Yes," she replied. "But one of them must pass the test if they are to learn of our world." She made eye contact with me. "And we all agreed it should be the one among them who is most warrior-like."

Me, a warrior? Pah-ha-ha, this chick clearly didn't know me.

"And if she fails?" asked Jamari, deadly serious.

"Then she will die, as will her family. Do not play the fool, Jamari. This is how it has been for centuries."

Jamari sighed. He turned to face me. "I'm sorry," he said, "but she's right."

"W-what?" I stammered. "You're going to agree with her just like that?"

"I have no choice."

"So let me get this straight. You all risked your lives to save me and my family—and now I have to pass a test. And if I fail, you'll kill us? Wow, you guys suck."

Jamari cringed. "Technically, they raided the warehouse to save me. You guys happened to luck out and get rescued, too."

I scoffed.

"Look, we're an old organization stretching centuries through time," Jamari said, as a nearby archer approached and handed him a bo staff. He inspected the weapon, then handed it to me. I accepted the bo staff absentmindedly, still trying to come to terms with what was going on. "It's not a brotha's place to question the Order's rules."

"Well, I'm questioning them," I said, glancing at the heavy and awkward bo staff now gripped in my hand. What the heck was I supposed to do with this thing?

Kamari removed the bo staff from her back. She began twirling it around in a Karate-style dance. Her moves were impressive. She clearly knew how to handle the weapon.

"Can we settle this without fighting?" I yelled at her. "Maybe play a game of Go Fish or Candy Land instead."

Archers chuckled.

Jamari winced. "Please don't embarrass me."

I laughed aloud, though my laughter was more from nerves than anything funny. "I might die and you're worried I might embarrass *you*?" I said. "Geez, and to think I thought you were cute."

"You think I'm cute?"

"Not anymore." I shoved past him to face off against Kamari. "So what's the challenge?" I shouted, loud enough for all the surrounding archers to hear. "Do I just beat Kamari senseless with this stick?"

Kamari smirked, brandishing her bo staff. "You can try," she said.

Chapter 52

I'VE ONLY SEEN ONE ROBIN Hood movie in my life, the 1990s version my dad loves so much. There's a scene in the movie where Robin Hood needs to cross a river, but to do so, he must fight a giant man with a quarterstaff. The two warriors battle viciously, striking each other as hard as they can and bloodying each other's noses. I enjoyed watching the fight scene from the comfort of my living room while eating popcorn.

But now—surrounded by archers shouting for blood as Kamari twirled her massive bo staff—I realized fighting in movies is fun, but fighting in real life kind of sucks.

"C'mon, Kamari!" an archer yelled from the crowd. "Show this twit the might of the Merry Men!"

"Geez," I chuckled nervously. "I'm guessing you guys don't want me to win."

Kamari lunged.

Startled, I leapt rearward as she swung. Her bo staff smacked the ground where I'd been standing mere seconds before. "Whoa," I breathed. "You could've killed me."

Kamari smiled. "That's the point."

She attacked again—this time jabbing with the end of her bo staff. I sidestepped the strike, but she swiped in my direction and walloped me on the back.

"OW!" I yelled, rubbing the spot where she'd struck me. Cheers erupted from the crowd of archers.

Kamari pressed the attack.

Jab.

Jab.

Jab.

And strike.

I darted rearward to avoid her jabs and dove to dodge the strike. I came out of the roll and sprang to my feet, then swung an attack of my own. But the bo staff felt heavy like weights were tied to my arms. The weapon could have been moving in slow motion for all the good it did me because Kamari avoided my attack with ease.

She darted forward and struck with her staff.

WHACK! I blocked her strike with my bo staff. Splinters flew from where the weapons smacked together. My hands vibrated painfully from the shock of the blow.

This whole scenario was so not cool. I wasn't a fighter. Unlike Kamari, who twirled her bo staff as if she were one with the weapon, entwined together in a dangerous dance. It was only a matter of time before one of her attacks landed a killing blow. How could I defeat her?

WHACK! WHACK! I defended two more strikes. Each time our bo staffs clashed together my hands stung from the impact.

Then it happened.

Kamari swung her bo staff toward my head, and when I ducked to avoid the blow, her weapon's shaft grazed the side of my head. White hot pain lanced through my ear. Stars blurred my vision. I leapt back from Kamari's attack range and felt something wet running down my neck. I touched the wetness. The tips of my fingers were covered in blood.

"Okay, this is getting serious," I said.

Kamari smirked, twirling her bo staff.

I swallowed, trying to spot a weakness in her stance, but I didn't know what I was doing. Kamari could be weaponless, yelling, "Attack me, I'll give you a free shot," and I still wouldn't be able to hit her. The weapon was too heavy for me to handle.

Kamari lunged an attack.

I darted left to get away—but I was so focused on my opponent that I crashed into a group of archers. Many of them spat insults in my bloody ear, but one of them surprised me by offering words of encouragement.

"Her left hand is injured," Jamari whispered. "Take advantage of it."

Then he shoved me back into the fight. I whirled toward Kamari, only to have my legs swept out from beneath me by her staff. I landed on my back hard. The wind got knocked out of me. She raised her weapon overhead, preparing to bring it down with all her might—and I noticed a bandage on her left hand with fresh blood seeping through the cloth.

"*Hiyaaa!*" Kamari shouted, swinging the bo staff toward my face.

My eyes widened in alarm, but I rolled away just as her staff *smacked* the ground. I jumped to my feet and kicked my black combat book into her wounded hand. Kamari cried out in pain, dropping her staff. She recoiled like a snake had bitten her, now realizing her opponent to be dangerous.

I pressed the attack.

Swinging the bo staff might not be an option due to its weight, but I could jab with its point with relative ease. And that's what I did. I jabbed my staff's point right into Kamari's wounded hand. She screamed and curled around her hand trying to protect it.

That's when I jabbed her in the nose.

Blood squirted. Kamari collapsed to the ground, gasping. She raised her good hand to defend herself. "I relent, please—no more!"

I raised my bo staff and shouted triumphantly, "Booyah!"

But I was the only one cheering. The crowd of archers all stood silent as they stared at their comrade, who whimpered over her hand with blood streaming from her nose.

Jamari rushed forward. "Come with me," he said, taking the bo staff from my hands.

"I won, right?" I asked, confused why everyone was glowering at me. Some of the archers looked like they wanted to throw me from the rooftop. "My family can live, right?"

Jamari didn't say anything. He opened the rooftop door leading to the stairwell and ushered me inside. Nobody tried to stop us. Light flickered on as he flipped a switch. An obsidian black staircase spiraled down with dark, oaken doors located on every floor.

Jamari whirled around to face me, smiling. "You did it," he said. "You passed the test!"

"Then why's everyone so glum back there?" I asked.

"Because you kind of cheated, bruh. Attacking Kamari's hand was a dirty move. Heck, they're probably plotting revenge as we speak."

"But you told me to do it," I protested.

"Well, yeah, but I didn't think you'd actually do it. My sister's gonna be ticked."

"Are you not mad that I bloodied her nose?"

"Are you kidding?" Jamari said. "She stole my phone charger and won't give it back. And by the way . . . *booyah?* Who says that anymore?"

"Shut up," I said, shoving him playfully. "Or I'll kick your butt like I did your sister's."

Chapter 53

WE DESCENDED THE SPIRALING staircase and entered a door on the third floor. My jaw dropped upon seeing the room. It was a huge, open space with leather recliners, plaid sofas, and colorful beanbag chairs—all positioned to face a dozen big-screen TVs mounted on limestone walls. PlayStation, Xbox, and Nintendo consoles were connected to each television. Vintage arcade machines filled a corner of the room: Asteroids, Pac-Man, Galaga, Mortal Kombat, Tekken 3, Cruis'n USA, and others I didn't recognize. There were also pool tables, dart boards, and even a bar with every kind of soft drink and snack you could imagine.

The room was amazing. I could easily spend the rest of my life here.

"Take that, ya noobs!" shouted Zac, sitting in a bean bag chair in front of a TV with an Xbox controller. He wore a headset and mic and appeared to be playing a first-person shooter game with players online.

What the fetch? I thought. *I risk my neck to save our lives and my brother is playing a frigging video game?*

Jason and Kleopatra sat at the bar, enjoying iced cold Coca-Cola and talking quietly. They were just as oblivious as Zac to the perils I'd faced. This was so not cool.

"What's up, Maddie?" Jason greeted me as I approached with Jamari in tow. I punched him in the arm. "Yeow!" he yelled, rubbing the spot. "What was that for?"

"Because you're enjoying a Coke while I fought to save our lives," I said. "These lunatics tried to kill me."

Kleopatra cleared her throat. "These *lunatics*," she twisted the word, "saved us from the sheriff and her men."

"Yeah," I said. "Then they challenged me to a duel on the rooftop and promised to kill all of us if I lost."

Jason's gaze darted to my bloody ear. "For real?"

Jamari stepped forward. "Yeah, bruh. Your sista just defeated one of our warriors in a bo staff fight."

"What? No way."

"It's totally true. Now if you'll give a brotha a sec . . ." Jamari walked away from the bar and disappeared into a side room.

Kleopatra watched him walk away. "Wow," she whistled. "That boy could model for Hollister, Abercrombie, Tommy Hilfiger, or whatever clothing line wanted to put clothes on him."

"Tell me about it," I sighed, sitting down on a barstool beside her. "But he totally threw me under the bus a minute ago."

"What'd he do?" asked Jason.

"Let's just say his ancient Order's rules are more important than girls."

"Been there, girlfriend," said Kleopatra. "So how'd you escape the sheriff?"

I inhaled a deep breath, then shared my story of opening the puzzle box, finding the rings, and discovering a strange deputy badge with an ominous engraving. I also told them how one of the deputies caught on fire for disobeying the sheriff's orders during the battle at the warehouse.

"That sounds like a curse," said Jason. "Like in China last year."

I nodded, agreeing with him. "Jamari rescued me shortly after," I explained.

"You said the rings have an engraving?" asked Kleopatra. "What'd they say?"

I reached into my jacket pocket and felt around until my fingers brushed against the two rings. I pulled them out and held them in my palm. Each ring had a tiny sentence etched on the inside of the bands. Together they appeared to form verses of a clue. The flowy script was cursive so I couldn't read it, so I handed the rings to Jason and he read the clue aloud.

Along a wayside road, where travelers pass,
the famed Robin of Loxley, rest deep in the grass.

"Welp," Jason groaned. "We're screwed. This clue is so vague, the road it's referencing could be anywhere."

"Maybe the rings themselves are a clue," said Kleopatra.

"What'd you mean?" I asked.

"The rings kind of look like wedding bands," she said. "And where do most people get married?"

"In a church," said Jason.

"Exactly, so maybe the road we're looking for is near a church where a wedding took place."

I was reminded of the Robin Hood sketch of the kissing

couple. "That's a pretty smart idea, Kleo."

"Thank you," she smiled.

The stairwell door burst open. Archers flooded in. They all went in separate directions. Some powered on game consoles and sat in recliners. Others wracked pool balls or hit the arcade. A few sat at tables already set up with Dungeons and Dragons books, pencils, and dice to resume games that must have been interrupted.

Their hoods and masks had all been removed. I was surprised to see that many of the archers were young, possibly early twenties or late teens, but I noticed a few archers looked older, in their late thirties or early forties. Most of the archers were guys, but I spotted a few women among the crowd. Many of them glared at me as they passed to spend time at their favorite hangout spots.

I motioned to Jason for the rings. He quietly handed them to me and I pocketed the clue before prying eyes could see our discovery.

Kamari came in last, her weight half-carried between two archers. They eased her onto a sofa. A nasty bruise purpled her eye.

Jamari reappeared with a first aid kit. He set it on the bar and pulled out some medical supplies. "Let's see your ear," he said, dabbing hydrogen peroxide onto a cotton swab.

He pressed the swab to my ear and I flinched, hissing at the sting.

"Easy," he said. "I gotta disinfect the wound. It doesn't look bad. A butterfly Band-Aid outta do it."

"Thanks," I mumbled as he bandaged me up, "but

shouldn't you be checking on your sister?"

"Nah, her boyfriend will take care of her."

I noticed a handsome man in his early twenties with a scruffy beard tending to Kamari's wounds.

"Besides," Jamari said. "She'd just dampen my swag. She scolds me whenever I don't follow the rules."

"You're a rule breaker, huh?"

"You have no idea, girl."

I smiled.

"Why the goofy grin?"

"Nothing," I said. "Just realized we have a lot in common, that's all."

Jamari's peppermint breath felt warm against my neck as he tended to my ear. Goosebumps formed on my skin. I tried to remind myself that Jamari wasn't fit to call boyfriend, not after witnessing his selfish demeanor firsthand on the rooftop. But my convictions quickly deteriorated as he placed both hands on the sides of my head and looked deeply into my eyes. His gaze was piercing, in a good way, and his dark ebony eyes were tinged with flecks of amber. Looking into his eyes sent a lurch to my stomach that had nothing to do with nerves.

"I don't think you've got a concussion," he said.

"Thanks, you've got gorgeous eyes too," I sighed.

"Excuse me?"

Kleopatra rammed me in the ribs with her elbow, snapping me out of my stupor.

"Ow," I said.

"I think what Maddie means is," said Kleopatra, "who are you guys?"

Jamari placed medical supplies back into the first aid kit. "Have you not figured it out yet?"

"I'm guessing the Merry Men of Sherwood Forest," said Jason.

"Sherwood Lumber," Jamari corrected.

"Right," I said slowly. "And that means one of you is the famous Robin Hood." I meant my comment to come across as sarcastic, but Jamari responded as though what I said was matter-of-fact.

"Nah, none of these losers are *him*. We're just misfits who were recruited to the cause."

"The cause?"

"Robbing from the rich and giving to the poor," he said. "You know, that sort of thing. But our missions have become more humanitarian lately. You might've seen our work. We recently saved a train full of people from a madman in Paris."

"Wait, that was you guys?" I said. "I saw that story on the news, but they said ex-soldiers stopped the terrorists from blowing up the train."

"Nah, it was us," Jamari said. "Everything we do is secretive. I'd love to go public, but the Order has to stay hidden."

"Why?"

"The Sheriff of Nottingham," he explained. "If she knew of our whereabouts—"

A horn suddenly sounded, interrupting our conversation. I turned toward the noise to see a strapping young man with broad shoulders standing atop a set of stairs, blowing a hunting horn. An intimidating iron door loomed behind him with a bronze plaque above it reading: WAR ROOM. The archer stopped blowing the horn. He stepped aside and the iron door swung open.

A towering black man emerged. His muscles were so big they bulged through a magnificent green and gold cloak draped around his thick neck. The guy's size reminded me of a WWE wrestler. I'm not making this up. He was extremely jacked. Pro Wrestler set hands on his hips and peered down at the room of archers.

All around the room, the Merry Men stopped what they were doing and knelt toward the man in strict obedience—as if he was a ruler and they were loyal subjects. Even Jamari hopped down from his barstool and took a knee. The man's dark eyes scanned the room. He spotted Kamari lying on the sofa holding a pack of ice to her face, and he frowned. Then his gaze darted over to me sitting at the bar with Jamari.

"Who is that?" I breathed out the corner of my mouth, feeling a sudden twinge of fear as the large man stabbed me with his eyes.

"He is the king of outlaws and prince of good fellows," Jamari whispered from the ground where he knelt. "A noble thief known the world over as Robin Hood." He took a deep breath. "And he is my father."

Chapter 54

OKAY, WHAT THE HECK WAS going on? First, we encounter a seriously old chick who appears to be the immortal Sheriff of Nottingham. Then one of her deputies catches on fire the moment she disobeys a command. Now I learn Robin Hood is alive and well and his son is the boy I'd been crushing on?

Geez, what did I eat today that gave me crazy cat lady syndrome?

"Archers!" Robin Hood bellowed. His voice boomed through the room like a war drum. "Tonight's rescue mission was a tremendous success. Not only did we save my son from the sheriff's evil clutches, but we rescued prisoners who would've died by morning."

Banging broke out, startling me. Archers pounded fists against whatever hard surface they happened to be near.

Robin Hood raised a hand for quiet. "We also won a trophy this night." He reached inside his cloak and revealed a black cord necklace with a mini-compass and lion-head key fastened to its end.

"Hey, that's mine!" I shouted.

But nobody heard me because a tumult of cheers erupted from the archers. Even Jamari pumped his fist triumphantly into the air. I made eye contact with Jason and

Kleopatra, and something unspoken seemed to pass between us: *We need that key.*

Robin Hood tucked the necklace back inside his cloak, hiding it from view. "Yes," he breathed after the archers grew quiet. "We are closer to finding Robert Fitzooth's treasure than ever before. And once we have the final clue—nothing will be able to stop us!"

Cheers broke out again.

I patted my jacket pocket to make sure the rings were still safely hidden.

"But it grows late," Robin Hood said. "And we have work in the morning. So get some rest, archers. You've earned it. As for the newcomers," he made eye contact with me as if singling me out from the crowd. "I have questions, and those questions will be answered soon . . ."

Everyone disappeared to their sleeping quarters. Jamari gave me, Kleopatra, and my brothers pillows and blankets, and we each claimed a different sofa in the living room. The lights were dimmed. I thanked Jamari for his hospitality.

"Son, a word," Robin Hood's deep voice called.

Jamari joined his father inside the war room for a private conversation. I watched the door close behind them, wondering how on earth we were going to get the lion-head key back.

"Can you guys believe it?" Jason said as he fluffed a pillow beneath his head. "Robin Hood and the Merry Men are *real.*"

Zac rested hands behind his head and stared at the

ceiling. "It's pretty crazy. And to think, you doubted it all along."

"Jason doubts everything," I said. "Remember last year when he refused to believe the terracotta warriors were all mummies, then they came to life and he nearly crapped his pants."

"Hey," Jason protested. "In my defense, mummies are gross and maggoty."

Zac and I chuckled.

"All right, kiddos," Kleopatra said. She reclined on a brown leather sofa and still wore a hijab. "It's been a long day so let's get some sleep."

I fluffed the pillow beneath my head and tried to get comfortable. My body ached from the fight with Kamari, and my eye stung from getting punched in the face with the sheriff's elbow crutch. I'd certainly earned a good night's rest, but sleep didn't come easy. I tossed and turned for nearly an hour.

Unsurprisingly, Kleopatra and my brothers fell asleep within minutes. Their breathing grew rhythmic and deep. Save Kleopatra's, of course, whose nasally snores wheezed from nostrils and echoed throughout the large room. I lay awake, staring at the blinking arcade games and lifeless mounted TVs. It was hard to believe we were having a sleepover inside the secret headquarters of the Merry Men.

Another half hour went by. I rolled over, the leather couch creaking and sticking to my skin. A TV remote rested on a coffee table nearby. I couldn't sleep, so I decided to see if they had Netflix. I reached for the remote—

—but the war room's door opened. Robin Hood and

Jamari walked out. They descended the steps down to the living room, speaking quietly. I yanked my hand back, closed my eyes, and pretended to be sleeping.

"Why you playin' me, bruh?" said Jamari, clearly upset about something.

"How many times must I tell you, son?" Robin Hood's voice reminded me of James Earl Jones—the actor who played both Darth Vader and Mufasa. "Speak naturally. Your slang sounds forced and it's unbecoming for someone of your station."

Jamari sighed. "I'm just saying, Dad. The girl fought fair."

"Was it *fair* to kick Kamari's stitched-up hand? Tell me, how did she know her hand was wounded to begin with? I was told the girl didn't attack Kamari's hand until after *you* shoved her back into the fight."

"I dunno," said Jamari. "Maddie seems to have street smarts. Maybe she saw the bandage and just went for it. My point is—she passed the test. By our laws that means she's free to join the Order."

Wait a minute. Were they discussing my enrollment in their weird Robin Hood club? What if I didn't want to join?

"In war, son," Robin Hood breathed heavily.

"In war, you do what it takes to survive," Jamari interrupted. "She thought we were going to kill her family, Dad."

"You know we would never do such a thing."

"Yeah, but she didn't."

"Okay," said Robin Hood. "I will consider your wisdom when I speak to her in the morning."

"Thank you."

"Now let us discuss plans moving forward . . ."

They continued their conversation as they walked toward the stairwell at the far end of the room, but their voices faded away as the door closed behind them. I opened my eyes and glanced at the war room. Its door appeared to be cracked open.

It's time I get my stuff back, I thought.

Chapter 55

I TIPTOED TO THE WAR room.

The door was indeed cracked open. I slipped quietly inside. A dark hallway stretched before me with dim light shining from a room up ahead. I peeked back into the living room to make sure I hadn't been spotted—no one in sight except for Kleopatra and my brothers snoozing away—so I closed the door behind me and crept toward the far room.

Framed portraits hung on the walls. They appeared to be paintings of men and women from different time periods of history. Each painting depicted a different person wearing the same magnificent green and gold cloak Jamari's dad had been wearing. In one painting, a middle-aged man donned the cloak *and* a white Colonial wig. In another, a beautiful Asian woman wore the cloak while holding a set of samurai swords. A third painting showed a weathered Native American man wearing the cloak, complete with a headdress of Indian feathers.

Beneath each portrait were bronze plaques. The plaque beneath the Native American read: CHIEF EAGLE WINGS, ROBIN HOOD, 1802-1813. I scanned the plaque beneath the samurai woman: ONNA GOZEN, ROBIN HOOD, 1587-1601. Portrait after portrait, plaque after plaque, seemed to show a different Robin Hood from a different era in history.

But that couldn't be right, could it? I mean, all the stories indicated Robin Hood had been *one* person who lived sometime around the 14th century. What mystery had I stumbled upon?

I made my way through the hall of portraits. I reached the war room, but a final portrait hanging on the wall caught my attention.

It was of Jamari's dad.

He wore the green and gold cloak, a severe expression, and he reminded me of a stern military general on the eve of battle—all serious and businesslike. The plaque beneath his portrait read: MALIK HONDO, PRESENT ROBIN HOOD.

This was all very strange, but I wasn't getting any answers standing around in the hall, so I entered the war room.

The place reminded me of my bedroom: messy and small.

Scattered on a large table in the center of the room were maps of England, Eastern Europe, China, and the United States. The walls were covered in black and white photographs of the sheriff and her deputies. I saw pictures of Ponytail, Blondie, and Merida—but there were pictures of other women as well. Several pictures had a big red X marked through the photographs, including the recently deceased Merida (the red-haired deputy who had caught on fire). Each photo included a colored pin with strings connecting them to newspaper clippings, which all indicated the women had gone missing, were presumed dead, or had been kidnapped. The sheriff's photograph was at the top of the wall.

Every string connected to her.

It was as though the entire room were a complex puzzle piecing people and places together, like a detective's office during a serial killer investigation.

I crept toward the table of maps. Similar to the walls, pins and strings connected cities from countries all over the world. There were pictures of people next to some of the cities—and my heart skipped a beat when I saw my hometown of Evansville marked on the map. A stack of photographs lay beside the orange pin. I leaned in close to inspect the top picture and—

Oh, my God!

It was a photograph of my dad. He stood on the steps of the Evansville History Museum on what appeared to be an early, foggy morning. He wore a brown tweed jacket with patches on the elbows, vintage-framed glasses, and a red dress shirt he'd gotten for Christmas. Hey, I remembered the day he wore this outfit. It was last week— the same day he left for New Mexico to attend the auction to acquire a famous artifact for the financially struggling museum. Someone else was in the photograph with him. I picked up the picture to get a better look—and I nearly had a heart attack and died right there on the spot.

It was the Sheriff of Nottingham. She leaned against elbow crutches as she spoke to my father. A jolt of fear punched me in the stomach.

Why is my dad talking to the Sheriff of Nottingham? I thought.

An object was being handed off between them—an iron box.

What the fetch?! It was the puzzle box we'd found after

sifting through museum rubble following the explosion. This mystery was getting stranger by the second, and I didn't like the direction it was going. I looked down at the stack of photographs. The next picture was of me and my brothers, waiting in the car pick-up line at school. I snatched up the photographs and rifled through them: Kleopatra, my brothers, Kleopatra, me. Picture after picture showed my family going about our daily routines.

Why are we being investigated?

"You aren't supposed to be here," someone said.

I dropped the photographs and glanced up.

Jamari stood at the end of the hall near the war room's entrance, and his bow was nocked with an arrow aimed right at me.

Chapter 56

JAMARI STALKED DOWN THE hall of portraits toward the war room, his bowstring creaking. How much longer could he hold the bowstring back before being forced to let go, sending the arrow hurtling to end my life?

"Anyone who sees this room must die," he said, deadly serious. "It's nothing personal, just one of our rules."

I swallowed to calm my nerves. "But you have pictures of my family—"

TWANG! He fired the arrow.

Its feathers brushed my cheek and I flinched. The arrow struck the wall behind me. It pierced a map of Eastern Asia and quivered from the impact.

"That was a warning shot," he said as he grabbed another arrow from a pouch on his hip.

My hands trembled, but I forced my voice to sound confident. "Or maybe you missed."

He chuckled. "My aim is perfect, bruh. You should know that by now."

He was right. Only a few hours ago, I witnessed him shoot two arrows at once while running and hit both targets with perfect precision.

"Step away from the table." He entered the war room with a new arrow drawn. The table of maps was between us. "Go back to bed and I won't tell my father you were here."

"Why? Will little Jamari get in trouble?"

"Probably, but not until after your execution."

I gulped.

THWACK! Another arrow struck the wall, piercing a map of the island of Japan.

I flinched again. "Will you stop doing that?!"

"Not until you leave." He nocked another arrow.

"Look, all I want is answers." I snatched up the photographs. "Who took these?"

Jamari's gaze flitted to the photographs in my hand. He glanced over his shoulder, down the long hall of portraits and at the war room's entrance.

"You don't have to tell your father I was here," I said. "Just help me understand what's going on."

Jamari returned his focus to me, his dark eyes gleaming. Dimples flared in his cheeks as he clenched his jaw. "If I tell you what I know," he breathed. "Do you promise not to say anything?"

"Of course."

Jamari lowered his weapon. "Okay. I'll answer your questions, but only because you defeated my sister and you've earned that much. Whaddya want to know? Let's make this quick."

I tossed the pictures of my family onto the table between us. "Who's the photographer?" I asked.

Jamari leaned weight onto his bow and peered at the picture of my dad meeting with the Sheriff of Nottingham. The bow's wood creaked but held firm. "I am," he said.

"*You* took these?"

"Yeah," he thumped the stack of pictures with his knuckle. "After your dad met with the sheriff, I was ordered to follow you guys. I kept tabs on your family to see if you were a threat."

"Are we?"

"Nah," he shook his head. "But I'm not so sure about your dad."

"Hey, my dad's not a bad guy."

"Then why's he working with the old hag?"

That was a good question. Why would my dad work with *her*? The mere thought made goosebumps crawl up my spine. The woman was vile and creepy.

No.

My dad wouldn't work with the sheriff, not unless she came to him needing help with something. "The iron box," I realized. "She contacted my father because of his expertise with ancient artifacts."

"The iron box once belonged to Robin Hood's wife," Jamari explained. "It was her jewelry box. She kept necklaces, rings, and brooches inside of it—but also Robin Hood's secret letters. After his death, the jewelry box went missing. Not even the Merry Men knew of its location. Until last spring, when the Sheriff of Nottingham found it inside the walls of a historic Catholic church in London."

"Let me guess," I said. "The sheriff couldn't open the box . . ."

"So she contacted your father," Jamari said. "We pursued the old hag to America. When we arrived in Evansville, she must've pressured your dad to open the box quickly, but he failed. She blew up the museum and tried to kill your father."

My eyes widened at the realization. "The sheriff sent the bomb?"

"It's got her signature style written all over it," he said. "Loud and deadly."

"But the jewelry box was still inside the museum when the place exploded," I said. "Why would she try and kill my dad, but forget to retrieve the box?"

Jamari shrugged.

"What the fetch is wrong with people? Why can't they leave my dad alone?"

"Hey, I get it," said Jamari. "The sheriff has tried to kill my pops too many times to count."

I shuddered. "What's up with her, anyway? Why can't the sheriff die?"

Jamari was quiet for a long moment before answering, almost as though he were afraid to share what he knew. "Do you believe in the supernatural?" he asked.

I nodded, explaining how I'd witnessed strange events last year in China.

"Well, I didn't believe," he said. "Not at first. But during a battle in London this past June, I put an arrow through the sheriff's chest and she didn't die. She ended up killing my best friend."

"I'm sorry."

"Nah, you didn't kill him," Jamari said quietly. "But to

answer your question, my dad thinks she's the original Sheriff of Nottingham—that her real name is Welma de Wendeval. She might've delved into witchcraft. Maybe she found a powerful artifact giving her long life." He shrugged. "The truth is, we just don't know."

"What about her deputies?" I asked. "Why do they wear those creepy badges?"

"The badges are the deputies' weakness," he said. "They tie their souls to the sheriff. If they're removed, or if a deputy disobeys an order—" he sighed heavily, "—well, you saw what happens. My dad takes it especially hard when a deputy dies. He has a personal vendetta to save them all."

I remembered how Jamari said the red-haired deputy was a stay-at-home mom. She wouldn't be returning home to her husband and child. Since I'd lost my mom at such a young age, the thought struck me like a semi-truck. Tears welled up in my eyes as I glanced at the photograph on the wall of Merida . . . marked through with an X.

"But the badges also give the deputies strength," Jamari said, his tone more serious. "As long as they wear them the women are invincible. You can shoot them, stab them, drown them, and it won't even matter. They keep on living just like the sheriff." He looked at me with a grim expression. "If a deputy is after you, don't hesitate. Don't think twice. Go for their badge and remove it if you can. If they've been ordered to kill, then they'll do everything in their power to follow the command. Otherwise, it's their life on the line."

I swallowed. "I'll keep that in mind."

Jamari paused long enough to glance toward the war

room's entrance. "Have I answered enough of your questions?" he asked. "I'd feel better if we left this room before my dad finds out."

I glanced past Jamari and at all of the paintings lining the walls in the hallway. "Actually," I said. "I still have one more question."

Jamari slung his bow onto his shoulder. "Lay it on me," he said.

"What's up with the portraits in the hall?"

Chapter 57

"THE SHERIFF OF NOTTINGHAM might be immortal," Jamari said, leading me to the hall of portraits beyond the war room. "But the Merry Men are not."

He stopped at a portrait and illuminated it with light from his cell phone. The painting was old with faded paint, a cracked canvas, and a splintered wooden frame. The portrait depicted a gruff-looking man with ginger hair. He wore a green and gold cloak.

"The first Robin Hood was a man named Robert Fitzooth," Jamari explained. "He was a supporter of King Richard the Lionheart. But when the king left on crusade in the holy lands of Jerusalem, England's government grew corrupt. Robert was forced to live life as an outlaw, along with his friends. Together they formed the Merry Men. They robbed from the rich to help out the poor."

He proceeded to the next portrait, a painting of an Englishman with brown hair and a scar across his cheek. "Meet Robyn Hode," said Jamari. "He took over the Merry Men after Robert Fitzooth passed away. It's from his name we got the title *Robin Hood*."

He walked to the next portrait, and then the next, and as he passed each painting he thumped their frames and spouted their names: "Roger Godberd. Onna Gozen. Chief

Eagle Wings. Jesse James."

"Whoa, hold up," I said. "Jesse James? The infamous American outlaw and gunslinger?"

"Yep, he served as Robin Hood from 1866 to 1882."

"Wow," I said. "I never knew."

"Most people don't. But several Robin Hoods have been famous. I'm talking Hollywood and White House famous."

"This is a lot to take in."

"I get it," he said. "When my dad told me he was Robin Hood, I laughed in his face."

I scanned the paintings Jamari hadn't yet introduced me to. There were dozens of them. "When you said the Merry Men have been fighting the sheriff for hundreds of years, you really meant it."

"It's our job to stop the Sheriff of Nottingham from terrorizing society," he said. "When a Robin Hood dies in battle, a new Merry Man steps forward to take up the charge—one deemed worthy to possess the mantle of noble thief."

"And the first Robin Hood was Robert Fitzooth?" I asked.

"Precisely," he said. "He's the one who hid treasure inside a grave."

"What'd you think the treasure is? I'm hoping it's gold and gemstones."

"That's where things get tricky," Jamari said. "No one knows for sure. Plus we don't know *where* it's hidden. What we do know is that Robert left clues to the treasure's whereabouts, hidden inside of his wife's jewelry box."

"And now that her jewelry box has been recovered," I said. "You guys are racing to reach the treasure before the sheriff does."

"That's the gist of it." Jamari adjusted the bow slung across his shoulder. "All right, I've answered your questions. Now it's my turn to ask one."

"If you're going to ask me to the prom," I teased. "My answer is still no."

He smirked. "You passed our test. In the morning, my dad's gonna ask you to join the Merry Men. When he does, I want you to say no."

"Excuse me, what? You don't want me to join?"

"It would be like joining the military. You'd have to do as Robin Hood says."

I scoffed. There was no way in H. E. double hockey sticks I'd willingly join an organization where I'd have to listen to authority.

"I figured as much," Jamari said.

"But if you didn't want me to join," I said. "Why were you arguing with your dad about my enlistment?"

His eyebrow with a stylish gash raised. "You heard that, huh?"

I nodded.

"Okay, yes, I convinced my dad to recruit you. But that was only so my ruse would work."

"Your what?"

He dropped his voice to a whisper. "I have a plan. However, the only way it'll work is if you refuse to join the Merry Men."

"I'm not following you."

"Anyone who refuses to join our Order must give Robin Hood a tribute—as a sign of surrender. The tribute acts as a promise not to reveal our identities to the public. If you refuse to join the Merry Men, my dad will demand a tribute. And I know what he wants—the next clue."

My hand started to shoot toward my pocket where I kept the rings, but I willed myself to stay still. "What clue?"

"Don't play dumb with me," Jamari said. "I know you've got two rings in your pocket. I already inspected them to confirm if they're real."

"What? How could you—"

"I'm a thief, Maddie. A hella good one."

My mouth hung open. "Well, if you already had the rings why didn't you just keep them? You could've given them to your dad and saved me the trouble."

"Because that's not how I work," he said. "I'm a *noble* thief, not a petty criminal."

"Seem like the same things to me."

"Look, I don't want my dad to have the real clue," he said. "And if I give him a fake, he'll know. He can read me like a book. But if a fake clue comes from *you* . . ."

I put a hand up to stop him. "I don't get it, why trick your dad?"

"Because I've lost friends and I don't want to lose more," he said. "My dad's plan to defeat the sheriff—well, let's just say I don't think it'll work. What I'm asking is that you refuse his offer to join the Merry Men, and when he asks for the clue you discovered, you give him *this*."

He held out his hand. Resting in his palm was a worn piece of yellowing parchment. Sprawling script had been written in faded ink. "It's the fake clue," he explained. "Give this to my father."

"What will a fake clue achieve?" I asked.

"When my dad deciphers the fake, he will lead the sheriff *away*. He'll have no choice. Then you can go after Robin Hood's treasure without worrying about the sheriff, or the Merry Men."

"Why would you do that?"

Jamari sighed. "Think of it like a crossover in basketball. Make it look like you're going one way, but juke in the opposite direction. If you give my dad those rings, he'll go straight toward Robin's tomb. The sheriff will follow, and since we can't kill her, we won't be able to stop her.

"But if he leads her *away*, you can get the treasure first." Jamari glanced toward the war room's entrance to make sure we were still alone. "The truth is, Robin Hood's grave might contain an artifact that can defeat the sheriff. I want you to get it for me. If you happen to find gold and gemstones, consider it a bonus. Keep them for yourself."

"You don't want any of the tomb's riches?" I asked, dumbfounded.

Jamari shook his head. "I just want this war to be over."

As strange as Jamari's request sounded, part of me liked the idea of resisting the authority of Robin Hood. Sticking it to the man. Doing the exact opposite of what the adults told us to do. It seemed Jamari and I shared more in common than I thought. Plus, Jamari was not only promising to clear the way for us to find the treasure, but he also didn't want any riches. We'd be guaranteed to save my dad's museum. In exchange, I'd give him anything *unusual* we might find—

which was likely nothing.

"Are you willing to do it?" Jamari asked. "Are you willing to lie to my dad so you can continue your quest?"

"You mean, am I willing to pull a prank on the infamous Robin Hood?" I said. "Of course!"

Jamari smiled. "Good, then here's what I want you to do . . ."

Chapter 58

I WAS EXHAUSTED AFTER being up all night.

After my conversation with Jamari, I attempted to get a couple hours of shut-eye on the sofa, but the sun rose before I could fall asleep and the living room grew busy with the hustle and bustle of Merry Men. Archers raided the bar's massive refrigerators, ate oatmeal, Raisin Bran, and blended fruit smoothies. The noisy blenders woke my brothers.

They didn't wake Kleopatra, though. She kept snoring.

The archers no longer wore cloaks. Now they all donned yellow overalls with SHERWOOD LUMBER embroidered on the front. Name tags were clipped to their breasts. Tool belts hung from their waists with hammers, tape measures, screwdrivers, and wrenches.

Work uniforms, I realized. The archers were getting ready for work.

I sat up. It looked like I'd be running on zero hours of sleep today. My eyes felt bloodshot and dry. There was no way I could sleep with all the noise, so I walked to the bar and poured a bowl of Cookie Crisp cereal. I started to take my first bite when the shadow of a towering figure loomed over me.

"Miss Jones," rumbled a deep voice like boulders tumbling down a mountainside. "Will you please accompany me on a tour of Sherwood Lumber's warehouse?"

I blinked up at Jamari's dad. He wore yellow overalls like everybody else. His name tag read: MALIK HONDO, OWNER. "Nah, I'm not interested," I said, and I took a bite of Cookie Crisp.

He stepped aside so I could see the stairwell door at the far end of the room. "This is not a request, Miss Jones. Meet me downstairs once you've finished breakfast." And he exited the living room. I suddenly realized everyone had gotten quiet to watch our exchange.

"What?" I snapped.

Movement began again at once. Chit-chat continued. Archers went back to eating breakfast.

"That's what I thought," I mumbled, milk dribbling down my chin.

A bell suddenly rang, loud and shrill like a fire station alarm. I jumped in my seat. Archers dropped what they were doing and rushed toward the stairs. They left their dishes and food out on the counters. I looked at my brothers, who were still in the process of heating oatmeal and buttering toast.

"Work," I shrugged.

Half an hour later, I found myself being led around by Robin Hood as he introduced me to the workings of Sherwood Lumber's warehouse. The sounds of power drills, hammering, and sawing made the place super noisy. Some of the workers wore respirator masks so they wouldn't breathe in sawdust, which reminded me of their archer masks from their "midnight" job.

"This is the table saw," said Robin Hood. "We use it to cut wood flooring before shipping it out for installation."

He gathered me around a metallic table with levers and blades, and started telling me how Sherwood Lumber provided wood flooring, two-by-fours, and sheetrock for home repair stores all over the world. He told me about the company's motto—*Build something rich even if you're poor*—and explained how the Merry Men now working for Sherwood Lumber started out like me.

As juvenile delinquents with criminal records.

I tried to listen to what he had to say because it intrigued me how he'd learned about my criminal history from my silly pranks, but all he did was drone on and on about his boring lumber store and my concentration drifted elsewhere. I was extremely tired. My lack of sleep was catching up. I'd probably be a walking zombie by lunchtime.

"And I believe you already met my daughter, Kamari," Robin Hood said.

I looked up to see Kamari standing in front of us with a clipboard. She wore a yellow uniform and tool belt. Her nose was swollen, and possibly a little crooked, but I wasn't about to say anything.

Kamari tapped the clipboard against her leg impatiently. "Please don't tell me you're thinking of recruiting her, father," she groaned.

"Ah, c'mon, Kamari," I said. "You know I'd be a real slugger in the company softball games."

She glared at me with a black eye.

Robin Hood cleared his throat. "This way," he said.

I followed him up a set of stairs to an office overlooking the warehouse. Robin Hood's office smelled of sawdust and fresh pine. Beyond the room's single window, workers cut planks of wood, packaged shectrock, and loaded crates onto shipping trucks. He closed the door. The warehouse's noises grew quiet, but I could still hear their muffled sounds through the door.

"Please, have a seat," he instructed.

Brown leather chairs faced an imposing oaken desk. Robin Hood sat behind the desk and folded his hands. He waited patiently for me to join him. Not wanting to appear like I was accustomed to following orders, I sat in one of the leather chairs and propped my feet up on his desk. My black combat boots knocked over his nameplate.

Robin Hood eyed my dirty shoes with distaste. He picked up the nameplate, opened a drawer, and placed it inside. I pointed at a cool decoration hanging on the wall behind his desk—a longbow with a set of crisscrossed arrows.

"Those real?" I asked.

He glanced at the longbow and arrows, then looked at me. "Yes," he said. "Carbon dating has aged them to be fourteenth century."

"Hey, isn't that the same century Robert Fitzooth lived?"

Robin Hood's eyes narrowed. He was probably wondering how I knew the name.

"My dad told me about him," I lied. "And you said his name last night during your big 'we won a trophy' speech."

Robin Hood nodded, accepting my story. He didn't say

more. Faintly, I heard a table saw cutting through wood and power drills whirring. "Miss Jones," he finally broke the quiet. "Last night you defeated one of my archers in a sacred trial. That trial was modeled after an event which occurred in the fourteenth century between—"

"Yeah, yeah," I interrupted. "Your stupid test was created because Robin Hood fought Little John, like, five hundred years ago."

"Ah, I take it you're a scholar of Robin Hood lore?"

"Nah," I said, picking beeswax from my ear and flicking it. "I saw a movie once."

Robin Hood scowled. "Hollywood often misinterprets the noble thief's storied past."

"And I'm sure you guys like it that way," I said. "Look, can we skip to the part where you offer me a spot in your nerdy archery club?"

"Straight to the point, as my son suggested you'd be." Robin Hood cleared his throat. "Okay, then. By our laws, your victory over Kamari means you're free to join our Order. If you accept, you will become a Merry Man of Sherwood Lumber. We would train you in the arts of warfare—archery, quarterstaff fighting, hand-to-hand combat, parkour, and the guises of stealth." He stood, and walked to the window overlooking the warehouse with hands clasped behind his back. "But we would also train you in the arts of carpentry—hardwood flooring, drywall, installations, and home repairs. All the skills an employee of this prestigious company needs for success."

"Here's the thing, Mr. Hood," I said. "May I call you Mr. Hood?"

Robin Hood inclined his head, but I saw the faintest hint of annoyance flash across his face.

"I'm just a kid. What do I know about fighting the immortal Sheriff of Nottingham or installing hardwood flooring?"

"We will train you—"

"Then there's school to think about," I said. "My dad isn't going to move our family to England."

Robin Hood waved my comments away. "Your family will not need to relocate. On the contrary, you will be allowed to stay home where a mentor can oversee your education. Once a month, we will fly you here to attend Sherwood Lumber seminars."

Hey, that didn't sound half-bad. I'd go to school by day, but in the evenings I'd learn how to shoot a bow and arrow. They'd even train me how to jump rooftops like a medieval ninja. How often did kids like me get invitations from the legendary Robin Hood?

Not very often, I thought.

But I was getting off course. Jamari had a plan, and I needed to follow through with it.

I scraped dry mud off the bottom of my boot onto the edge of Robin Hood's desk. "As tempting as it sounds to become a construction worker," I said. "I think I'm gonna pass, Mr. Hood."

Robin Hood sighed. He walked back to his desk and sat. "Then I have no choice but to demand a tribute," he said, and he explained the whole process. I tried my best to pretend like the information was new, nodding every so often and grunting in annoyance when he told me what he wanted.

"The tribute I request is the clue you discovered." He held out his hand, palm up.

"What clue?" I played dumb.

Robin Hood's open hand clenched into a fist. "Come now, Miss Jones," his voice rumbled. "My son has confirmed you found something. Hand it over, or I can hand *you* over to Detective Murphy—I believe that was her name. She sounded quite pleasant when I spoke to her on the phone."

My heart jumped to my throat. He spoke to the detective?

Oh, man, if he handed me over to *her* then I'd be blamed for the museum explosion. Dad would lose his job. I'd go to juvie until I was probably eighteen. There was no telling what would become of my brothers.

"You have one minute to decide," Robin Hood said, his deep voice pleasant despite the shady business he was dealing.

I wracked my brain for what to do. The answer seemed obvious enough—give Robin Hood the clue. But should I give him the *real* one, or the *fake* one? Robin Hood struck me as the kind of man who could see through deception.

"Your time is up."

I reached into my jacket pocket. My fingers brushed against the rings *and* the yellowing parchment Jamari had given me. Which clue should I choose, the fake or the real? Slowly, I removed the clue from my pocket and showed it to Robin Hood.

"You're making a wise choice, Miss Jones," he said.

Chapter 59

ROBIN HOOD UNFOLDED THE counterfeit clue. As he read the lines of verse Jamari had created, I held my breath in anticipation. Would he believe it was real?

"Where did you find this?" he asked.

"Inside a golden container I pulled from Little John's grave," I answered.

He scrutinized the yellowing parchment more closely with a magnifying glass. "Was anything else inside the golden container?"

"Nah, just dirt and that piece of paper," I said. "Is something wrong?"

"It looks real," he mumbled, his eyes raking over the fake clue's sprawling script. "But there's something *off* about it. I'll need a second opinion." He set the clue down and looked up. "Thank you, Miss Jones. Your actions today will save countless lives."

"Are you still going to call the detective?" I asked.

He shook his head.

"Then I'm free to go?"

"Of course."

Robin Hood stuck out a meaty fist for me to shake. As he reached across the desk, the lion-head key and mini-compass necklace came free from behind his yellow overalls and dangled from his neck. He noticed me staring at them.

"Did the sheriff take this from you?" he asked.

"The compass was my mom's," I explained. "She gave it to my dad before she passed away."

Robin Hood's expression softened. "Then I'd like you to keep it."

He untied my mom's compass from the thin, black cord. My eyes tracked the lion-head key, and for the briefest moment, I thought about snatching it from his neck and darting out the door, but with all of the Merry Men in the warehouse, I doubted I'd get very far. Duping Robin Hood into believing a fake clue was one thing. Prying a precious artifact from his neck was going to be another challenge altogether.

Robin Hood reached across the desk to hand me the compass. I opened my palm to accept it, but right when he was about to drop it into my hand . . .

BOOOM! An explosion rocked the warehouse.

The office window blew. Glass shards blasted everywhere. The force of the blast sent a shockwave throughout the building. I was thrown from my chair and into the wall opposite the window. My back punched a hole in the drywall. The breath was knocked from my lungs and I slumped to the floor. My ears rang. Blood trickled down my arms from where I'd been cut by flying glass. Dark smoke billowed into the office through the busted window, wafting in from the warehouse.

Robin Hood lay slumped beside me, unmoving. I wasn't sure if he was dead or alive.

Shouting sounded from the warehouse. I climbed to my

feet and staggered toward the busted window. The smoke made me cough. I used the hem of my shirt to cover my mouth and nose. Downstairs, fires waged and black smoke curled into the air. A large gaping hole now loomed in the side of the building. Through the haze, I could see a sunlit street outside and overturned cars, which were also on fire.

Holy cow! Whatever caused this explosion had been powerful.

Flames flickered throughout the warehouse . . . and there were bodies. Corpses. Merry Men in yellow overalls were strewn about the room, their limbs twisted in unnatural angles. I recognized several of them from breakfast this morning.

I suddenly felt sick.

A commotion broke out near the gaping hole. One of the sheriff's deputies entered the building. Ponytail. She stepped across busted rubble and flames, shouldering an AK-47. One of the Merry Men who hadn't died from the explosion stirred, lifting a hand into the air.

Ponytail shot him dead on sight.

I flinched, and ducked back from the busted window so she wouldn't see me.

Then I noticed a Merry Man with braided hair and a black eye rousing from the ashes. It was Kamari. She clambered to her feet with a hammer. It looked like she was about to attack Ponytail.

Don't do it, I thought.

But she charged, screaming a war cry as she attacked. Ponytail looked up to see Kamari rushing her, but she didn't pull the trigger. Instead, she waited until Kamari closed the distance between them—and pistol-whipped her with the butt of her AK-47. Kamari collapsed to the ground.

Then something shiny appeared in Ponytail's hand. When Kamari saw it, she scrambled to get away. But Ponytail stabbed a silver badge into her heart before she could run. Kamari screamed and writhed, then fell limp. Words were spoken, but I couldn't overhear. Slowly, Kamari stood to her feet. Ponytail handed her a Glock pistol.

No, she'd been deputized!

Click. *CLACK!* The Sheriff of Nottingham appeared from the smoke. She leaned heavily against elbow crutches and held a device with a blinking, red button—the detonator for the bomb. She glanced around the destroyed warehouse and glared at the corpses.

"Find the g-g-girl," she croaked at her deputies. "Bring me the key!"

Chapter 60

"MADDIE," A VOICE croaked.

I whirled around to find Robin Hood slumped against the wall. He clutched his side where fresh blood seeped through his yellow uniform.

"Pull the crossed arrows," he said.

"Huh?" I asked.

"The arrows on the wall," he pointed at the decorative longbow and crisscrossed arrows hanging behind his desk. "Pull the left one."

Gunshots rang out from down in the warehouse. I darted from the busted window to where Robin Hood motioned and grabbed the left arrow's fletch. I pulled down hard. A trapdoor fell from the ceiling and a rope ladder tumbled out.

"Climb," Robin Hood said. "I'll be right behind you."

I didn't wait to be told a second time. The gunshots sounded like thunder. It seemed the sheriff and her deputies weren't taking prisoners.

The rope ladder's metal rungs felt cold as I ascended into the ceiling. The sounds of gunshots and flickering flames muffled as Robin Hood's office disappeared beneath me, and the passageway's darkness swallowed me. For the space of a minute—which felt like forever as my thoughts trailed to Kleopatra, my brothers, and their safety—I climbed blindly, one rung after another, until my head hit something solid. I reached up and pushed. A trapdoor opened. I climbed out and into Robin Hood's war room.

Kleopatra, Jason, and Zac were already there.

"Oh, Maddie—thank goodness you're safe," said Kleopatra. Tears blurred her eyes and ruined her mascara. She embraced me in a fierce hug. When she let go, my brothers hugged me just as hard.

"What's going on?" asked Zac, letting go. "We heard an explosion."

Before I could answer his question, Robin Hood appeared from the trapdoor. "I set some traps. It should buy us time." He hurried to a bookshelf and pulled a book with a purple spine. Immediately, the bookshelf swiveled to reveal a hidden room with an armory of weapons.

Robin Hood entered the room of weapons and grabbed a sawed-off shotgun, a longbow and quiver of arrows, throwing knives, and a bo staff. He handed me the bo staff—as if I'd be any good with the thing. I guess since I defeated Kamari with one, he figured I could handle the weapon. Boy, was he wrong. Besides, the sheriff and her men had assault rifles and Glock pistols. How could I defeat them with a stick?

The door to the hall of portraits burst open. I startled and brandished my bo staff, but it was Jamari. He was covered in sweat, soot, and blood.

"Son, you're bleeding." Robin Hood stopped what he was doing and grabbed a first aid kit.

"It's not my blood," Jamari said, gasping for breath.

Two arrows were nocked in his bow, ready to fire at the first sign of trouble. "The blood is from . . . it's from . . ." tears welled up in his eyes. "They're slaughtering us, Dad."

Robin Hood darted the distance to his son. He grabbed Jamari by the shoulders and forced him to look him in the eyes. "I know," he breathed. "And they will kill us, too. Unless we flee."

"You want us to run? What about the others? What about *Kamari*?"

"She was deputized," I blurted out. "I saw the whole thing. They got her."

"What?" Jamari said. "She's *turned*. That can't be true . . ."

"Jamari," Robin Hood bellowed. "Quiet your fear. If your arrows are going to fly true, you must remain calm."

"But, my sister—"

"Is now the enemy. Kamari knew the dangers when she took up her bow."

"You can't mean that, Dad," Jamari said.

"I mean every word, as much as it pains me," Robin Hood said. "We are warriors, and warriors fall in battle." He paused to wipe his son's eyes dry. "We will worry about Kamari when the timing is right. But now, I need you to calm your emotions. Your bow can save us, boy. It can save Maddie and her family." He motioned to the rest of us standing in the war room. "But only if you're calm."

Jamari looked at me, then at my brothers and babysitter. He must have seen the fear splayed across our faces because a quiet resolve seemed to harden his eyes. "All right," he said, tightening the grip on his bow. "I can be calm."

Robin Hood turned and grabbed a black duffel bag. He crammed pistols, bullets, grenades, maps, and newspaper clippings into it. When it was full and bulging, he shouldered the bag, grimacing from the movement. Then he loaded ammunition shells the size of my thumb into a shotgun and cocked the weapon. "There's a truck out back," he began.

A mini explosion rocked the floor we stood on. The building quaked. Dust rained down from the ceiling. We all flinched—well, everyone except Jamari and his dad.

"That was the booby trap in my office," Robin Hood said.

"The truck, Dad."

Robin Hood grabbed a set of car keys from the table. He tossed them to Jamari. "The truck's behind the warehouse. We'll cross the living room, descend the stairs, and escape in the vehicle. Son, lead the vanguard."

Jamari nodded.

"I'll cover the rear," Robin Hood said. "The rest of you, stay between us. Deep breaths everyone. We go on three." Both Jamari and his dad closed their eyes and inhaled large gulps of air. I figured they were doing some sort of Merry Men meditation mumbo jumbo. Then their eyes snapped open, and before I could say ready, Robin Hood counted to three.

Jamari burst into the hall of portraits, his bow aimed and deadly.

Chapter 61

ROBIN HOOD SHOUTED, "GO! GO! GO!"

I rushed after Jamari while Kleopatra and my brothers followed on my heels. Portraits of Robin Hood from various parts of history swept past my peripheral vision. My heart pounded fiercely and I squeezed the bo staff with sweaty fingers.

Jamari reached the end of the hall and kicked the iron door wide open. He dashed forward—and gunshots rang out, igniting sparks on the door. Jamari ducked, then fired two arrows at once.

The gunfire ceased.

Jamari popped his head out and looked around. "All clear," he said.

Then he darted down the stairs to the living room. As he ran, he shouldered his bow and drew a hidden dagger from his cloak. I sprinted after him—and saw Blondie pinned to the wall with Jamari's fired arrows. The arrows pierced the deputy's clothes and nailed her to the wall like a stuffed animal at the state fair. Her gun lay on the floor out of reach. She squirmed to break free, but the arrows held her prisoner.

Geez, Jamari was good.

We sprinted past the kitchen with cereal bowls still left

out on the bar. Arcade machines *beeped* and *booped*. A table had been knocked over, scattering a Dungeons and Dragons game across the floor. We burst into the stairwell at the far end of the room. Black smoke made me cough. The temperature felt like a furnace as flames licked up the walls. The sound of boots stomping on metallic stairs sounded from below. I peered over the railing and saw Ponytail climbing up to kill us.

"The rooftop," Jamari said.

We raced up the stairs. Robin Hood now led the way and Jamari covered the rear. I felt an overwhelming sense of fear as Ponytail chased us. She reminded me of the Terminator—unstoppable and impossible to kill. How could we escape her?

A dark oaken door flung open. Kamari appeared on the other side. She was splattered in blood and her eyes were wild like a feral dog. For the briefest second, she seemed startled to see us—because she didn't raise her weapon right away. But then her expression hardened and she raised the gun. She pointed it at me, the closest person to her.

My stomach lurched, but I walloped her in the head with my bo staff.

Kamari stumbled back, blinking away stars. At the same time, Jamari stepped in front of me and threw a throwing knife. The blade dinged into Kamari's newly pinned deputy badge. The badge didn't come unpinned, but Kamari clutched her heart and yelled in pain.

Jamari tackled his sister. They went sprawling to the ground. Kamari tried to fight back, but her father, Robin Hood, removed a pair of twist ties from his duffel bag and handcuffed her wrists to the staircase.

Jamari broke free and stood. "Remember," he scolded me. "Go for their badge. Hitting a deputy in the head won't do anything."

"I'm sorry," I said. "She was about to shoot me and I panicked."

Kamari struggled against her restraints. "Lemme go!" she shouted, tears streaking her cheeks.

"You know we can't do that," Robin Hood's voice sounded pained. "If we did, the curse might kill you."

"We're sitting ducks here, Dad," said Jamari.

Boots stomping up the stairs reminded me that Ponytail was still after us.

Robin Hood knelt beside his daughter. "Baby, we have to go, but I swear I'll do everything in my power to save you." He kissed Kamari's forehead, wiped tears running down her cheeks with a dirty thumb, then stood and sprinted up the stairs.

Jamari lingered behind. He stared at his sister with fresh tears blurring his eyes. He mouthed the words *I love you.* I think he tried to say it aloud, but his voice came out choked.

Kamari wriggled the restraints. "Then let me go, brother," she cried.

Jamari turned to the rest of us. "Keep moving," he said.

I coughed and waved away smoke. I stepped past Kamari and ascended the stairs. Kleopatra and my brothers followed right behind me.

"Baby brother," Kamari shouted. "Don't leave me here!"

"I wish I didn't have to," Jamari said.

Kamari's cries of anguish grew more distraught as we fled up the stairs. I couldn't imagine leaving behind someone I loved, knowing they might die and it could be the last time I ever saw them. How horrible. I hoped I never had to experience what Robin Hood's family was going through.

We reached the rooftop.

Bright sunlight stung my eyes after the smoky stairwell. Fresh air filled my lungs. Jamari barred the stairwell door with a lead pipe. Then he and Robin Hood led us past air conditioning ducts to the rooftop's edge. I peered over the side and spotted a yellow van five stories below.

"How do we get down?" I asked.

Jamari pulled a grappling hook from his quiver. Robin Hood pulled one from his black duffel bag.

Kleopatra scoffed. "Tell me you're joking."

Jamari smirked, then he latched the grappling hook to a chimney and threw the rope over the side. Robin Hood did the same.

"I'll take the girls," Robin Hood said. "You take the boys."

Jamari nodded.

Robin Hood motioned for me and Kleopatra to join him. "Climb on my back," he instructed.

"Can you carry both of us?" I asked.

He flexed a beefy arm, just as the stairwell door rattled as Ponytail attempted to break through.

"Good enough for me." I dropped my bo staff and hopped onto Robin Hood's back, wrapping my arms around his neck.

Kleopatra was reluctant, but the lead pipe holding the

stairwell door rattled again, so she jumped on beside me. Robin Hood grabbed the grappling hook's rope. He swung a leg over the edge of the roof. Beneath us, a five-hundred-foot drop loomed to an asphalt parking lot.

Don't let go, I told myself, squeezing Robin Hood's neck tighter.

"Ack," he gasped. "Girls—you're choking me."

The stairwell door burst open. Ponytail rushed out. She scanned the rooftop, and as her eyes settled on our group preparing to repel down the building, she raised her pistol and fired, fired, fired—

Robin Hood and Jamari kicked off the wall. My stomach did a somersault as wind rushed by. My grip slipped, and for a fraction of a second I thought I was going to fall, but then Robin Hood's boots hit the pavement. We were on the ground level.

"That was *awesome,*" said Zac.

"Let's go!" Jamari said.

We rushed to the Sherwood Lumber van. Its horn bleeped as Jamari hit a key fob. He hopped into the driver's seat. Kleopatra climbed into the passenger side. Robin Hood opened the van's rear doors and he ushered me and my brothers inside.

"Do you have a driver's license?" Kleopatra asked as Jamari cranked the engine.

"Nah, but I've got a learner's permit," he said.

"You're kidding, right?"

"Nope."

Kleopatra fumbled for her seat belt.

"Drive!" Robin Hood shouted.

Jamari punched the gas. The rear tires squealed. Robin Hood reached out to shut the van's rear doors, but a bullet ricocheted off its yellow metal. He ducked inside as sparks flew. I glanced out the back of the van and saw the Sheriff of Nottingham exiting the warehouse, her six-shooting revolver aimed right at us. She fired three more rounds.

Jamari yanked the wheel, and the open doors swung wildly as the van swerved onto the street. The sudden change in momentum flung me into a metal shelf bolted to the floorboard. Tools went flying from the shelf and a bucket of screws was knocked over. Most of the screws skittered across the floorboard, but a few fell out the back of the van and clanged, bounced, and tumbled against the road. Robin Hood reached out and slammed the doors closed. We raced onto the highway and away from the burning Sherwood Lumber building.

"Is everyone okay?" Robin Hood panted when it was clear nobody chased us.

I checked myself to make sure I hadn't been shot, which might sound crazy, but you'd be amazed how adrenaline can blind your senses in the heat of battle. I didn't see any Maddie holes, thank goodness.

"We're good up here," Jamari said, accelerating the van to fifty, sixty, and then seventy miles an hour. Kleopatra gave us a shaky thumbs-up.

But my brothers didn't respond.

"Boys . . ." I said slowly.

Jason looked at me. Tears filled his eyes.

"What's wrong?" I asked as my heart dropped to my stomach.

Jason's voice was more terrified than I'd ever heard before. "Zac's been shot."

Chapter 62

IN ALL MY LIFE, I'D NEVER felt fear like I felt now.

Not when I dangled from a fifty-story skyscraper while Tamora Rose—my dad's former work colleague and the woman who murdered my mom—crunched her boot into my knuckles to make me fall. Nor when a 2,000-year-old mummy rose from the grave or when giant scorpions swarmed a tomb to kill me. All of those scary moments paled in comparison to now.

"Nggghh," Zac grimaced, holding his side where he'd been shot. Blood was splattered on his shirt. "Ow, ow, it hurts."

I rushed to my brother's side and pulled back the bloody garment to see the gunshot wound.

It was a scratch.

Nothing more than a thin, red line across his ribcage—no wider than a papercut. And his shirt wasn't covered in blood. It was red paint. A can had been shot and its contents had splattered onto his clothes.

"You big baby," I yelled, my hands still shaking. "You were barely even wounded!"

"What?" Zac said.

"Look at it."

He glanced at his meager wound, probably caused by a

flying screw instead of a bullet. Even so, the cut needed a Band-Aid or medical tape to stop the bleeding. Robin Hood appeared by Zac's side with a first aid kit.

"So he's okay?" Kleopatra said, tears streaking her cheeks as she watched from the front seat. "He's not gonna die?"

Jason sat back and sighed. "No, thank God. Sorry for overreacting."

"No apologies needed," said Robin Hood, pouring hydrogen peroxide onto a cotton swab and applying it to the cut.

Zac hissed.

Robin Hood pressed a bandage firmly over the wound. "At least now you'll have a cool scar," he said.

Zac smiled weakly.

Jamari changed lanes to pass a slower vehicle. "Where am I driving to, Dad?" he asked.

Robin Hood gathered up his medical supplies and tossed them back into the first aid kit. "Isn't it obvious? We must pursue Robert Fitzooth's treasure before the sheriff does."

"But what about our comrades back at the factory?"

"They knew the escape plan. I trust most made it to the safe houses."

"Not all of them," Jamari's voice came out pained.

"Not all of them," Robin Hood conceded. "But we must think of Kamari now. I believe we can save her if we find Robert's tomb."

Jamari scoffed. "What are we gonna do, bruh? Buy her freedom with treasure?"

"The old hag is after *something*, and I don't think it's jewels and golden goblets," he said. "She doesn't care who she kills to get it, and that's what puts fear in my heart. Let us follow the clues so we might acquire this artifact first."

Jamari cleared his throat. "Erm, Dad. About that. The clue Maddie gave you—"

"Is fake, I know."

Jamari took his eyes off the road long enough to stare at his dad. "What? How'd you know?"

Robin Hood reached into his pocket and pulled out two rings. Wait a minute! Those were *my* rings—the ones I discovered inside the golden container. I felt inside my jacket pocket, but it was empty.

"They tumbled out of your jacket," Robin Hood explained. "When the explosion threw you into the wall in my office." He tossed me something shiny.

I caught it. It was my mom's compass.

"I'm sure you want that back," he said.

"Thanks," I mumbled, tucking the compass into a jacket pocket. I zipped it up this time.

Robin Hood scrutinized the rings. He read the writing engraved on the insides of the bands aloud:

Along a wayside road, where travelers pass,
the famed Robin of Loxley, rest deep in the grass.

"We think the rings are wedding bands," Kleopatra said.

"Wedding bands," Robin Hood repeated. "Then that would mean—"

Jamari banged the dashboard. "We were right!" he

hooted. "The treasure is where we thought it might be. I'll head to Witchford then drive north up the A-10 Motorway."

"Wait," I said. "You know where to go?"

"He does," Robin Hood said, smiling. "Part of our boot camp training requires reading up on Robin Hood lore. Any Merry Man could've deciphered the clue once they knew the poem was related to Robert Fitzooth's wedding."

"Where are we going, then?"

"To a church in Sandringham, Norfolk. It's where Robin Hood married the love of his life." He tucked the rings back into his pocket. "The tomb must be near the church. When we find it, we'll have to be especially careful. It's likely littered with booby traps."

I shuddered. Last year, my brothers and I barely survived a booby-trapped tomb. Sometimes I still had nightmares of poisonous gasses, giant killer scorpions, and deadly spikes made of sharpened bone.

Robin Hood must've noticed my worried expression. "It's not too late to turn back," he said. "If you kids don't want to go, we can drop you off on the way."

"There's an exit for an airport coming up," Jamari said. "Just say the word."

We were quiet for a few minutes. The smell of first aid disinfectant from Zac's bandage drifted beneath my nose. His wound was a subtle reminder of what could happen if we continued our quest. Next time the bullet might not miss.

"Whaddya think, kiddos?" Kleopatra asked. "Do we keep going? Or do we take the exit and fly back home?"

I thought about what would happen if we traveled back to Evansville. How much longer would we keep our home if Dad lost his job? Would the museum close in one month? Two? Next year? It was only a matter of time.

No.

I was determined to finish what we started.

"Keep driving," I told Jamari. "We'll help the Merry Men find the grave of Robin Hood."

Chapter 63

AFTER SEVERAL HOURS OF DRIVING, Jamari pulled over and parked on the side of a lonely road. I'd gotten a little bit of sleep during the trip, and it had done wonders to restore me after staying up all night. I felt somewhat normal, and that was saying a lot.

Robin Hood opened the van's rear doors and we all hopped out. It now neared midday, but I couldn't see the sun overhead because gray clouds hung low in the sky. Brisk winds whipped my jacket and hair. The air felt damp.

"Is it always cold and gloomy in England?" I groaned.

Jamari appeared from around the driver's side of the van, his green hoodie pulled up over his head. "Pretty much," he said, shouldering a bow and quiver of arrows. "You get used to it."

I rubbed my arms for warmth, thinking I'd never get used to weather like this, and scanned our surroundings. A grassy field was to our right. A quiet church was perched on a hilltop in the distance. I thought it looked a lot like the church from the drawing.

"That's the Church of Saint Mary Magdalene," Robin Hood said, noticing me staring at it. "Local legend says Robin Hood and Maid Marian were married there, with King Richard the Lionheart presiding over the ceremony."

"*Supposedly* married," interjected Jamari. "We don't know if Robin and Marian got hitched. He might've married somebody else."

Robin Hood shook his head. "We on about this again?"

"Always," said Jamari.

I glanced back and forth between father and son. "I take it you guys have had this argument before?"

They both nodded.

"It's not important," said Robin Hood. "The first line of the clue said to seek a road where travelers pass." He motioned to the road we were now parked beside. "This is that road. When Robert Fitzooth—the first Robin Hood— died, the prioress who killed him buried his body beside a road. She did this to warn robbers who might prey on helpless travelers, but also to let travelers know they needn't fear getting mugged because Robin Hood was dead."

"Hold up," Jason chimed in. "I thought Little John buried Robin Hood after he shot an arrow from an open window. Where the arrow landed became Robin Hood's grave."

"That's one story," Robin Hood conceded, "but there are other accounts. In this version, the prioress buried him."

"In 1665," Jamari picked up the story. "A drawing by Nathaniel Johnston showed a slab of stone beside a lonely road, decorated with a cross and an inscription carved around the stone's edge: HERE LIES ROBERT HUDE, WILLIAM GOLDSBOROUGH, AND THOMAS."

"Not much is known about William Goldsborough and Thomas," said Robin Hood, "but we believe they were Merry Men who the prioress also murdered."

"Geez," whistled Zac. "That chick sounds like a serial killer."

"What about Robert Hude?" I asked.

"Simply a different spelling for Robin Hood," Jamari answered. "Anyway, the story goes that Little John, and a select few Merry Men he trusted to keep secrets, dug up their friends' graves so they could give them a proper burial. But they feared thieves might spoil the tomb's riches, so they kept its entrance plain and simple—hence the stone with names engraved on it."

"So we're looking for a stone beside the road?" I asked.

"Not exactly," Robin Hood shook his head. "Hundreds of years have passed since the stone would've been placed here to mark the tomb's entrance. It has disappeared. No, we're looking for something else."

"What?"

He pointed at the church on the hilltop. "A hidden entrance somewhere inside the cathedral." He grabbed the black duffel bag filled with weapons from the rear of the van, and slammed its doors. "Let's hike up to the church and see what we can discover."

Chapter 64

THE CHURCH'S SANCTUARY WAS beautiful, rustic, and grand.

An arched wooden ceiling had been intricately carved overhead. Dark oaken pews faced an altar with black and white checkered tiles on the floor. Behind the altar, a stunning stained glass window depicted Jesus Christ hanging on a cross while a gathering of mourners milled about his feet. More stained glass windows lined the walls, showing various events from the Bible and the life of Jesus. They cast a myriad of colors as the setting sun's rays gleamed into the room.

A few church visitors sat in pews, knelt in prayer, or lit candles at the altar. We didn't want to disturb anybody's time of worship, so the six of us quietly slipped into the sanctuary. The place smelled of incense, wine, and the yellow beeswax candles burning throughout the room gave off the summer scent of honey.

"Look around," Robin Hood instructed.

We all went in different directions in search of a clue. I walked to a golden font filled with holy water near the entrance, and knelt to inspect its base. Beside me, Kleopatra tapped her high-heeled shoe impatiently.

"Another boring church," she groaned. "At least this time we're not digging up someone's grave."

"Not yet," I teased.

She rolled her glitter-painted eyes. "For once, I'd like to visit a royal location. Somewhere the Prince of Wales visited, or even better, the Queen herself."

I suddenly felt guilty. "I'm sorry we never made it to Windsor Castle, Kleo."

She shook her head. "Don't worry about it, kiddo. Our adventures in England have been more memorable than a lame tour of a dusty castle."

"Still, though. I hope I can make it up to you."

Nearby, Robin Hood inspected a plaque on the wall. "You know," he whispered. "The royal family *has* attended church services here."

"Really?" said Kleopatra.

He nodded.

"Well, look at that," I said. "You get to tour a royal location after all."

Kleopatra smiled. Then she swept off to explore the sanctuary, suddenly interested in every little detail.

I stood up from the font of holy water, having not found anything of importance, and joined Robin Hood as he finished reading the plaque. "What are we looking for?" I asked.

"Names from the Nathaniel Johnston rock," he said. "There should be something here with their names on it— an engraving, statue, or pew. Honestly, their names could be on anything."

I scanned the magnificent architecture of the church, and sighed. The sanctuary was filled with so much pomp and flair, there were thousands of places to search. Not to mention the church likely had rooms we'd have to sneak inside to check.

Robin Hood walked away to inspect a framed painting. I strolled down the middle aisle of pews, glancing at the beautiful colors streaming through the stained glass windows.

I reached the pews right in front of the altar. An elderly man sitting in the front row greeted me with a warm smile. I sat across from him, and as he went back to his prayers, I studied the stained glass window of Jesus Christ. The stained glass was filled with gorgeous blues, reds, and turquoise— made even more beautiful by the slanting sunlight. Jesus looked to be surrounded on both sides by angels. But I didn't see anything that screamed *clue*, so I craned my neck to stare at another colorful stained glass window located beneath a decorative arch.

My jaw dropped to the floor.

No, it couldn't be that easy, could it? I thought.

The stained glass window was a replica of the Robin Hood treasure map. But instead of being shaded in the blacks and grays of pencil lead, the image was pockmarked in an explosion of color. I rushed to the window, accidentally alarming the elderly man as I abruptly stood.

"Sorry," I said, sweeping past him.

Every detail in the stained glass window mirrored the details in the drawing. Even the small details like the tombstone with RIP and an arrow sticking out of the ground. The kissing couple was embraced in a fierce kiss as if they'd just spoken their vows and were now husband and wife. Even the letters R.W.T. were carved into the tree trunk beside the man's boot, just like in the drawing.

Whoa, hold the phone.

R.W.T.

Robert Hude. William Goldsborough. And Thomas. The first letter in each man's name. This was it. This was what we were looking for!

"Guys," I called the others. "I found it."

Kleopatra, my brothers, Jamari, and his dad rushed to my side. I showed them the stained glass window and pointed their attention to the initials.

"Excellent work, Maddie," Robin Hood said. "There must be a secret lever or switch nearby. Search."

Excited at my discovery, I studied the stained glass window for tiny details. I scanned each colored pane in hopes one might be a button to press. When that came up short, I checked the arch and pillars framing the stained glass window, but nothing stood out.

My initial excitement started to fade.

A priest with gray hair combed over to hide his baldness came by to ask if we needed help, or if we could use prayer for anything. Robin Hood growled at him to bugger off. As the priest scampered away, I leaned heavily against one of the pillars and looked around.

And I saw it.

Across the room.

Sunlight gleamed through the window, casting a colorful reflection on a marble statue of two knights on horseback . . . and the shadow of R.W.T. rested on their shields.

"This is some Indiana Jones bull crap," I said.

"What?" asked Jamari.

I led everyone to the statues and showed them how the letters cast a shadow on the knights' shields. The shields were both decorated with crosses.

"Temple knights," Jamari said. "The stories are true."

"It seems so," said Robin Hood.

"What're you guys talking about?" asked Kleopatra.

"Rumors, mostly," said Robin Hood. "But a few stories have suggested that the first Robin Hood was a member of the Knights Templar."

"A knight of the cross?" said Jason.

"The very same," Robin Hood nodded.

"There's a hole between the shields," Zac pointed out.

He was right. And the hole was big enough to fit a key. I looked at everybody, and I could tell from their expressions that they were thinking the same thing I was.

The lion-head key.

Robin Hood took off the necklace. He held it up by the black cord, and as the key dangled, I saw R.W.T. etched into its metal teeth. "Miss Jones," he rumbled. "Would you care to do the honors? After everything you've done to solve the clues, it seems only right that you unlocked the tomb."

I thought about it for a moment. "Nah," I finally said. "You can do it. You're the current Robin Hood, after all."

Robin Hood smiled, then he jammed the lion-head key into the hole and twisted the handle. The statue of mounted knights began rumbling. Sand and dust fell from cracks of plaster at the base of the statue. The statue slid back—heavy marble grating against the tiled floor—and a secret passageway appeared.

A narrow stairwell with worn, stone steps spiraled down into the gloom.

Chapter 65

WE ENTERED THE SECRET passageway.

Unlit torches rested in iron sconces lining the walls. Robin Hood grabbed two of them and handed me a torch. As I gripped its splintered handle, rumbling sounded from the way we came. I turned toward the noise to see the statue guarding the entrance slowly grinding closed. Before it shut completely, I caught a glimpse of the partially balding priest scampering toward us.

"What in Heaven are you people doing—" he demanded, but his words died away as the statue closed over the entrance with a resounding bang.

Darkness hugged us.

"Looks like there's no turning back," whispered Zac.

"Guys, this is crazy," Kleopatra's voice sounded panicked. "We shouldn't be here."

Light flared in the darkness. Robin Hood had lit a match. He touched the match to his torch's cloth wrapping, and flames flickered to life. Shadows shifted and the strong stench of pitch and tar filled my nostrils. He handed the torch to Jamari, then adjusted the strap on his duffel bag of weapons. "All right, gang," he said, his deep voice muffled in the confined space of the stairwell. "Time to get your game faces on. This tomb will be crawling with traps."

Kleopatra groaned.

I swallowed. Tombs were dangerous places often filled with puzzles, death traps, and labyrinthine passageways.

Jamari moved closer and helped light my torch. "You ready?" he asked.

"Not even a little," I said as my torch sparked to life, crackling and spitting, its flames hot against my face.

"Me neither, but we'll survive if we all stick together."

We descended the spiraling stone steps carefully. They were worn and narrow, and sometimes difficult to see with the torchlight shifting shadows at our feet. Step after step we delved deeper into the earth. I tried to count the number of steps as we went, but after about three hundred, I lost track. We were so deep beneath the church my ears started to pop.

"The construction of this place is magnificent," Robin Hood whispered.

He was right. The curved, stone walls must've taken years to build. Decorative crosses had been etched into the stonework, reminding me that an ancient order of holy knights once walked this path hundreds of years before.

The stairs leveled out. A chamber opened up.

The room was unlike any place I'd ever seen. Gnarled roots from some great tree wove in and out of the stonework. Two iron doors were located to our left and right, both sealed shut. At the foot of the left door was a large, weathered stone. To my right, the door was guarded by a rusty set of knight's armor. In one of the armor's gauntleted fists was a halberd—a fancy axe with a ten-foot handle. Gripped in the other fist was a shield with a red cross, the paint so faded its color was almost pink.

Jamari and his dad entered the chamber. They walked to the door on the left and inspected the weathered stone.

"Hey, don't leave me." Kleopatra rushed after them, almost as if her survival instincts screamed to stay with our group's warriors.

"It's the Nathaniel Johnston rock," breathed Robin Hood. "Do you see the names?"

"Amazing," Jamari gasped.

"Guys, we need to leave. I have a bad feeling about this place." Kleopatra hugged herself for warmth with trembling hands. Her eyes darted nervously about the room.

Meanwhile, my brothers and I lingered at the chamber's entrance, cautious and alert. Our experience in Emperor Qin's tomb taught us to be wary of places like this.

"Look," Jason pointed at the knight's armor. "Words are etched onto the shield."

"Do we risk walking over there?" asked Zac. "One of the cobblestones could be a hidden switch."

Last year, I accidentally stepped on a hidden floor switch in Emperor Qin's tomb, springing a death trap. We only survived because we solved a puzzle before poisonous gasses could fill our lungs.

I studied the uneven floor. None of the tiles appeared discolored or like they didn't belong. "The floor looks safe," I said.

We risked entering the chamber and walked carefully toward the knight's armor. None of the cobblestones depressed into the floor. No razor-sharp blades flew out of the walls to sever our heads. Off to a good start. I held my torch high to see more of the knight. Spiders skittered from the sudden illumination. The rusting armor was covered in cobwebs and dust. I brushed cobwebs away from the shield, then read its cryptic message:

> *Uplift the stone, and there ye should find,*
> *A tomb full of riches, but be wary of mind.*

> *The path moving forward, is not what ye think,*
> *One false step, and ye die in the brink.*

"I knew it," Jason groaned. "This chamber is a trap."

"Look," Zac whispered. "Another message is written on the door."

> *Only the heart of a lion, may enter unharmed,*
> *All else must perish, consider ye warned.*

The door's handle was shaped like a lion with a regal mane of hair and a king's crown. Beneath the handle was a keyhole. Its size looked to be a perfect match for our lion-head key.

Suddenly, the chamber reverberated with the noise of stone grinding against stone. Jamari and his dad were moving the Nathaniel Johnston rock. I reread the warning on the knight's shield, and realized our mistake a split second too late.

"*Wait!*" I shouted.

But it was done.

Grinding gears sounded from the door Jamari and Robin Hood stood in front of. It rumbled open. A new chamber appeared. Jamari's torchlight lit up the entrance, and I could see gold—everywhere I looked I saw the glint of gold. Golden statues, jewelry, goblets, and crowns. Mounds of golden coins with red and green gemstones sparkling throughout. It was a treasure worth billions, maybe zillions. And I could only see the treasure room's entrance. Imagine what wealth lay hidden in the dark.

Kleopatra gasped. She started to walk forward.

"*Don't move!*" I yelled.

Again, too late.

Her foot stepped past the threshold of the treasure room, and a thunderous *crash* sounded as the entire floor collapsed into a deep pit.

Chapter 66

KLEOPATRA SCREAMED AS THE floor caved in.

I watched in horror as my babysitter plummeted down alongside huge slabs of stone. Jamari and his dad tumbled down with her, shouting in alarm. A deafening *boom* quaked the chamber. Dust shot up from the collapse. When the dust settled, a gaping hole was left in the floor.

Half of the chamber's cobblestone floor had fallen into the pit—the half with the Nathaniel Johnston rock. The other half—the side my brothers and I stood on with the knight's armor—remained intact. However, while we hadn't fallen into the pit, we weren't completely safe. The cobblestone floor in front of the entrance had also collapsed, and the gap between us was too wide to jump.

I coughed and waved away dust. Then I knelt and shone my torchlight into the pit for signs of life. Even with my torch, the bottom of the pit was shadowed in billowing dust and darkness. "Kleo!" I shouted. "Jamari! Are you guys okay?!"

No one answered.

"Can anybody hear me?!"

Faintly, I heard grunting and what sounded like the shifting of stones. "Yeah," Jamari's voice called up from some great depth. "We must've fallen fifty feet."

"What about Kleo and your dad?"

"Ngggh!" came the painful reply of Robin Hood. "My leg is trapped beneath stone. It might be broken."

"Fetch," Jason swore.

"Kleo—are you there?" I shouted.

"I—*coff*—*coff*—"Kleopatra coughed, probably from all the dust lingering in the air. "I'm fine, kiddo. A little bruised, but fine."

I blew out a breath. This could have been worse. If the knights who built this tomb had wanted, they could've lined the pit with deadly spikes to impale anyone who fell.

"Do you see a way out?" Zac called down to them.

"It's too dark to see anything," said Jamari. "So to answer your question—nah, bruh."

"Can you use one of your rope arrows to climb out?" I shouted.

"Not with my dad's leg pinned. He's gonna need help."

Jason knelt beside me. "There's gotta be another way down into the pit," he said. "A secret entrance or something?"

"Where, Jason?" I said. "If you haven't noticed, we're trapped, too."

He looked at the iron door behind us. "We might find another entrance if we go deeper into the tomb."

I glanced at the door, then closed my eyes and thought for a moment. If we traveled farther into the booby-trapped tomb, the chances of getting hurt or killed increased significantly. We were lucky we hadn't fallen into the pit with the others, but next time we might not be so fortunate.

But we have to do something, I told myself.

I opened my eyes and stood. My torchlight illuminated the destroyed chamber. The entrance loomed to our left across a gaping hole we couldn't jump. Directly across from us, the treasure room's entrance loomed with gold and gemstones glinting from the light. Seeing the treasure across a chasm we couldn't cross filled me with an awful emotion—an emotion that ruined people's lives and made them do stupid things.

Greed.

The treasure taunted me like a serpent in a garden. I wanted that gold. There was enough moolah in there to save Dad's museum *and* set us up for a life of leisure. We could travel the world, buy a bigger house, own rich cars, and pretty much never have to work a day in our lives. Money wouldn't be a problem ever again.

But I knew if we attempted to reach the treasure, then Kleopatra, Jamari, and his dad would likely die. The gold would become blood money. Every dollar spent would damn our souls for all eternity.

"What'd you say, sis?" asked Jason. "Do we risk exploring the tomb?"

I peeled my eyes from the glinting gold, swallowing my desire to be rich. "Yeah," I said. "Let's see where the door leads."

Chapter 67

"JAMARI!" I CALLED DOWN INTO the pit. "Can you toss up the lion-head key?"

The key came hurtling out of the dark chasm. It clanged against the iron door behind us and clinked onto the cobblestone floor. I snatched it up, then jammed its teeth into the keyhole. I twisted the handle.

CLICK!

Hissing sounded from inside the walls like steam being released from a locomotive engine. A rumbling noise made me turn around. The treasure room's door slowly grinded closed, sealing the riches within.

Then the craziest thing happened.

All the gnarled roots weaving in and out of the chamber's stonework began *moving*. They withdrew out of the room like a squid's tentacles releasing its prey. It was a strange sight. I shifted my torchlight so I could inspect a root as it retracted itself from the wall, and noticed that it was mechanical. The root was made of brushed metal designed to look like wood. Whirring gears and spinning belts must have powered its movement because now I heard the clunky sound of medieval machinery.

"What's happening up there, you guys?" shouted Kleopatra from down in the pit.

"It appears the tomb is Optimus Prime," Jason called down.

"What does that even mean?"

"Geez," whistled Zac. "Has she never heard of Transformers?"

"We'll have to fix that later," I said. "Look."

The iron door swung inward, its rusted hinges screaming in protest. Inside, just visible from my torchlight, a dangerous set of stairs appeared—formed from the gnarled roots that had disappeared into the walls. The stairs had no handrails, and it appeared a misplaced step could lead to a deadly fall. To make matters worse, the stairs were curved like branches of a tree with lengthy gaps between each step.

"Another trap," Jason groaned. "Why can't tombs ever be easy?"

I knelt near the edge of the pit. "We're going deeper into the tomb!" I shouted. "Will you guys be okay until we find an exit?"

"Don't worry about us," Jamari called up. "I'll keep watch over Kleo and my dad." I started to rise, but Jamari shouted, "Hey, Maddie . . ."

"Yeah?"

"Be safe, all right?"

I smiled. "You, too, Archer Boy."

I stood and faced our newest obstacle. Anxiety, anticipation, and a hefty amount of fear churned in my stomach like rocks in a washing machine on the spin cycle. I swallowed to try and calm my nerves, then I raised my torch and set my foot cautiously onto the first step. The stair felt awkward beneath my black combat boot since the stair was curved like a tree branch. I tested the step by bouncing a little weight on it. It held, as solid as concrete and steel. I peered ahead and saw that the next step loomed several feet away, a little lower in the air, and the stair after, several feet farther and even lower. We'd have to hop from stair to stair, all while maintaining our balance.

Even worse, the place was pitch black. I couldn't see walls or a ceiling or where the gnarled roots protruded from. On the plus side, we wouldn't have to deal with any dizzying heights because the ground under the floating stairs was also shrouded in darkness. All I could see were the few stairs on the cusp of my firelight.

"Do you have your flashlight?" I asked Jason.

"Yeah." He removed his cell phone from his pocket and harsh, white light glared.

Zac didn't have a flashlight so I told him to stay between us. He nodded. Then, with my heart pounding in my throat, I leapt to the next stair. For a fleeting second, cold winds brushed my cheeks as I hurtled weightlessly through the air.

My feet stuck the landing with a solid thud, but my momentum kept going forward and I was forced to jump to the next stair even though I wasn't ready. I flung my arms out to try and regain my balance—more wind swept by— and as the heel of my boot touched down, I slipped.

And I fell.

My chest smacked the stair hard, knocking the breath from my lungs. My arms wrapped around the stair and I hugged the gnarled root for dear life. One of my legs was draped over the root, the other dangling beneath me. Somehow, I held onto the torch, but its fiery heat singed the hair on my arm. I hissed and yanked the flames away from my flesh.

"*Maddie!*" yelled Jason.

"I'm okay—" I panted. "Just gotta get back to my feet."

It was difficult, but I managed to straddle the gnarled root and sit. I blew hair from my eyes. "This might be harder than I thought."

"We don't have to do this," said Jason, still standing in the doorway.

"Yeah," Zac agreed. "Maybe there's another way."

"There isn't." I set a foot beneath me and stood. "Stay if you want, but I'm going ahead."

"We're not letting you go alone."

My balance wobbled like I stood on slippery ice. "Good, because I don't think I can do this alone."

I glanced at the next stair. It was narrower and the gap to reach it even farther. This was going to be a stressful trip. Behind me, I heard Zac grunt as he jumped and then landed on the stair I'd just left.

"Cool, parkour," he said.

Oh, brother. Leave it to Zac to relate our situation to those YouTube videos he liked watching, the ones with crazy people doing handstands on the edge of skyscrapers and leaping buildings like Jamari.

I leapt to the next stair. My boots touched down, and thankfully, I didn't wobble or teeter this time. "All right, guys. Let's take it slow."

We descended the treacherous staircase one jump at a time, hopping from one mechanical tree branch to the next. Every so often, Jason cursed from nearly losing his balance or I stumbled and felt like I walked a tightrope until I regained control. Despite the occasional hiccup, it seemed like our descent was going pretty smoothly.

Until a loud *bang* startled us.

"What was that?!" I demanded.

"Erm, guys," said Jason, glancing back the way we came. "The steps we already crossed are falling."

"They're what?!"

"They're *falling*—like dominos. RUN!"

Throwing caution in the trash, I leapt onto the next stair, and the next, and the one right after. I moved quickly, feeling like my boots barely touched the gnarled root stairs as I leapt between steps. Behind us, the bangs grew louder and sounded closer as the stairs plummeted into darkness.

"Faster!" yelled Jason.

I picked up my pace. My legs felt like they were on fire. Note to future self: don't skip leg day. Ahead, I saw that the stairs leveled out to a cobblestone floor and a chamber beyond. My bouncing torchlight also revealed what doom awaited us beneath the stairs if we fell—a sea of sharpened broadswords, their tips pointing straight up. I gulped and glanced back up just as I reached the final stair. I leapt from it toward the chamber with all my strength . . .

I soared across a five-foot gap.

The torch's flame crackled in the wind.

My boots stomped down onto the safety of the chamber's floor, but my legs were weak from jumping from stair to stair, and they buckled beneath me and I went sprawling. The torch went flying from my grasp and skittered across the cobblestones.

I looked up to find my brothers. Zac soared across the chasm of swords. He landed inside the chamber, but then tripped over me sprawled across the ground, and went stumbling past. I whirled to find Jason. He was leaping from step to step, but the gnarled roots were falling away behind him quicker than his pace.

"He's not going to make it," I realized.

I scrambled to my feet and raced toward the edge of the pit. Jason landed on the final stair and started to jump—

—but the stair fell away beneath him.

Chapter 68

I REACHED OUT AND CAUGHT Jason by the collar of his shirt.

One of his hands gripped my arm as he slammed into the pit wall. We both grunted in pain. It felt like my shoulder was being pulled out of socket from holding Jason's weight. His fingernails dug into my flesh and stung. His sneakers kicked and scrabbled against the wall. The toes of his shoes were inches from the sharpened swords. I grimaced and tried to lift him up, but I wasn't strong enough.

Zac rushed to my side. He skidded onto his belly and reached down to grab Jason's arm.

"Quick, pull me up!" Jason yelled.

"What'd you think we're doing?" I said through gritted teeth.

We pulled Jason up over the edge and onto the cobblestone floor. He sprawled on his back, gasping for air. "Tombs—seriously—suck—" he panted.

I rubbed my arm where his nails had left a mark. "For real. Let's pray that's the worst this place has to offer."

Zac got to his feet and picked up my fallen torch. He swept its flickering light around to illuminate our new surroundings. My eyes tracked the light. It appeared we were in a cavernous chamber. Part of it looked manmade with stonework, but most of it looked natural with limestone walls and columns of stalagmites rising from the ground. The room was huge with a ceiling so tall the torchlight couldn't touch it. It's an eerie feeling having nothing but blackness over your head.

"Fetch!" Jason swore. His voice echoed throughout the damp cavern. "I lost my cell phone."

"That's the least of our problems," I said. "Look at this place."

A series of passageways led out of the chamber, all in different directions. There must have been a dozen hallways for us to choose from.

"A maze?" Zac complained. "We have to navigate a labyrinth?"

"And without a map," Jason said. "At least we had Dad's map when we explored Emperor Qin's tomb."

"How will we know which way to go?"

"We won't. We'll have to navigate this maze the old-fashioned way. With nothing but our wits."

"Guys, look—" I pointed at a stone table in the middle of the room. "There's something on it."

We approached the stone table cautiously. Our footsteps sounded wet as we walked through puddles of cave water. When the torchlight illuminated the table's flat surface, we found a black strip of cloth with frayed ends. The tattered cloth looked really old. Rot pockmarked the cloth with holes in the fabric. Jason picked it up.

He turned the cloth over to inspect it. "What is this thing?"

I caught a glimpse of writing embroidered on the back. "Lemme see it."

He handed me the cloth. I flipped it over to read the writing, but holes made the writing almost unreadable:

D_rk_s sha_ lig_ _he wa_.

I couldn't make it out. Jason scrutinized the writing over my shoulder while Zac held the torchlight high.

"It's a word problem," Jason said.

"What'd you mean?" I asked.

"There are missing letters," he explained. "Similar to the riddles I enjoy solving when I play word games online."

I gawked at him. "Why do my friends have crushes on you? You act like an old man."

He blushed. "Really, your friends like me?"

"Guys," Zac interrupted. "Focus."

"Right," I said. "So what does this riddle say?"

Jason squinted at the pockmarked writing. After a few seconds, he said, "I think it says, *darkness shall light the way.*"

"Well, that's not vague or anything," Zac scoffed.

Jason shook his head. "I know, right? The cloth kind of reminds me of a blindfold, though."

An idea suddenly struck me like lightning. "Oh, you've got to be kidding," I groaned.

"What?"

"Don't you get it? Darkness shall light the way." I waved the black strip of cloth in Jason's face. "They want us to solve this maze blind!"

Chapter 69

I PUT THE BLINDFOLD ON and tied it tightly around my eyes, being sure to fold the fabric in half so none of its holes created opportunities to peek.

My world became dark.

The first thing you notice when you lose your sense of vision is sound. Every noise is louder, clearer. You get combinations of sounds in tombs like this. Dripping water, screeching bats, and cave beetles are obvious, but you also hear more ambient sounds like wind creeping through small cracks of stone. Other sounds are a toss-up, depending on where you're standing. Jason's nervous breathing. Zac's sneakers stepping in a cave puddle. The torch crackling with fire.

Smells attack your senses, too.

Some pleasant like the dampness of the cavern. Others pungent like my brothers' sweaty armpits. Or was that me? Probably. Please don't judge me.

"Can you see anything?" asked Zac.

I craned my neck to *look* around. "Nah, just blackness," I said. "Maybe I was wrong about—"

A flare of light sparked to life on the edge of my vision. I turned toward the source of light and saw a golden glow far away in the distance. The light reminded me of a miniature sun with gleaming rays on its edges. Unlike actual sunlight, though, the glow was gentle and pleasant to look at.

I pointed. "The path through the maze is that way."

"How'd you know?" asked Jason.

"There's a star over there, it's beautiful. Don't you see it?"

"No," said Zac. "All we see is the tunnel you're pointing at."

"Ah, I get it now," said Jason, and I could hear a grin in his voice. "By wearing the blindfold Maddie can *see* which direction to go. *Darkness shall light the way.* This is gonna be easy."

"Since when have tombs ever been easy," said Zac.

"He's right," I said. "We need to be careful. Can one of you guide my steps?"

A sweaty hand interlaced with mine. The touch was gentle and the hand felt small. "Is that you, Zac?" I asked.

"Yeah," he said, and he tugged my hand, forcing me to take a blind step forward. "Stay with me. I'll guide you through the maze."

It felt awkward walking without sight. Zac led me left and right, maneuvering me through the stalagmites on our way to the tunnel's entrance. I was thankful for his guidance. While the star pointed me in the right direction, I couldn't see any of the obstacles blocking our path.

"We've entered the maze," Jason whispered from somewhere up ahead, the crackling of fire coming from his direction. He must have held the torch now. "I'll let you know when there's a fork in the path."

"Sounds good," I replied.

It didn't take long. Zac stopped me in my tracks, and Jason explained how three new tunnels branched out from our current location. "Can you see where to go?" he asked.

I studied the darkness. The glowing light gleamed in the far distance straight ahead, but when I explained this to my brothers, Jason said none of the new tunnels led that way. I glanced left and right, noticing that when I turned my head toward the left, the miniature sun's rays stretched with me in that direction.

"That way," I pointed.

Zac tugged my hand and we went down the new tunnel, traveling deeper into the maze. We moved slowly, partly because I was blind, but also so my brothers could watch for booby traps. The tunnel twisted and turned, and every now and then, Jason asked which direction to go. Each time he asked, I stopped and studied the glowing light until I found which way its rays pointed.

I started hearing a strange sound the farther we traveled into the maze.

Howling wind.

"Why can I hear wind blowing underground?" asked Zac.

"I was just wondering the same thing," Jason said.

"Just stay close and don't touch anything," I said.

We navigated the maze for nearly half an hour, the glowing light steadily growing bigger beneath my blindfold as we moved closer toward it. Eventually, the howling wind started wafting through the tunnels, whipping the tips of my hair and snapping the ends of my clothes and blindfold.

It blew so fiercely that Jason shouted to be heard: *"Which way? There are two tunnels?"*

I pointed toward the tunnel all the wind was gusting from. We went down it. With my free hand, I held the blindfold pinned to my face to make sure the wind didn't knock it free. Zac led me around a corner, but as soon as we emerged onto the new path he shouted in alarm and yanked my hand.

I stumbled back and fell on my butt. "What's wrong?!" I yelled, unable to see anything other than the glowing light on the horizon.

"It's a chasm," Jason described. "A massive cliff with a drop so deep we can't see the bottom. Wind from its depths is funneling into the maze."

"Is there another tunnel nearby?" I asked.

"Not based on your directions," he said. "Where is the light now?"

I pointed.

Zac gulped. "I told you this wouldn't be easy. How the heck is Maddie going to cross that thing blindfolded?"

"Cross what?" I asked.

Neither of them answered.

"Guys—I can't see *anything*. What obstacle do we have to cross?"

"It's a bridge," Jason said.

"Oh," I sighed in relief. "That's not so bad."

"The bridge is only as wide as my hand and there aren't any railings."

Chapter 70

HAVE YOU EVER SEEN *The Fellowship of the Ring?* There's a scene toward the end of the movie when Gandalf, the fellowship's powerful wizard, leads the party across a narrow bridge in the realm of Moria while goblins fire arrows at them. Because the bridge is so narrow, they have to run across it one at a time. A misplaced step could cause them to fall into a great chasm. It's a dramatic moment in the movie because—spoiler alert!—Gandalf sacrifices himself to save the others.

I never thought in a million years I'd ever do something remotely close to that movie scene. But here I was, placing one foot in front of the other as I felt blindly for solid ground with the toes of my combat boots. Imagine walking across a gymnast's balance beam, and you'll have a good idea of what we were dealing with. Do it with a blindfold, howling winds, and a thousand-foot drop to sharp stone and death, and you'll have an even better idea.

"This is crazy, Maddie!" yelled Jason from somewhere in front of me. "At least take off the blindfold."

I took another cautious step forward, making completely sure my boot touched down on the bridge before shifting my weight. "No way," I shouted back. "If I remove the blindfold we might lose the light."

"It won't matter if you fall and die."

"This maze is a test, Jason. Without the light, we won't make it out of here alive."

I focused on my footing and took another step. A gust of wind swept through me and snapped my jacket like a billowing flag. My balance wavered. I felt myself tilting. I thrust my arms out to try and regain control, but the blindfold disoriented me and I kept swaying.

"Maddie!" yelled Zac.

A quick scuffle of feet sounded behind me. Strong hands grabbed my leather jacket and pulled me upright. "Easy," Zac said, not letting go of my jacket until I regained my balance.

"Thanks," I panted.

"No problem, but please be careful. That was really close."

I inhaled a deep breath to calm my jittery nerves, then I scooted a foot forward. My boot touched down on the narrow bridge, and I resumed my blind hike across. It was a slow walk. Each step required my focused concentration.

Halfway across the bridge, something strange occurred.

The glowing light on the horizon vanished. I stopped in my tracks and *glanced* around. To my left and right I saw nothing but darkness, but when I looked down—the miniature sun gleamed beneath me.

"Why'd you stop?!" yelled Zac, his words muffled by the howling wind.

"The light changed direction," I shouted.

The gentle glow of the light's rays started throbbing, almost like the miniature sun was trying to tell me something.

"What's going on?" Jason called.

"Maddie says the light changed," said Zac.

"Where is it now?"

I pointed.

"Beneath us? Maddie—that's crazy!"

"He's right," said Zac. "Where you're pointing is nothing but empty air and mist."

"C'mon," Jason said. "It's just a little farther to the other side. I can see a tunnel leading deeper into the maze."

I didn't move. The miniature sun pulsed, stronger and stronger the longer I stared. Wind gusted, a harsh reminder that we stood on a thin strip of stone so high in the air it might have been the same height as a skyscraper, maybe higher.

But the light seemed like it was beckoning me.

"We have to jump," I realized.

Jason scoffed. "Do you hear yourself, Maddie? If you could see what we see, you'd know that would be suicide."

"It's the only way through the maze," I said. "We're being tested. Remember what the door to this place said: *Only the heart of a lion may enter unharmed.* We have to prove that we're worthy."

"No, we don't," Zac protested. "This isn't an Indiana Jones movie where we take a leap of faith to show how brave we are."

"I think that's exactly what's going on."

Jason laughed, but not because I'd said anything funny. "If we jump and you're wrong, Maddie—we're dead."

The light throbbed, matching the tempo of my heartbeat. This was too crazy to ignore. How could the light be synced to me? Even crazier, how could I see light if I was blindfolded? The rational part of my brain said to follow Jason to the tunnel, but another part of me said we'd be trapped in the maze if we didn't follow the light. What should I do? Walk to the tunnel, or leap from the bridge? As scary as it sounded, the choice seemed simple.

"I'm not wrong," I finally said. "Let's jump."

My brothers groaned.

"Maddie," Zac began.

"If we can just check out this tunnel—" Jason started.

I stepped off the edge of the bridge before they could finish their sentences.

Chapter 71

"MADDIE!" MY BROTHERS screamed.

I fell blindly from the bridge. Cold winds brushed my cheeks. My stomach did a somersault as my body started flipping uncontrollably. Wet air pressed against my skin as I broke through the mist. My brothers' terrified shouts faded away. In the back of my mind, for a fraction of a second, I thought I might've made the wrong choice—that I was about to slam into sharp stones and painfully die.

But an impact never came.

Instead, I felt myself freefall into a slide. I know it sounds crazy, especially falling from such an insane height, but one minute I was plummeting to earth, and the next, I thumped into a gentle curve and went speeding down a slippery slope.

It was a rough ride. The slide banked left and right, and during sharp curves, I bumped at the corners. The glowing sun grew bigger on the horizon the faster I sped down the slide. An unexpected turn banked hard, and I smacked my head. Stars flashed behind my blindfold. I rubbed the spot where it hurt, and felt wetness on my fingertips.

Ouch. That was going to leave a mark.

I prayed the end of this ride didn't conclude with a battered Maddie Jones lying broken at the bottom of a vast pit. Another curve came upon me unexpectedly, and I attempted to use my hands as leverage so I didn't smack my face again.

No luck.

I struck the turn hard, and not only did my jaw take a hit, but a loud *pop* sounded from my forearm. I cried out in pain as white, hot agony lanced from my hand up to my shoulder. The pain was excruciating. My whole arm went numb.

The turn leveled out and I shot down an even steeper slope. The speed and wind caused my blindfold to partially come undone. I reached up with my good hand to keep it pinned to my face—

—just as the slide fell away beneath me. I plummeted down.

SPLASH!

I landed in a pool of deep water. My face went under. The water felt like ice. The cold sent a shock to my nerves. For a few seconds, my body wouldn't respond. I simply kept sinking. Then my boots touched down on a muddy bank, and I was able to coax my body into movement. I kicked off the muddy ground and floated upward.

Still blind, I must note. Somehow the blindfold still covered my eyes.

I surfaced and caught my breath. My teeth chattered from the cold. It was difficult to tread water with only one arm, but I managed to stay afloat. My other arm dangled uselessly at my side, aching like I'd been stung by a wasp the size of a pterodactyl. I'd never broken a bone before. If this was what it felt like, I never wanted to experience it again.

A stench attacked my nostrils.

It smelled like rotten eggs. I could taste the odor in the back of my mouth. Yuck!

My legs and good arm were getting tired from treading water. I swam to one side, hoping to find a platform or solid ground to rest on, but all I discovered was what felt like a slimy stone wall. I treaded water beside the wall, groping blindly to see if it led anywhere, but I must have been swimming in circles. There didn't appear to be a way out.

Wait, where's the glowing light? I thought, trying not to panic.

I *glanced* around. The light wasn't above or beside me. I looked down, and when I did water went up my nose, making me cough. I got my breathing under control, then craned my neck to *peer* beneath the water's surface.

Ah, fetch! The glowing light was underwater, angled as if a tunnel was beneath the wall I'd just searched.

This scared me.

If I swam down there, how long would I need to hold my breath? How far would I have to swim? What if I got turned around in the dark and couldn't tell which way to go? Even worse, what if my brothers showed up after I swam down there? They might be sliding down to join me if they were brave enough to leap from the bridge. Without the blindfold to guide them, they'd get stuck in this room and likely drown.

I decided to wait a few minutes before taking the plunge.

Treading water became more and more difficult. My mouth and nose sank beneath the surface a few times, making it hard to breathe. Several minutes passed, and I realized I needed to go now or I wouldn't have enough strength to make the swim. Jason and Zac had yet to fall into the pool of water, and this worried me. If they didn't jump from the bridge, what would happen to them in the maze?

"You gotta g-g-go, Maddie," I said to myself through chattering teeth.

I hated to do it, but it was time. I inhaled a huge lungful of air, faced the direction of the glowing light, and dove beneath the water.

Little did I know, the swim would nearly kill me . . .

Chapter 72

THEY SAY THE AVERAGE SWIMMER can hold his breath for two whole minutes, but that's insane. My all-time best record—recorded last summer in my grandmother's pool—was one minute and seventeen seconds. Now, I realize you can probably hold your breath longer, but you know what I have to say to that?

Man, I wish I were you right now.

Seriously. The weight of frigid water pressed in around me, and my lungs felt tight from all the air I'd stored. My brain screamed to take a breath, but I forced my feet to kick frantically and swim toward the light. I raked at the water with my good hand in a feeble attempt to surge forward. My injured arm was limp at my side, throbbing in pain.

I ignored the discomfort and swam, counting the seconds in my head. Somewhere around thirty seconds, the light leveled out. I changed direction and swam horizontally toward it while my boots scuffed the muddy ground. Each time they did, I kicked off the ground to give me an extra boost.

Forty-one seconds.

My chest ached. Involuntarily, I released a bit of air from my lungs. Bubbles brushed my cheeks on their way to the surface. For the space of a heartbeat, I felt a fierce desire to exhale all of my stored air and inhale a lungful of fresh air.

No, don't do it, I told myself. *SWIM!*

One minute passed.

My head throbbed at the temples. Part of me wanted to kick off the ground and rise to the surface, but I feared the tunnel I swam through would be completely submerged.

One minute and twenty-two seconds.

I'd beaten my record! But how much longer could I hold my breath?

Faster, Maddie!

My hands brushed against a hard surface covered in algae, probably stone. Oh, no! Did I just hit a literal brick wall? I needed to swim forward—the miniature sun was gleaming straight ahead of me—but no matter where I set my hands I couldn't find a way through the wall. I searched frantically for a gap or a new tunnel.

One minute and fifty-three seconds.

Panic started to set in. I needed air. I kicked off the ground to rise to the surface, and I smacked my head against the roof of the tunnel. The blow not only hurt, but it startled me, sending out an angry burst of air from my lungs.

I shook off the daze as bubbles drifted past my face. Then I continued feeling along the wall with trembling hands. The tips of my fingers brushed against slimy stone and rough grooves, but I didn't feel anything other than—

Wait, my hand broke through a gap!

Not wasting another second, I squeezed through a space no bigger than the width of my waist. It was a tight fit, but I didn't care. I shimmied and pushed, kicked and scrabbled, trying desperately to get my body through . . .

. . . my belt buckle got snagged on something.

Now I was definitely panicking. I thrashed to break through the gap. I kicked to propel myself forward. I needed to breathe. Desperately. More air left my lungs despite my efforts to hold it in. I felt myself convulsing. My muscles were betraying me. My body was going to inhale a large gulp of air one way or another—even if it meant swallowing water.

I was about to drown.

It hurt like hell, but with my injured arm, I managed to unclasp my belt buckle. As soon as it came undone, I felt myself break free—and I shot through the gap. The last reserves of air stored in my lungs exhaled in a blurp, blurp, blurp. Behind my blindfold, the glowing light shifted upward, and I kicked *hard* off the ground.

I torpedoed through the water. My head broke the surface.

And, as I inhaled large gulps of air, I found a stone floor to rest my broken and exhausted body, thankful to be alive.

Chapter 73

AFTER THE DEADLY WATER tunnel, I found myself in utter darkness. I could still see the glowing light, so that's not what I mean, but my brothers weren't here to guide my steps anymore.

I was literally blind.

Plus, it was extremely cold. The tomb was a miserable place, made even more wretched after my dip in the icy water. My hair and clothes were sopping wet. My body shook uncontrollably from the cold. Or did I tremble from the shock of injuring my arm?

Maybe it was both.

I told myself to keep moving. Each minute lying halfway in the water was another minute of energy I couldn't afford to lose. So with what little strength I had remaining, I pulled myself out of the water and climbed unsteadily to my feet. My legs quivered and threatened to give out, but I managed to stand by placing my uninjured hand against a rough stone wall. A migraine throbbed at my temples.

Ignore the pain, I thought. *Focus on the light.*

The miniature sun pulsed in my peripheral vision. I turned toward the light, now glowing bigger than it had since I first put the blindfold on, and staggered toward it using the wall to guide my steps. Surely, the maze's end must be near since the light had grown so big.

My teeth chattered. My boots squished as I walked. I wasn't a hundred percent certain because my ears felt numb from the cold and were clogged with water, but it sounded like torches crackled with fire nearby.

A noise startled me.

I stopped dead in my tracks. It sounded like cave bats flapping their wings. Normal sounds for a cavern, I supposed. I took another step—but a colony of bats swarmed right past me. Their shrieks were high-pitched. Their wings slapped my face. A few claws scraped my cheeks, stinging. I ducked and covered my head until the last of them were gone.

Like I said, the tomb was a miserable place.

Panting, I rose and brushed away fresh blood trickling down my cheek. I hoped the scrape wouldn't give me rabies—or worse, turn me into a vampire or something stupid like that. The glowing light throbbed faster, matching my quickening heartbeat. I continued my blind hike toward it.

Until I bumped into something hard. My knee took the brunt of the blow.

"Son of a—" I cried in pain, rubbing my kneecap to try and ease the suffering.

The pain subsided, and I reached out to feel what I'd stumbled into. The object felt smooth and cold—and the moment my hands brushed its surface, the glowing light behind the blindfold flared like sunshine on a summer day.

"This is it," I breathed. "I've reached the end of the maze."

With trembling hands, I peeled off the blindfold. Torches crackled nearby in iron sconces set into stone walls, illuminating the chamber in flickering light. My eyes took a minute to adjust after being blindfolded for so long, but once they came into focus, I peered down at what I'd slammed my knee against.

A coffin.

It was made of polished white marble with little blue veins running through it. The lid had been sculpted to look like a person. The sculpted figure depicted a bearded man wearing a tunic and trousers. Gripped in his closed fists was a broadsword, a real one, covered in rust. By the figure's side was a wooden, weathered longbow with a quiver of arrows made of cracked leather. Etched beneath the figure's feet were the words:

ROBERT HUDE

THE PRINCE OF THIEVES

Holy fetch, it was the grave of Robin Hood! Two more coffins flanked Robin's. They didn't have sculpted figures on their lids. Just simple names carved into the marble: WILLIAM GOLDSBOROUGH, and THOMAS, THE MILLER'S SON.

Footsteps startled me.

I glanced up, taking in the rest of my surroundings as I searched for the source. The coffins rested beside the cave pond I'd emerged from. Torches hung throughout the chamber on walls that were a blend of natural rock formations and manmade stonework. The chamber was a crypt, half cave, half Knights Templar church. Beyond the trio of coffins, a set of stone stairs spiraled upward into the gloom.

And it was from those stairs the footsteps approached.

Whoever was coming must've carried a torch because firelight bounced around the stairwell creating a monstrous shadow on the wall. For a fraction of a second, I thought about ducking behind Robin Hood's coffin to hide.

But a slender woman in a gray, woolen cloak appeared before I could.

Her pale eyes gleamed from the torchlight. She looked me up and down as she walked into the room, her expression appearing unsurprised to find me there. I suddenly felt guilty like I was trespassing on sacred ground.

"H-hello," I stammered, still trembling from the cold and my injured arm. "I know what this looks like, but it's not what you th—"

"Hush, child," the woman rasped, her voice thin like fragile winds passing through time. "Your honor has been tested. The bravery of your heart has been found true. Step forward and claim your reward."

Chapter 74

I STARED AT THE WEATHERED woman.

Her skin was leathery like she'd spent way too much time in the sun. Wiry black hair stretched to the small of her back. A crow's feet of wrinkles framed her gray eyes. She looked older than her years, almost as if her life had been filled with so much hardship the trials had aged her.

"What'd you mean, my reward?" I asked.

The woman touched Robin Hood's coffin and caressed the sculpted figure's cheek. "Long years ago," she said. "My husband devised a plan to hide an artifact of power from the Knights Templar. He was once a knight of the Order himself, honored amongst their ranks. But the Order's corruption and betrayal led him to seek a different path. He became a prince of thieves, an outlaw who robbed from the rich and gave to the poor. The peasants called him Robert Hude."

"Wait, your husband was the *original* Robin Hood?" I asked.

She inclined her head.

"But that would make you, what, seven hundred years old?"

"I am far older than that," the woman said.

I scoffed.

She went on as though her age wasn't a big deal. "I first met my husband in the year 1191 after I was captured by the Knights Templar. The Order had been raiding Jerusalem in search of holy relics. I was the protector of one such relic, a traveling cloak worn by a man named Jesus the Nazarene. Before his betrayal in the Garden of Gethsemane, Jesus entrusted the cloak to me. I was only twenty-seven at the time.

"I wore the cloak for over a thousand years," the woman continued. "The healing power of Jesus must have affected the cloak's fabric because it cured deadly diseases and healed mortal injuries. It granted me long life."

"That's a cool story," I said, trying to make my voice sound like I didn't think the woman was crazy. "I've got Band-Aids at home with pictures of Jesus on them. They heal, too."

"This is not a laughing matter, child. We are talking about the Klok Kyoor, the traveling cloak of Jesus Christ."

"Hey, I'm not laughing," I said. "It's just that this tomb nearly killed me, like, a thousand times already. I'm exhausted and my arm might be broken. Your story is interesting, promise, but please forgive me if I'm too worn out to process it."

"I understand," she said. "You need proof."

"No," I groaned. "That's not what I'm saying. Maybe you can point me to the tomb's exit, or help me find my brothers? They're about yay high." I used my hand to indicate their height. "Super annoying. Probably still lost in your maze."

The woman unclasped the gray, woolen cloak from her neck. She removed it from her shoulders, revealing a black gown beneath with a white cloth draped across her neckline.

"You're a nun?" I said.

"I have been for many years," the woman said. "Ever since my husband died. I serve the Church, it is true, but secretly I keep watch over Robert Hude's tomb and the treasure it protects."

"You mean all that gold I saw earlier?"

She shook her head. "No, child, not the materialistic wealth of this world. That is treasure of a different sort. The wealth I guard is much more . . . substantial."

And she draped the woolen cloak over my trembling shoulders. Warmth flooded my body. I stopped shaking immediately. The migraine in my temples vanished, just like that. I felt my injured arm tingling with pinpricks, the same feeling you get when your foot falls asleep. I pulled my jacket sleeve up to the elbow to glance at my arm. The skin was swollen and bruised purple where the injury had occurred, but as I stared, the swelling went down and my skin transformed to a healthy color. I felt normal again. No, I didn't feel normal. I felt *amazing*, like a frigging superhero who could lift cars and sprint lightning-fast.

"Now do you see?" the nun asked. "The Klok Kyoor *heals*. That is the reward you have won."

I touched the cloak's scratchy fabric, trying to figure out how the heck it healed all my injuries in the blink of an eye. After coming up short of an answer, I looked up at the nun's weathered face.

"But, why me?" I asked.

"I have lived far too long," the nun said. "It is time the cloak passes to someone worthy of its healing powers. The trials in my maze served this purpose, to test your honor, and to judge your bravery. When you didn't peek through the blindfold, you proved your honor. When you jumped from the bridge in the face of death, you showed unrelenting bravery. You truly have the heart of a lion, child."

"B-but I could've died," I stammered.

"Many have."

"Don't you think that's a bit harsh?"

"It is reality."

I was silent for a long moment, contemplating all the ways I could've been killed in the maze. Finally, I asked, "So what now? I'm free to just take the cloak and go?"

She inclined her head.

"What will happen to you?"

"I will die."

My eyes widened in horror.

"Not today," she added with a chuckle, "but in a few years. I will age quickly. Time will catch me for all the years I shouldn't have lived. But do not mourn my passing." She brushed the tips of her fingers across the coffin and touched the closed hands of Robin Hood. "I look forward to my reunion with Robert."

Something the nun said wasn't adding up. "Can we back up a second? There's something about your story I don't understand."

"What confuses you, child?"

"You said the Knights Templar stole the cloak from you?"

The nun nodded. "Yes, by a woman who disguised herself as a knight. She was a cousin of King Richard the Lionheart."

"A woman knight," I said. "That's pretty cool."

"No," the nun said. "The knight was not *pretty cool*. She was dangerous and deadly. And it is because of her I must issue you a warning."

"A warning?"

"The woman knight—" she rasped, her tone sounding as though her strength was already fading since she no longer wore the cloak, "—is still alive."

An image of the old hag appeared in my mind.

"Yes," the nun breathed. "You know of whom I speak. The Sheriff of Nottingham lives because she possesses a torn piece of fabric from the cloak." She showed me where the cloak had been ripped.

I touched the tear. "But if she stole the cloak from you, how'd you get it back?"

"My husband was a talented thief."

If I hadn't spent the past couple of days with Jamari, I would've scoffed at her matter-of-fact comment. But in retrospect, it made total sense that Robin Hood would've been able to steal the cloak from the Knights Templar, and then make it nearly impossible to find unless you solved complex clues while trekking across England on a dangerous scavenger hunt.

"However," the nun continued. "The torn fabric is not enough to restore the sheriff's vitality. It only keeps her alive, hence her decrepit state. Even so, the sheriff is dangerous. She will stop at nothing to obtain the Klok Kyoor. I believe she thinks stealing it back will win her a measure of revenge for what I stole from her."

"You mean the cloak?"

"No, I stole something else. Something more precious."

"What?"

She glanced at Robin Hood's sarcophagus. "Her lover," she said. "They were betrothed to marry."

"Oh," I said. "Oh, this just got juicy."

The nun smirked. "My Robert was in love, I cannot deny this, but once his bride-to-be possessed the cloak, she *changed*. It became addictive like a drug for her. She coveted its power for herself, even refusing to heal others if it meant removing the cloak. Robert sought solace in my wisdom during this time, hoping to bring his love back from the brink. But it was too late. Her heart had been corrupted." She stared longingly at Robin Hood's coffin. "Our relationship blossomed. Their relationship died. Thus the twisted love triangle began, spanning centuries through time."

"Wow," I said. "And I thought Netflix had all the best dramas."

"What is Netflix?"

"Seriously, you've never heard of Netflix?"

She shook her head.

"Not important," I said.

"In that case, I have one last word of advice for you," the nun said. "Do not let the cloak corrupt your heart. Use it for good and help those in need."

I touched the hem of the gray cloak and felt its weight pressing down onto my shoulders. "I—I will," I promised.

"Good," she said. "Now you must begone. At the top of those stairs, you will find the tomb's exit. Your brothers are there, waiting for you now."

"And my friends?" I asked. "The ones trapped in the pit?"

The nun smiled. "They are with them as well. Though the *new* Robin Hood has broken his leg, but I am confident you will figure out how to heal him." She winked.

"Erm, thanks—" I said. "Thanks for everything."

"You are most welcome."

I started for the stairs, but stopped myself. "I just realized you never told me your name."

The nun smiled again. "Deborah of Nazareth."

"Nazareth? Isn't that where Jesus was from?"

Deborah nodded. "We were childhood friends. But enough about me. What is your name, child?"

"Maddie," I said. "Maddie Jones."

"Well met, Maddie Jones," Deborah said. "May the cloak of Christ help you weather any storm."

Part Three

THE SHERIFF OF NOTTINGHAM

Chapter 75

AFTER A LONG HIKE UP a spiraling stone staircase, I found my brothers, Kleopatra, Jamari, and his dad waiting for me in a torch-lit chamber. Large framed paintings of Jesus and other important figures of the Church hung on the walls. A threadbare carpet ran down the center of the room. At the far end of the chamber, a wooden ladder led to a closed trapdoor in the ceiling. Organ music sounded from the room above us, its muffled notes ominous yet somehow cheerful.

"Oh, my God!" gasped Kleopatra when she saw me.

She rushed forward and threw her arms around my neck in a fierce hug. Glitter mascara ran down her cheeks as though she'd been crying. "The boys were saying that you—that you jumped—" she couldn't finish the sentence. Instead, she buried her blotted face into my shoulder and wracked with heavy sobs.

"Ack, Kleo, I'm fine," I said, trying to unhinge her from my neck. "I jumped off a bridge. It was stupid, but I survived."

She let go, then snorted as she wiped wet cheeks with the back of her hand. Geez, talk about attractive.

My brothers both hugged me next. "I can't believe you jumped," Jason said; and Zac added, "Don't *ever* do anything like that again."

"Hey, it's not the stupidest thing I've ever done," I said.

Jason arched an accusing eyebrow.

"All right, it *was* the stupidest thing I've ever done. But I was right, Jason. A leap of faith was the only way through the maze."

Zac let go of our hug. "The maze trapped us. We explored the tunnels beyond the bridge, but no matter which path we explored it turned out to be a dead end."

"How'd you guys make it out?" I asked.

"A nun," Jason said. "She appeared out of nowhere and guided us here. Afterward, she left and brought Kleo, Jamari, and his dad. All of us were so thankful to get out of the tomb alive, we didn't ask questions when she told us to stay put."

"That must've been Deborah," I said.

"Deborah?" asked Zac. His eyes fell upon the gray cloak draped across my shoulders. "Wait a minute, you're wearing her cloak."

"Yep," I said. "I'll explain later."

I faced Jamari and his dad. Robin Hood sat in a rickety wooden chair that creaked when he moved. His broken leg was propped up on an adjacent chair, and his face was contorted in pain as Jamari leaned over his wound. It appeared Jamari was trying to create a makeshift splint out of a trio of arrows (the arrowheads removed) and a roll of bandage.

I knelt beside father and son. "Need a hand?" I asked.

Jamari looked up at me and smiled. "Bro, am I happy to see you."

"Why, were you worried about me?"

"Nah, more like I was worried about your babysitter. She promised me a slow death if something bad happened to you."

I blew out a breath. "That's all? You weren't concerned for a cute girl."

The dimple in his cheek deepened. "Well, maybe a little."

I blushed.

Jamari finished wrapping the bandage around his dad's leg, and pulled it tight. Robin Hood cried out in pain. "Geez, son, have a little care," he complained.

"Sorry, Dad, but the brace has to be tight if it's gonna work."

"Can I help?" I asked.

"Do you have medical experience?" Jamari pocketed the three arrowheads he'd removed from the shafts to create a splint. "Because the Merry Men have been trained for situations like this."

I took off the gray cloak. "You might be surprised," I said.

Then I draped the cloak over Robin Hood's leg. He gasped. None of us *saw* the healing power of the cloak, but there was a shift of energy in the room, almost as though a presence had joined us. Torches sputtered and spit as if wind stirred them to life. Warmth filled the chamber. The scent of summer wine and baking bread wafted beneath my nose.

The wonderful smells reminded me of a famous painting by Leonardo da Vinci called The Last Supper.

Call it magic.

Call it the Holy Spirit.

Call it what you will.

All I know is that one minute Robin Hood was grimacing in pain, and the next, he rose to his feet and bellowed, "Hark, the sick and wounded touched the fringe of His cloak—and they were healed!"

Jamari stumbled back. "Whoa, Dad, did you just cite the Bible or something?"

"I dunno." Robin Hood's expression was filled with wonder and awe as his gaze flitted to the gray cloak. "The words just came to me."

I removed the cloak from his leg and clasped it back around my neck. The cloak's warmth and thrumming energy enveloped me, making me feel invincible. "I bet you guys would like an explanation?"

"Er—duh," said Jamari.

I inhaled a deep breath, then explained everything I'd learned from Deborah, the nun who had protected the cloak for thousands of years before I came along and passed her test. None of them believed someone could live so long, or that the cloak once belonged to Jesus Christ, but no one could deny the miracle we'd just witnessed when the cloak healed Robin Hood's broken leg.

"This is what the sheriff is after," Robin Hood realized. "She needs the cloak to keep her immortal."

"She has a torn piece of the cloak," I explained. "And Deborah told me she wants the cloak because she's addicted to its healing powers. Plus, she's out for revenge."

"Revenge?" asked Jason.

"It turns out the Sheriff of Nottingham is a scorned lover of Robin Hood."

"Been there, kiddo," Kleopatra said. "A punk boyfriend once ghosted me."

"Ouch," said Zac.

Jamari slung his bow across his shoulder. "Then we must keep the cloak away from the sheriff," he said. "We've witnessed her brutality firsthand. Imagine how scary life would be if she could terrorize people forever."

I shivered. The thought of the old hag's unending cruelty sounded dreadful.

Robin Hood glanced up at the trapdoor in the ceiling. "Let's escape this place," he said. "We'll figure out a plan once we're somewhere safe."

Chapter 76

ORGAN MUSIC GREW LOUDER as we ascended the ladder to the trapdoor. Thankfully, the door wasn't locked or barred by heavy furniture resting on top of it. Robin Hood nudged it open, and the musical notes of the song came into clear focus. I recognized the song, kind of. It was either a high school graduation piece or some other important ceremonial song.

We all climbed out. I closed the trapdoor. A carpeted rug had folded at the corner when we opened the trapdoor, so I folded it back so it looked undisturbed. As I stood up, I realized the trapdoor was hidden behind the altar of the church. The stained glass window of Jesus being crucified loomed right over my head. I turned around to join the others—

—and stopped dead in my tracks.

A man in a rich tuxedo stood in front of the altar, along with a priest. Hundreds of people sat in pews. Everyone was dressed in tuxes and shimmering dresses. Except for the bride, who wore a magnificent white dress with lace and a sheer train fanning out behind her. She stood frozen halfway down the aisle, gaping at us with a horrified expression across her beautiful face. Organ music came to a screeching halt—of course, it was the wedding march song—and a tumult of murmurs went up from the pews.

"Oh, fetch," I swore.

"We just crashed a wedding," Kleopatra groaned.

The priest and groom turned around to see what everyone was gawking at. We must've been a strange sight— a couple of dirty teenagers, a Muslim woman with a torn hijab and smeared mascara, a black boy in a green cloak armed with a bow and quiver of arrows, and a huge man the size of a WWE wrestler in Sherwood Lumber overalls. I felt awful interrupting their beautiful wedding ceremony. The bride had probably dreamed of this day since she was a little girl. Yet here we stood, looking like we'd just emerged from the sewers.

We probably smelled like it, too.

Jamari nodded toward the open doors at the front of the church, where ruddy sunlight streamed inside. "C'mon," he said, then he brushed past the priest and groom and descended the altar steps.

The rest of us followed.

"Congratulations," I said to the groom as I swept by.

"You look beautiful," Kleopatra said to the bride halfway down the aisle. "I absolutely *love* your makeup!"

"Don't mind us," Zac shouted to the wedding guests gaping from the pews. "We're just a couple of bug exterminators. A huge cockroach was found in the basement—ate somebody's dog. But no worries, we killed him good!"

I palmed my face. Why was my brother such a dork?

Chapter 77

I WISH I COULD SAY OUR little interruption was the worst thing to ruin the couple's wedding. I wish I could say the bride and groom kissed and lived happily ever. But wishes hardly come true when life isn't a fairy tale.

We never made it out of the church.

Before we could exit, the Sheriff of Nottingham limped into the cathedral. The old hag's elbow crutches *clicked* and *clacked*. Her wrinkled and pockmarked face scanned the sanctuary. As her milky eyes settled on me wearing the gray cloak, a sneer darkened her expression.

"The cloak belongs to m-m-me," the Sheriff of Nottingham croaked.

Two deputies walked in behind her. Ponytail wearing a suit. And Kamari, who still wore her bloodied Sherwood Lumber uniform. They both gripped automatic assault rifles. A murmur of confusion swept across the wedding congregation, but Ponytail pointed her rifle into the air and fired. The din of gunfire was deafening. Bullets sprayed into the rafters.

Wedding guests screamed. Many of them ducked for cover.

I flinched and ducked into a pew myself, joining a young couple whose eyes were wide with fear. The gunfire ceased.

My ears rang from the loud rifle *pops*. Across the aisle, my brothers were crammed into a pew alongside wedding guests, hiding like me. But I didn't spot Jamari and his dad.

Then I heard them.

"The cloak doesn't belong to you," said Robin Hood. I peeked out from my hiding spot and saw him and Jamari squaring off against their longtime nemesis in the middle of the aisle. "It belongs to the girl with the heart of a lion."

"Yeah, bruh . . ." Jamari nocked an arrow into his bow. "And that ain't you."

My heart swelled with pride. The Merry Men were protecting me. Talk about a cool hero moment.

BANG! Robin Hood cried out in pain and collapsed to the ground. Little wisps of gunpowder smoke curled from the sheriff's revolver.

"DAD!" shouted Jamari.

"NO!" Kamari cried out.

The sheriff cackled, her maniacal laugh sending chills down the back of my neck.

The sight of someone getting shot sent wedding guests into a panic. They screamed, climbed over pews, and each other to escape the church. The bride darted to her groom, but tripped on her train and fell to the ground. The groom rushed to her aid and helped her stand. Together they ran into a side room.

During the chaos, I unclasped the cloak and prepared to throw it to Jamari so he could heal his dad's gunshot wound—but the sheriff saw what I was doing. She aimed her revolver at me.

"Ah, ah, ah," she rasped, spittle flinging from her lips. "Toss the cloak to me—or *she* becomes my next victim."

I glanced to where the sheriff motioned. Somehow in the chaos, Kleopatra had been caught. Ponytail held her hostage, but it wasn't a gun she threatened her life with. It was a silver deputy's badge.

My babysitter whimpered. "J–just do what they ask, Maddie."

Chapter 78

IT WAS CHECKMATE.

If I gave the cloak to the sheriff, then Jamari's dad would bleed out and die. If I gave the cloak to Jamari's dad, then Kleopatra would be deputized. What should I do? How could I save them both?

"Maddie," said a weak voice. I glanced at Robin Hood. His hands were pressed against his stomach, attempting to stop the bleeding. "It's okay, give the sheriff the cloak."

"But you—" I began.

"Don't worry about me," he grimaced. "Save your friend."

I was torn, but Robin Hood's bravery gave me strength. I tossed the cloak at the sheriff's feet. Kamari picked it up. She handed it to the old hag.

The sheriff clamped bony fingers around the gray cloak. "The relic's power tingles. Long have I missed this feeling," she rasped. "Too many years have I searched for this relic, barely alive. But now, I will be free of p-pain. Free of d-death. I will be *healed*."

And she dropped her elbow crutches and worked the cloak over her stooped shoulders with trembling hands. She gasped a raspy breath as the cloak settled onto her feeble form. A summertime breeze flitted by, ruffling my hair and warming the sanctuary. The wind swirled around the Sheriff of Nottingham as scents of honey and cinnamon drifted beneath my nose.

Right before our eyes, the sheriff's wrinkled and pockmarked skin slowly metamorphosed to that of a younger woman. She didn't grow younger, so much as she grew *healthier*. Her balding scalp with wisps of thin, white hair transformed into a lush head of auburn locks streaked with gray. Her bent posture changed from hunched over to standing tall. An old hag no longer stood before us.

A beautiful, older woman did.

The sheriff blinked, and her eye color changed from cloudy white to vibrant brown. She took in the sanctuary and its stained glass windows, almost as though she were truly seeing for the first time.

"The colors," she said, and her voice no longer rasped or stuttered. It was a gentle voice with hints of authority and confidence. "How long has it been since my vision faded?" She inhaled deeply. "And the smells. My God, the scents are wondrous."

"Erm, I'm glad you're healthier now," I said, drawing the sheriff's crystal gaze onto me. "And that you can see and smell stuff, too. But my friend's gonna die unless he gets medical attention, like, right now. Please, help him."

The Sheriff of Nottingham glared at Robin Hood writhing in pain. "If you think I would remove the cloak now, after all these years," she laughed, its notes ringing with youthfulness. "The scum can die for all I care. He isn't even the *real* Robin Hood."

"But he's bleeding—"

"Not my concern," the sheriff snapped.

She looked around the sanctuary and studied its overturned pews from the wedding guests' mass exodus, the raised altar, marble statues, and paintings lining the walls. "God, how many years has it been since I last visited this place? The fabled church where Robert Hude wed Maid Marian." She spit on the ground. "Lies. He rejected me in favor of the heretic from Nazareth."

"Hold up, bro," said Jamari. "*You* are Maid Marian?"

The sheriff inclined her head.

"So the stories are—"

"Lies," she finished. "The stories are lies. Yet one story must be true since you found the cloak in this place. Where is the entrance to Robert Hude's tomb?"

Nobody answered.

The sheriff's revolver clicked as she pulled back the hammer.

"There's a trapdoor behind the altar," I blurted out. "Please, let my babysitter go."

The sheriff—AKA Maid Marian—tucked the revolver into a hip holster. "No," she said. "Good help is hard to find. Bring the woman."

She stepped past Robin Hood lying wounded on the ground and strode toward the altar, the gray cloak swishing in her wake like great wings. Ponytail followed as commanded, dragging Kleopatra along with her. My babysitter's expression was one of horror and confusion. I wanted to leap to her aid, but what could I do? Kamari still stood guard with her gun.

The sheriff found the trapdoor. She pulled back the rug and opened the latch, but she barked one last command before descending the ladder. "Kill them all," she ordered Kamari.

Kamari aimed her automatic assault rifle. "Kill," she cried, her expression crazed as tears streaked down her cheeks.

Chapter 79

KAMARI LOCKED AIM ON HER brother, but she didn't squeeze the trigger right away. She hesitated for the briefest moment.

Enough time for Jamari to grab a hidden dagger from his cloak and throw it at his sister.

The dagger struck Kamari's rifle. The weapon went flying from her hands. Jamari reached for another hidden blade, but Kamari lunged. She was blazing fast, like a sharp-fanged hyena pouncing on its prey. The full weight of her body crashed into Jamari and they went sprawling to the ground. He dropped his bow from the force of impact.

Kamari's sharp fingernails dug into Jamari's flesh. He cried out in pain as she grabbed his arm and twisted, locking Jamari into some kind of jiu-jitsu hold. Part of me wondered if Kamari was faster and stronger because of the deputy's badge, but I knew she'd spent much of her life training alongside the Merry Men.

Maybe she was simply a better fighter than Jamari.

He needed help. Robin Hood reached for the bow Jamari had dropped, but I was willing to bet he couldn't shoot an arrow with such a serious injury in his abdomen. Plus, I couldn't believe he'd actually shoot an arrow at his daughter.

So.

I tackled Kamari, forcing her to let go of her brother.

Our fight went to the ground. We grappled, wrestled, and slapped at each other. I tried to overpower Kamari, but she was stronger than me and much much quicker. Fingernails raked across my nose and cheek, drawing blood. I yelled a battle cry, something that resembled an "Agghhh!" or a "Waagghhh!" but more than likely it sounded like, "Somebody get her off me!"

Kamari's fingers wrapped around my neck, squeezing. I clawed at her hands, but I couldn't get them unhinged. I couldn't breathe! What was up with people choking me in fights?

WHACK! She was struck across the head with a hardcover Bible. The hit staggered Kamari, forcing her to release the grip on my neck. She stumbled off of me. I climbed to my feet and gasped for air.

Another Bible went hurtling by. Then another. And another. A few thumped into Kamari, but most missed her completely. I whirled around to see Jason and Zac grabbing Bibles from the back of pews and throwing them wildly— something that under normal circumstances they'd never do in a million years.

But if they didn't do something, Kamari might've murdered me.

Kamari swatted a Bible out of the air before it could hit her. She bared teeth at my brothers. "Stop—throwing— books—" she growled.

"Stop trying to kill our sister!" shouted Zac, and he flung another Bible.

Kamari ducked the hurtling book. Then she charged at my brothers—but a blur of green came out of nowhere and tackled her. Jamari sprang to his feet, his green cloak flowing with his movements, and he hopped spryly like a boxer light on his toes. He lunged a roundhouse kick.

Kamari rolled aside and dodged the kick. Then she lunged like a Kung Fu warrior and threw a right hook at Jamari's head. He blocked the punch with his elbow.

And brother and sister were locked in a vicious brawl.

Their fists were a blur they moved so fast. Their kicks knocked over pews when they missed. I'd never seen anyone fight like Bruce Lee or Jackie Chan in real life, but here were two karate masters going at it with everything they had.

"Robin Hood just passed out!" shouted Jason.

Jamari glanced sideways at his dad, and the brief distraction cost him. Kamari roundhouse kicked his legs. He fell onto his back and Kamari elbow-punched him in the chest.

"Ooomph!" Jamari wheezed.

Kamari threw a punch, but Jamari recovered his wits and swatted it aside. He rolled away to get free of her strikes. "Get my dad outta here—" he yelled, striking at Kamari with a series of jabs. She blocked each one. "He needs a doctor!"

A doctor? Where the heck could we find a doctor?

Now Jamari was on the attack, pushing Kamari back on her heels.

He's distracting her, I realized. *He doesn't want to kill his sister, but he also doesn't want her to stop fighting.*

If Kamari gave up the fight, then hellfire would destroy her because she had disobeyed the sheriff's command.

I rushed to Robin Hood's side. He'd lost so much blood he was unconscious. His large chest rose and fell, so he still breathed, but how much time did he have left? There was no way I could carry him out of the church. The man was huge with massive knots of muscle.

But I don't have to carry him.

"I'll be back!" I shouted to my brothers. Then I darted for the altar.

"Where are you going?" Jason called after me.

"To get help!" I yelled back.

There was only one thing that could heal Jamari's dad before he bled to death. The cloak of Jesus Christ.

Chapter 80

I RUSHED TO ROBIN HOOD'S crypt.

When I reached the bottom of the stairwell overlooking the chamber with the trio of coffins, I crouched in the shadows to hide . . . and to watch. The coffins were illuminated by flickering torchlight. Murky water from the pond I'd almost drowned in an hour earlier lapped onto a cobblestone shore.

And Maid Marian loomed over the sarcophagus of Robin Hood, caressing the sculpted figure's face.

Geez, Robin Hood must've been a player. I had now witnessed *two* women pine over his dead body.

I spotted Ponytail. The deputy stood guard behind the sheriff, watching and alert. Her automatic assault rifle was strapped to her shoulder, hanging at her side, but ready. The fact that she no longer held Kleopatra hostage sent a sinking feeling to the pit of my stomach.

Where was my babysitter?

I peeked out so I could see more of the chamber. Just on the edge of firelight, I spotted Kleopatra near the cave pond. Darkness shrouded most of her features, but when she turned away from the ominous water, I caught a glimpse of light gleaming off her chest.

A silver deputy's badge.

No, I thought. *She's been deputized.*

How could I save her? If the badge was removed by anyone other than the sheriff, she would die. If she didn't follow the sheriff's orders, she would die. No matter how I tried to imagine the next few minutes, they all ended in Kleopatra's death. I tried to shake the horrible thoughts aside. If I was going to save my babysitter and Jamari's dad, then I needed a clear head . . . and a plan.

A loud bang startled me.

Maid Marian had pushed the lid off Robin Hood's coffin. The heavy stone lid with its sculpted figure carved to resemble the dead man inside clanged onto the floor. The rusting broadsword gripped in the figure's hands went skittering across the ground.

Maid Marian gasped when she saw the corpse. "My Robert," she said with longing in her voice. She reached inside to touch the corpse's face.

I gagged. So gross!

Although the sheriff had said she would never remove the cloak, it appeared there was one exception—for her dead lover. She shimmied out of the gray cloak and draped it across the corpse.

"Time for you to wake, my dear."

A heavy silence settled. Would the corpse of Robin Hood rise from the grave? I'd seen a mummy come to life before, and let me tell you, it was absolutely disgusting.

Minutes passed, but nothing stirred.

"Why isn't it working?" said Maid Marian.

I noticed that her hair was thinning. Its color was also slowly transforming back to ghost white.

"The Klok Kyoor is supposed to *heal.*"

I realized something in that moment. The gray cloak couldn't raise the dead. It could only heal the *living.* Which meant the cloak could possibly heal Kleopatra of her deputy's curse. I also realized the cloak was the only thing maintaining the sheriff's vitality. And I was willing to bet a healthy sheriff was far more dangerous than the old hag.

The cloak was the key. If I could just get my hands on the relic. But how?

Maybe.

Just maybe.

I could outwit the Sheriff of Nottingham.

It seemed worth a shot. After all, there was no way I could overpower three women—two of them armed with guns no less. But a battle of wits, now that was something I could possibly win. A plan started to form in my mind. A dangerous, suicidal plan. Part of me didn't want to go through with it.

But you have to try, I told myself. *Otherwise, your friends will die.*

With my heart hammering in my chest, I stepped out from my hiding spot and walked into the torch-lit crypt with my hands held up. Ponytail saw me approaching. She grabbed her rifle and aimed.

"Whoa, don't shoot," I said, trying hard to keep my voice steady so it didn't reveal my fear.

Kleopatra wrapped her arms around herself for warmth. "M-Maddie?" her voice trembled. It sounded like she'd been crying. "You shouldn't have come here."

I didn't look at my babysitter. If I did, my confidence would waver and I might not have the courage to go through with what I had planned next.

Maid Marian looked up from Robin Hood's corpse. Pockmarks had formed beneath the surface of her skin again. "T-talk?" she croaked, her voice now hoarse without the healing power of the cloak. "For your sake, I hope you've something worthwhile to s-s-say. You're interrupting my r-reunion."

"Yeah, erm," I hesitated, giving Ponytail a sidelong glance to see her gun still aimed at me. "I noticed the cloak isn't working. I think I know why."

"W-why?" the sheriff rasped.

"The cloak has to be *worn*," I said. "You can't drape it across someone like that, it won't work."

Maid Marian's brown eyes narrowed, and right before my eyes, they transformed to a blind, milky white as the old hag continued aging. "L-liar," she growled.

"No, it's true," I said. "The nun who gave me the cloak told me all about it."

"The nun?" the sheriff said. "What was her n–name?"

"Deborah," I said. "Do you know her?"

Maid Marian snorted and spat. Yellow snot splattered on the cobblestones near my feet. "Of course I know that w-witch. She stole my Robert. But if Deborah says the cloak must be worn . . ." She pointed at Kleopatra. "You there. P-put the cloak on my love, but be gentle with the body. I don't want his head f-falling off."

Kleopatra's cheeks puffed, probably from stifling a gag reflex. I'd spent enough time with my babysitter these past few weeks to know she had an aversion to anything gross. Despite her revulsion, Kleopatra moved to obey. Her life depended on it.

"I also came to ask a question," I said, trying to draw the sheriff's attention. "How can I become a deputy?"

Maid Marian drew her revolver. She loaded fresh bullets from her gun belt into the chamber, her hands now trembling from old age once more. "You want to j-join us?" she stuttered.

"Oh, of course," I said, as Kleopatra lifted the skeletal corpse while mouthing ew–ew–ew. She began working the corpse's bony arms into the gray cloak. "I mean, your deputies are hot and super powerful. What girl wouldn't want to join you guys?"

"They are young and b-beautiful, aren't they?" the sheriff said. "I suppose I longed for youth so I started deputizing pretty women to be n-n-near it."

"Exactly," I said. "And I'm young. Not as pretty as you when you're wearing the cloak, but I think I might make a good deputy."

Kleopatra finished putting the cloak on Robin Hood's corpse. Nothing happened, so I knew the next part of my plan needed to speed up.

"Another thing Deborah said about the cloak," I informed the sheriff. "Is that it takes longer to heal the dead than it does the living."

"Is that so?" Maid Marian studied my dirtied face.

I tried not to break eye contact. Otherwise, she might catch me in my lie. A bead of sweat ran down my temple. I hoped she didn't notice.

"Then let's play a game while we wait," the sheriff rasped. "You want to become a d-d-deputy . . . prove it. Because we have a little problem that must be dealt with first."

"What?"

"I gave my last badge to *her*," she pointed her revolver at Kleopatra. "But I've had an idea. If you want to join our ranks, then you must p-pass a test."

"Anything," I said. "You name it and I'll do it."

She smirked. "Kill your babysitter."

Chapter 81

FETCH, MY PLAN BACKFIRED big time.

"Erm, say what now?" I said.

"Kill your babysitter," the sheriff said matter-of-factly. "And you," she spoke to Kleopatra now. "Kill this b-brat. Winner of the fight becomes my d-deputy."

Gulp! This meeting didn't go down how I foresaw. What the heck should I do now?

Kleopatra's mascara-smeared eyes flitted to me, and I could see in her expression that she was trying to work out a plan, just like I was. She walked around Robin Hood's sarcophagus. I didn't see any weapons in her hands, but as she got closer, she squeezed them into fists.

To say that Kleopatra's fighting stance was laughable is an understatement. She was the biggest girly girl I'd ever met, so it was hard to be intimidated by her meek demeanor. In contrast, I'd survived loads of fights over the years—at school, in juvie, even against Tamora Rose, my dad's former work colleague who tried to kill my family last year.

All this to say, Kleopatra didn't stand a chance. She might be older than me by several years, but none of that mattered once the pummeling commenced.

"You sure about this?" I said, balling my hands into fists.

Kleopatra closed her eyes and inhaled deeply. After releasing a long, quivering breath she did something that surprised even me.

She lowered her fists.

"I won't kill you, Maddie Jones," she said. "You're like a little sister to me and I love you too much."

Whoa, her words punched me in the stomach like an emotional brick.

Kleopatra *loved* me? I'd grown quite fond of my babysitter over the past few days. If I was being completely honest, I'd probably grown to love her, too. Life and death moments will do that to people, I suppose. Talk about a cool hero moment for Kleopatra. She was *choosing* to disobey the sheriff's command, knowing the decision would end her life.

Wait a minute! I couldn't let that happen.

"I hate you," I growled. "I hate everything about you."

Kleopatra looked confused. "What?"

"That's right," I said. "You think you can just swoop in and become my mom? She died, and nobody can replace her. Not even *you*, Kleo. All you've been good for is free rides and your daddy's credit card."

"You don't mean that, Maddie."

"I mean every word. So there's no point sacrificing your life for me because I'm not worth it. You better kill me, Kleo. I'm sure as hell about to kill you."

Kleopatra's expression looked truly hurt. My words had stung deeply.

"No," she said. "You may not like me, Maddie. But that doesn't change how I feel about you."

"But Kleo—" I said, and tears welled up at the corners of my eyes and streaked down my cheeks. "You're gonna die."

"I know," she said. "And I'm okay with it."

Well, I sure as heck wasn't. If Kleopatra didn't attack me, she would burst into flames and die in agony and pain.

So.

I flung myself at my babysitter and decked her in the face.

Chapter 82

I'D FOUGHT PEOPLE WHO deserved to be fought. I'd brawled with chicks who hated my guts. But never, ever in my short years of life had I punched, kicked, and scratched someone I cared so deeply for.

Kleopatra was surprised by my unexpected attack.

She didn't have time to put up her hands to defend herself, and my punch clocked her on the jaw. She reeled from the blow and went sprawling on her butt. I didn't relent. I leapt on top of her, screaming and punching, hoping Kleopatra would at least fight me back.

For those of you who have never been in a situation like this before, there's a sort of primal instinct that kicks in when your life is on the line. For Kleopatra, that moment occurred when I ripped the silk hijab from her head. A tangle of black hair came with it, clenched in my fist.

Muslim women keep their hair hidden for a reason. The hijab is a symbol of faith, sure, but there is also beauty found in the headscarf. It embodies modesty, how you talk, and the way you treat others. Muslim women take pride in the beauty of their hair, many seeing it as a crown to be worn with pride and uniqueness. For some, their hidden locks are for a lover's eye only—not worthy of the public's attention.

So when I exposed Kleopatra's hair *and* ripped strands of it right off her scalp, I'd done more than tear a headdress. I'd unveiled her beauty. And if there's one thing I'd learned about my babysitter these past few days, it was this.

You don't mess with Kleopatra's beauty.

"You *witch*!" my babysitter growled.

She reared back and smacked me in the face with an open palm. I went sprawling, my cheek stinging from the strike. Before I could get to my feet to face my now enraged babysitter, she flung herself at me.

And the fight was on.

Kleopatra was surprisingly strong. She grabbed me by the hair and pulled back hard, then proceeded to slap me in the face. I blocked a couple of her blows, but a few stray hits got through my defenses and smacked me on the ear, my forehead, and right on the chin. If Kleopatra was pulling her punches, it didn't show. Each strike stung worse than the hit that came before it.

I elbowed Kleopatra in the gut. She let go of my hair and doubled over. I leapt rearward to put some distance between us, panting heavily from the viciousness of my babysitter's assault.

Holy cow, where did Kleopatra get all this pent-up rage?

The sheriff cackled.

I glanced over to see her watching the fight with a sort of maniacal glee. Long years must've messed with her brain if she thought young women fighting to the death was a form of entertainment. No wonder Robin Hood had ditched her for Deborah. The chick was insane.

Something moved in the background, catching my eye. For the briefest moment, I thought I saw a nun entering the crypt.

Then Kleopatra yelled and attacked, drawing my attention. She threw a clumsy punch, but I ducked it easily. When I sprang back up, I glanced toward the stairwell to find the nun, but no one was there.

What the heck?!

My babysitter whirled around and charged. She didn't seem to have the same level of energy and hate she'd had at the start of our skirmish because I swatted her hand away with ease. She couldn't stop her momentum as she went running past, and I stuck out a boot and tripped her. Kleopatra went sprawling to the ground.

The sheriff yawned. "Your fight b-bores me," she hissed as she cocked the hammer of her revolver. "One of you end this or I'll shoot the both of you."

Kleopatra climbed to her feet, breathing deeply. I faced her with clenched fists. We circled each other like two boxers in a ring. My brain was working overtime, trying to figure out a plan to get out of this mess, but no matter what thoughts crept in, none of them were helpful. Every scenario seemed to end with one of our deaths, maybe both.

"Do you remember last week's prank, Maddie?" asked Kleopatra. "The one Principal Watson called to complain about?"

I didn't understand why Kleopatra would ask about this now, of all moments. Maybe she was trying to tell me something without the sheriff knowing.

"The one with the pigs?" I asked.

She shook her head.

"The one with the dog poop brownies?"

"No, kiddo, the one with the mannequin."

Oh, yeah. That was a good one. I swiped sunglasses right off Principal Watson's head and ran before she could catch me, then I bought a wig and decorated a mannequin to look just like her. I hid in a locker and mimed her voice as students walked by, issuing detentions and yelling at kids to get to class. And the funny thing was, the students I gave detentions to actually showed up.

How would I know? Well, I ended up serving detention with them.

Principal Watson found me inside the locker.

Even though I remembered the prank, I didn't understand what Kleopatra was trying to tell me. Her eyes implored me to follow along, but her meaning just didn't click. We continued circling one another. The sheriff was now behind me and I could hear the revolver tapping against her leg.

That's when Kleopatra lunged.

I dove out of the way, but my babysitter didn't aim her attack at me.

Instead, she lunged at the sheriff and dug fingernails into her chest. And it was then that I understood what my babysitter had meant. She wanted to *swipe* something off the sheriff.

Her badge. She ripped it out of her chest.

Chapter 83

THE BADGE CAME OUT OF the sheriff's chest in a bloody mess.

Just like the deputy badges, it had a metal spike that had been stabbed into her heart. A torn piece of cloth was pinned behind the badge. I vaguely recalled that the deputy badge I'd found had a piece of cloth glued to the spike, albeit much smaller.

Of course.

They were torn pieces from the cloak of Jesus Christ.

That's how the sheriff had lived all this time. She had kept the cloth pinned to her body, hidden from prying eyes. But now that the cloth wasn't touching her skin, its healing power couldn't keep her vitality healthy any longer.

The sheriff's eyes widened in shock. She glanced down at her chest where the badge had been, and gasped. Blood spit up onto her lips. She lunged for Kleopatra, but my babysitter turned and threw the badge as far as she could—right into the cave pond. The badge splashed into the water and sank.

"N-n-no," the sheriff stammered. She whirled around to grab the gray cloak from Robin Hood's corpse—

—but Deborah, the nun, now held it tightly in her hands. During my fight with Kleopatra, she must've snuck into the chamber and removed the gray cloak from the body.

"Yeeeeuuuuu," yelled the sheriff, pure hatred oozing from her lips. "You stole everything from m-me. Robert was *my* life. *My* love. Why'd he choose yeeeuuu?"

Deborah's expression was darkened in sorrow. "Because you loved power, Marian," she said. "Robert tried to save you from yourself, but even then, you chose the cloak over him."

The sheriff let out a screeching yell that dwindled into a strangled gasp. Without the badge, without the cloak, her immortality couldn't last. Her health deteriorated rapidly. She grew even older, which I know sounds crazy because the old hag already looked like a walking corpse, but she aged like a withered flower losing pedals in the sun. The aging didn't stop until she was nothing more than a gruesome heap of rotting flesh and bone. An odor hit my nostrils. A stench so foul it threatened to knock me to my knees—the bloated ripeness of a corpse.

I swallowed to keep from vomiting.

Ponytail dropped her gun. It clanged onto the floor. I glanced her way and saw that she held the deputy badge in her hands. "The curse—" she said breathlessly. "It's gone!"

"It is," said Deborah, "but it will take time to mend your mental health after all you have experienced. For now, I think it wise if you stayed with me here at the church. When you're ready, we'll reunite you with your family."

"I have a husband," said Ponytail, tears streaking her cheeks. "We were married for only a month before I crossed paths with . . . with . . ."

Deborah draped the gray cloak across Ponytail's shoulders. The moment it touched her skin, the former deputy let out a deep sigh, almost as though some of her troubles had been lifted from her chest.

"What is your name, child?" asked Deborah.

"R-Raine," she stammered.

"All right, Raine. Let's draw you a warm bath and get you something to eat."

Raine nodded, the tears flowing freely.

Deborah removed the gray cloak, then approached and offered it to me. I accepted the cloak with trembling hands. "Try to take better care of it this time," she said with a smirk.

"S-sorry," I said.

"Don't be, the sheriff was a formidable foe."

I put on the gray cloak. It felt warm like a father's hug after a long day of school. "There's still something I don't understand," I said.

Deborah nodded. "Let me guess. You are wondering why the cloak wouldn't raise Robin Hood from the dead."

"Yeah."

"It's a mystery even to me." Deborah glanced at the open sarcophagus and her late husband's skeletal remains. "I tried countless times to raise Robert after he died . . ." she sighed. "But the cloak heals only the living."

"And there's another thing," I said. "Why'd the sheriff die like that? You are far older than her, but you're still alive even though you're not wearing the cloak."

"I wore the cloak for a long time," Deborah said. "Meanwhile, the sheriff only had a piece of the cloak. Perhaps that is why. Now, there is a lot of commotion going on upstairs in the sanctuary."

"Oh, fetch! Jamari's dad. He needs serious medical attention."

"Then it's time we say our farewells." Deborah stepped aside so I could see the stairwell behind her. "Take the cloak and do all the good you can, Maddie Jones. Remember to keep it hidden. Keep it safe. Heal others often, but don't let the artifact corrupt your heart."

"Thanks," I said. "I won't."

Kleopatra stood near the cave pond. A deputy badge was in her hands.

"Kleo," I said. "You coming?"

Kleopatra wiped tears from her eyes. My babysitter was a strong-willed woman, probably more so than me. Having to obey corrupt authority wasn't something girls like us were accustomed to. The ordeal with the sheriff must've shaken her deeply.

She looked up. "Of course, kiddo. I just have to do one thing first." And she chucked the badge into the cave pond. "Now let's go heal Robin Hood."

Chapter 84

THE CHURCH'S SANCTUARY was chaotic.

First responders were everywhere. Policemen. Firefighters. Paramedics. You name it. Outside, nighttime had settled across the land, but flashing red and blue lights streamed inside through the open front door. The place looked like an earthquake had hit. Pews were overturned. Marble statues had been busted. Framed pictures had fallen from the walls, many of their frames broken and lying among shards of destroyed stained glass windows.

Holy cow, the fight between Jamari and Kamari had been fierce.

I made my way through the mess toward Jamari and his dad. They were between the pews in the middle aisle, right where Robin Hood had fallen after getting shot. He was still on his back and unconscious.

And paramedics conducted CPR.

"No," I said when I saw what was going on.

"C'mon, Dad . . ." Jamari knelt beside his father. Tears flowed down his face. One of his eyes was swollen from a punch he likely wasn't able to block. "Don't die, please don't die."

Kamari stood beside Jamari with a hand on his shoulder. She had a purple cheek and a busted lip. Tears blotted her eyes as she watched. I noticed the deputy badge was no longer pinned to her chest.

Nearby, my brothers were huddled together watching in horror. They'd most likely never seen something like this before.

I took off the gray cloak and knelt to help.

"Back up," the paramedic doing chest compressions barked. "I need room to work."

I blanketed Robin Hood with the cloak. Nothing happened. My heart sank.

"Young lady, give me space or—"

A summertime breeze flitted by. It ruffled the tips of the paramedic's shaggy, brown hair. The scent of red wine filled me with images of church and communion.

Robin Hood's eyes snapped open. He gasped.

"Jesus!" said the paramedic, stumbling back.

If you only knew, I thought.

I removed the gray cloak and put it back on, hoping I hadn't drawn more attention to it than necessary.

"H-how did you—" the paramedic stammered.

"He was just cold," I said.

Robin Hood stood, to the bewilderment of the paramedics. He thumped his chest. "Hark, I feel as though I could defeat an entire army single-handedly!" he bellowed.

"Let's start by sitting down and taking your vitals," said the paramedic.

"Get your grubby hands off me," Robin Hood shouted. "I feel fine—better than fine, actually."

"Please let them do their job, Dad," said Jamari.

"All right, all right." Robin Hood sat in a pew that hadn't fallen over. The paramedics took his pulse, checked his temperature, and did a few tests.

Jamari rushed over and gave me a huge hug. "Thank you," he said, his breath smelling like peppermint. He was sweaty and the rest of him stank, but part of me wanted to keep my arms wrapped around his muscled body. "I didn't think my dad was gonna make it."

"Don't mention it," I said, letting go of our hug. Then I dropped my voice to a whisper. "I mean it, don't mention the cloak. Keep it secret."

"Of course, bruh."

I slumped into a pew. The exhaustion of the last few days felt like it was finally catching up with me. Jamari sat beside me.

"So," he began. "How'd you defeat the sheriff?"

"I didn't. My babysitter did."

He eyed Kleopatra as she stood near the church's entrance and talked on the phone, probably to her papa. "Wow, I need to get myself a babysitter like that."

"Well, you can't have her," I said. "She's out of your price range, anyways."

He chuckled. "You're probably right."

I eyed Kamari. She spoke to Robin Hood while the paramedics continued running tests. "How's your sister doing?" I asked.

"Dunno," Jamari sighed. "I'm worried about her. What if she killed someone while under the sheriff's orders?"

"Look at it this way," I said. "She wasn't a deputy for very long, so most likely she didn't have enough time to go full Darth Vader yet."

Jamari chuckled, but the laugh didn't sound genuine. He clearly cared for his sister.

"There's a nun here who might be able to help," I said, hoping to offer words of encouragement. "I'll talk to her before we leave."

"That would be great," he said. "Thanks."

We were quiet for a moment. Usually, when I'm attracted to a boy I find not talking awkward. My brain races for something interesting to say. But sitting beside Jamari in silence felt . . . good. It felt normal.

"How about you?" he broke the quiet. "Will you be okay after all of this?"

"Well," I sighed. "We didn't save my father's museum, so that's a bummer. But maybe there are more important things in life than a museum full of relics."

"Like what?"

Kleopatra finished her phone call. "I love you, too, Papa. I'm sorry for all of the credit card charges."

I smiled. "Like family. They're the real treasure."

Jamari glanced at his dad. "I think you're right." He looked at me. "You know, the offer still stands."

I raised an eyebrow. "What offer?"

"To join the Merry Men. You passed our test, remember? Sherwood Lumber will be rebuilt and we're always looking for fresh recruits. We could use someone like you."

"I don't know . . ."

"Will you at least think about it?"

"Are you guys gonna keep robbing from the rich?" I asked.

"Probably."

"Give money to the poor?"

'Definitely."

"What do you think about healing the sick?"

Jamari didn't seem to understand at first, but then his gaze darted to the gray cloak.

"If I'm going to join you guys," I said. "Then I'd want to start a new branch of Sherwood Lumber, one focused on *healing*. I want to help people who are beyond the reach of medicine."

Jamari smiled. "I think that's brilliant, bruh. Do you have any idea where you'd like to start?"

I thought about it for a moment. Who did I know in need of healing more than anyone else? A smile touched the corners of my eyes when I realized just the right person.

"Can Sherwood Lumber fly us to Boston?" I asked.

Chapter 85

AMIRA RAJA'S HOSPITAL ROOM was exactly how I remembered it.

It was white and sterile with bright, morning sunshine streaming through the blinds of a single window. Tiny dust particles floated in the rays. Flowers, get-well cards, and framed photographs decorated the tables. There was even a picture of me, which Amira must've taken during one of our lengthy FaceTime conversations. My picture rested beside a photograph of Amira and her dad during one of their hiking trips through the mountains. In the photograph, Amira's complexion was dark, of middle-eastern descent, and long black hair bounced beautifully off her shoulders.

But Amira Raja no longer had hair.

Cancer treatments stole her gorgeous locks long ago. And her dad, well, he died last year in a failed attempt to find a cure for his daughter.

I entered the room with Jamari in tow, surprised to find Amira asleep. The nurse had warned us that Amira's health had declined in the past month, but seeing firsthand how pale and thin she looked knocked the breath from my lungs. The spunky teenage girl I had grown to love was losing energy by the day.

But I'm here to change all of that, I told myself.

"So this is Amira, huh?" Jamari asked as we approached the bed. I'd told him all about her during our flight from England. "Do you want to wake her first?"

I did.

There was no way Amira should miss this miracle.

So I gently nudged her arm and whispered her name. "Amira, there's someone special here to see you."

She blinked open her eyes. Her bleary gaze settled on Jamari. "Oy," she said sleepily. "Have I died and gone to heaven? Oh, gosh, you're gorgeous."

"Erm—" Jamari spluttered.

"Amira," I scolded. "It's *me*—I'm the someone special."

"No, you're not. Look at *him*."

I palmed my face.

Amira sat up and rubbed her eyes. "Sorry, Maddie, but he's even prettier in person."

"Hold up, bruh, have we met?" asked Jamari.

"The distraction in the sheriff's warehouse," I explained. "Amira was the person I called to act as a decoy so we could escape."

"Oh, yeah."

Amira reached for me. "Come here," she said, and I embraced her in a fierce hug. "I'm so happy you're safe."

I squeezed her back. Her grip around my neck felt extremely weak. "Me too," I said, letting go.

"Why are you here?" she asked. "Did you come to watch Harry Potter movies? Oooh, are you two on a date?"

"What? No—" I said.

"Wow, you sure answered quickly," said Jamari. "Am I not datable?"

"No. I mean, yes. Man, is it hot in here?"

Amira smirked. "Your face is red, Maddie."

I set my backpack onto her bed, unzipped it, and took out the gray cloak. "Let's just this over with. Here—put this on."

"What is it?"

"It's what your dad should've been looking for. It will cure your cancer."

"How?"

"Put it on. You'll see."

Amira shimmied into the gray cloak. As soon as it was draped across her shoulders, strange winds swirled around the room, blowing the get-well cards on her bedside table onto the floor. Artwork taped to the walls billowed like flags. The breeze brought with it hints of bread and wine—you know, the usual smells I was growing accustomed to every time the cloak healed someone.

Amira gasped.

Dark hair sprouted on her balding scalp. It grew right before our eyes, past her shoulders, and to the same length it was in the photograph with her dad. Her sickly complexion also brightened from pasty white to a sun-kissed olive color.

As the winds stopped swirling, Amira snatched up one of the framed pictures and studied her reflection in its glass. She ran fingers through her dark hair, smiling so big I thought her cheeks might explode.

"I can't believe it!" she said, tears rolling down her cheeks.

"It's amazing, isn't it?" I said.

She looked up. "Can the cloak heal others? There's a little boy next door. He's only four, but—"

"Oh, my God," I interrupted, an idea forming in my mind. "Let's heal the whole hospital."

"The whole hospital?" said Jamari. "Won't that put the cloak in jeopardy?"

"Ah, we'll keep it hidden," I said. "C'mon!"

I grabbed his hand and pulled him out of the room. Amira jumped out of bed and rushed after us into the hall. And for the next couple hours, we snuck into every hospital room and healed all of the kids.

It was the best day of my life!

Chapter 86

ONE WEEK LATER, I WAS IN my bedroom preparing for my first-ever date while my insides churned like bricks in a washing machine. In the background, my small TV streamed a Netflix show, but I was so nervous I didn't pay much attention to it.

"You nervous?" asked Kleopatra as she swept a makeup brush across my eye.

"Who? Me?" I said. "Nah, you're talking to Maddie Jones. I've raided tombs and put bad guys in their place. Why would I be nervous?"

Kleopatra shifted her makeup brush to my other eye. It tickled as she applied mascara. "I dunno, kiddo. Dating is a lot different than surviving booby-trapped tombs. I'd say it's even more dangerous. Don't squint or you'll smear your makeup."

"Sorry," I said. "So your dad is seriously okay with it?"

"He is, actually." She set the mascara brush aside and picked up a pink rose lipstick. "Starting tomorrow, I begin cosmetology school. I'll get my certification, then work toward opening my own beauty parlor. I'm gonna YouTube the whole thing."

"No more archaeology?"

"Kiddo, I've had enough archaeology to last a lifetime."

I smiled. "I'm happy for you, Kleo. You deserve it. You're gonna do great."

"Thanks, Maddie. Now no more talking so I can do your lips."

She started to apply lipstick, but my brothers burst into my bedroom, startling both of us.

"You aren't going to believe this!" said Zac. He was dressed in a track and field uniform and wore a gold medal around his neck, having won first place in a school meet earlier today.

"It's on all the channels," said Jason. He adjusted the glasses perched on his nose, then grabbed the TV remote. He changed my Netflix show to live television.

The President of the United States was holding a news conference.

"Look, we don't know how it happened," the President said. *"Can we roll the footage again for the public to see?"*

The video switched from the President behind a podium to doctors in white lab coats. They appeared to be scrutinizing CAT scan photos and X-rays. In one of the CAT scans you could clearly see an abnormal growth, but in another image, the tumor was missing.

The video footage changed.

Now it showed the parking lot outside of the Dana-Farber Children's Hospital in Boston. A sea of people overflowed the parking lot and into the streets. They appeared to be from all different walks of life and religions, as some prayed with rosaries while others knelt on prayer mats.

Everyone was celebrating.

The video footage changed again to show kids in hospital gowns embracing their parents, siblings, and friends. They were all smiling and crying.

Happy tears, I noted.

The sight of such cheerfulness made my heart swell. The gray cloak would do marvelous things.

"Stop crying, or you'll ruin your mascara?" said Kleopatra.

"I'm sorry." I grabbed a Kleenex to dab my eyes. "It's just so amazing to see those families healed. I want to use the cloak again. I want to help more people."

"And you will," she said. "But not tonight. You've got big plans, remember?"

"Yeah, yeah," I said.

"As for the cure," the President continued. *"Doctors are flabbergasted and cannot figure out how their patients were healed. By all accounts, this event appears to be a miracle. I assure you we are working tirelessly to replicate the results. But we need your help, America."*

The television footage changed yet again. Now it showed grainy images from hospital security cameras of me, Jamari, and Amira as we walked from room to room. Our faces had been covered with emojis. Jamari's and Amira's were both big yellow smiley faces, but mine was a stinking poop emoji.

What a dweeb, I thought.

But I had to admit, Jamari's computer hacking skills were pretty sweet if he was able to hide our identities, even from the government.

"If you have any information regarding who these people are," said the President. *"Then please contact your local authorities. Their faces have not only been hidden, but all hospital sign-in records have vanished as well."*

Jason turned off the TV. "Well, that's *that*," he said. "But something else happened just a few minutes ago."

"What?" I asked.

"As Dad was going through the mail, he got a letter from Sherwood Lumber."

"Seriously? What'd it say?"

"Nothing, but there was a check inside."

Kleopatra's interest was piqued by the prospect of *money*. "Oh, yeah, how much?"

"Two-hundred-fifty-thousand dollars."

Kleopatra spluttered. "A quarter million?"

Jason nodded.

"You should've seen Dad's face when he saw the amount," said Zac. "He spit coffee up all over his clothes."

"Holy cow," I said. "So the museum is going to be saved?"

"Looks like it," Jason said.

I sat back and smiled. Robin Hood and the Merry Men had struck again, this time coming through for my family in a big way.

"All right you two," Kleopatra said. "Time to get out. We need to finish getting Maddie ready for her big date."

My brothers made kissing sounds as Kleopatra shooed them away and shut the door. She returned and painted my lips, then blew dust from a makeup brush and swept it across my cheeks. After she applied the finishing touches to my makeup, I glanced into a mirror.

"Wow, I look . . ."

"Beautiful," Kleopatra finished. "Now get dressed and I'll drive you to Turoni's Pizzeria."

"Erm, do *you* have to drive?" I asked, wincing at the idea of sitting in a car with Kleopatra again. "My dad can take me."

"No way, kiddo. I want to see the guy's reaction when he sees how gorgeous you look. What'd ya think he has planned?"

I didn't know. Maybe dinner and a movie. Perhaps coffee or an arcade afterward. I had no idea what to expect. I bet you're wondering who the lucky guy was.

Well.

Let's just say he's a stylish construction worker who robs from the rich and gives to the poor.

Epilogue

THE MAN WITH AN EYEPATCH answered the phone on the first ring.

"Hello?"

"Was the bomb a success?" said a woman's cold voice.

"No," the man grumbled. "The museum was destroyed, but the target wasn't eliminated."

"And the girl?"

"She survived."

"Blasts," the woman cursed. "All right, I'll plan a new attack. In the meantime, a package has been sent to your PO Box. You'll find instructions and enough money to carry out your orders."

A wicked smile touched the man's lips. "Thank you. When the time nears just send word. I'll be ready."

"I'd accept nothing less from a hired mercenary."

"My revenge isn't about money," he growled. "I wear an eyepatch now because of Maddie Jones."

"Oh, yes," she rasped. "I remember."

"And her brothers," he grunted. "They shot me in the hand with a crossbow bolt. I can barely grip a gun because of them."

The woman chuckled, her laugh hissing like a serpent with fangs.

"It's not funny," he barked into the phone.

She stopped laughing immediately, her tone serious once again. "I do apologize, Lynch. We both have our reasons for wanting the Jones family eliminated."

"What was your reason?" Lynch asked. "Did Maddie's dad really kill your son?"

Static sounded on the other end of the line. "Yes," she breathed, and there was pain in her voice. "Do not remind me. Or I'll dock your pay."

"Sorry," he said. "It won't happen again."

More static sounded. "I must go."

"When will I hear from you next?"

"Soon. Take care of yourself, Lynch. It's a dangerous world out there."

"You as well, Tamora Rose."

"I'll be in touch," Tamora said.

Click.

The End

Continue reading Maddie's story in Death Mask of Tutankhamun: A Maddie Jones Mystery, Book 3!

Don't miss updates on new releases from Mark Douglas, Jr. Sign up for his mailing list at <u>www.Mark-DouglasJr.com</u> and receive a FREE Maddie Jones mystery!

If you enjoyed reading this book, I would sincerely appreciate it if you would give me a review! It only takes a few words, but it means so much. Thank you!

Join Mark's Newsletter

Want to be notified the minute Mark's next book is released? Sign up for his newsletter at www.Mark–DouglasJr.com to get cover reveals, exclusive content, and new release announcements. Plus, you'll receive a FREE Maddie Jones mystery for signing up!

About the Author

MARK DOUGLAS, JR. finds inspiration from history and cranks it up to eleven. After graduating college, Mark went on to teach history to teenagers. Each day, the kids participated in a program called Drop Everything and Read. However, many of Mark's students hated reading, so he began reading aloud to them. Mark read Wednesday Wars, Treasure Island, and the Egypt Game. But the kids enjoyed Percy Jackson & the Olympians most. Several kids checked out the series from the library so they could read ahead.

Inspired, Mark embarked on his own storytelling journey. And a decade later, he's telling stories about the exploits of spunky teenage heroine Maddie Jones.

Want More?

Love Mark's books? Join his mailing list at <u>www.Mark–DouglasJr.com</u> to be notified of new releases and giveaways!

You can also hang out with him on Facebook, Instagram, Twitter (X), and Goodreads.

Want even more? Subscribe to Mark's YouTube channel or join him on TikTok to get insider information on his writing process, how he finds inspiration for his stories, and what it's like to be an author. He also creates fun games and challenges for his viewers.

Connect With Mark Online:
<u>www.Mark–DouglasJr.com</u>